SAQI BOOKSHELF

Saqi has been publishing innovative writers from the Middle East and beyond since 1983. Our Saqi Bookshelf series brings together a curated list of the most dazzling writing from this kaleidoscopic region. From bold, original voices to modern classics and contemporary bestsellers, begin collecting your Saqi Bookshelf and discover the world around the corner.

For reading recommendations, new books and discounts, join the conversation here:

X @SaqiBooks
◎ @SaqiBooks
f SaqiBooks

www.saqibooks.com

ABDEL RAHMAN AL-SHARQAWI (1920–1987) was born into a peasant family in the Egyptian province of Menoufia. His first works were published while he was a student at the law school of the University of Cairo and he became widely known after the publication of his novel *Egyptian Earth* in 1953. The author of four novels as well as numerous short stories, poetry collections and plays, his work is highly regarded for its realism and commitment to social issues of the day. Al-Sharqawi also took part in the antimonarchy struggle and founded the progressive journal *Al-Katib*, which advocated peaceful cooperation among peoples. In 1974, al-Sharqawi received the State Appreciation Award in Literature by the Egyptian government. He died in 1987.

Abdel Rahman al-Sharqawi

EGYPTIAN EARTH

Translated from the Arabic by
Desmond Stewart

Foreword by
Robin Ostle

SAQI

SAQI BOOKS
Gable House, 18–24 Turnham Green Terrace, London W4 1QP
www.saqibooks.com

First published by Saqi Books in 1990
This edition published 2024

First published in Arabic in 1954
First English publication in 1962 by William Heinemann Ltd

ISBN 978 0 86356 968 5
eISBN 978 0 86356 722 3

A full CIP record for this book is available from the British Library.

Printed and bound by Clays Ltd, Elcograf S.p.A

CONTENTS

The author and the translator wish to express their thanks to Towfik Hanna, whose help and advice proved invaluable.

FOREWORD

ABDEL RAHMAN AL-SHARQAWI (1920–87) published *Egyptian Earth*, his first novel, in 1954, just two years after the Free Officers' Revolution of 1952 had inaugurated a new era in the modern history of Egypt. It was an era which seemed to offer fresh hope for the disinherited millions of Egyptians in both town and country, but in particular for the peasants, the *fellahin*, who still form the majority of the population. Until that time, Egypt's experience as a modern nation state had seen a progression from great hope and heady aspiration to an ever-increasing sense of deception and disillusion. At first the path towards Egyptian independence had been marked by great and significant achievements: Saad Zaghloul (1860–1927) created the first organized mass party in modern Egypt, the Wafd Party, and via the Egyptian Revolution of 1919, events moved swiftly towards the British Declaration of 1922 which created an independent sovereign Egyptian state. A new Constitution was proclaimed in 1923, and after elections were held in January 1924 Zaghloul and the Wafd formed the first parliamentary government of independent Egypt.

This 'liberal experiment' was to prove sporadic and shortlived: the royal dynasty which had ruled Egypt since the days of Muhammad Ali (reigned 1805–48) was restored by the British after the First World War, and the new Constitution gave powers to King Fuad I which seemed designed to undermine the fabric of parliamentary government. The British themselves were far from relinquishing crucial control over Egyptian foreign and military affairs, and the political behaviour of both the Wafd and their opponents led rapidly to a fatal degeneration in public affairs which played into the hands of those who had no interest in seeing the triumph of liberal democracy.

Egyptian Earth is set in the early 1930s, the years that seemed to destroy all hope of a genuine development of parliamentary government. The monarchy had just mounted its third campaign against the democratic process in less than seven years. In 1930 Ismail Sidky assumed the premiership; within a short time parliament was dissolved, the 1923 Constitution was suspended and Sidky had formed his own ironically named People's Party. New electoral laws ensured that large sectors of the Egyptian population were effectively disenfranchised, the Omdas or village headmen were used increasingly as corrupt instruments of government control and violence became an endemic feature of political activity.

The plot of the novel thus unfolds in a milieu of oppression and corruption in which the fellahin are the constant victims: the Omda holds on tenaciously to his power, acting as the agent of the government and aided by the immoral brutality of the chief of police, Mahmud Bey. The Pasha is a shadowy figure who symbolizes the exploitation of the peasants by the government and the capital city and whose palace will be linked by the new road to Cairo, destroying much of the villagers' valuable land in the process. Ranged against these inimical forces is the sense of solidarity of the villagers, led by Abdul Hadi and Abu Suweilim who personify in quasiheroic fashion the traditional virtues of the rural community. Although the divisions between town and country appear to be unbridgeable, Sheikh Hassouna, the schoolmaster from Cairo, is an important character who is able to deploy his urban skills and knowledge to the advantage of his relatives in the village. It is worth recalling that the period 1930–34 was one of grave economic difficulty in which cotton prices dropped to an all-time low, and when the market for agricultural goods was extremely depressed. The debts of farmers, both large and small, rose dramatically, as did the interest rates to service their loans. In such conditions it is obvious that the harshness of the existence of the majority of fellahin became even more acute.

Egyptian Earth is one of a series of landmarks in the development of the modern literature of Egypt. In the history of this literature to date, the representation of the fellahin has been one of the dominant motifs. The rise of the novel form in Egypt is closely associated with the mood of romantic nationalism which was to guide Egypt towards the first phase of its independence. *Zaynab* (1913) by Muhammad Husayn Haykal (1888–1956) is one of the first examples of this genre, although it was inspired by an ideological commitment quite different from that of Abdel Rahman al-Sharqawi. Haykal's vision of the Egyptian countryside and the fellahin is one of pastoral idyll rather than social criticism, although the book is not altogether devoid of a sense of the harsh realities of peasant life. *Zaynab* was also written at a time when it was important to emphasize Egyptian national identity, both in political and in artistic terms. Even though the peasants suffered from poverty, disease and ignorance, they constituted the majority of the population of the newly emerging Egyptian nation and were the guardians of traditional cultural values and virtues. In fact, the peasants and the countryside were a constant dilemma for politicians, writers, artists and intellectuals in the period between the two World Wars. After the initial burst of romantic enthusiasm which Haykal expressed in *Zaynab*, it became increasingly clear that the cultural gulf which existed between the small city elites and the teeming masses of the countryside was impossible to bridge. Haykal's major contribution was to establish the novel as a respectable genre in both modern Egyptian and modern Arabic fiction; he also placed the fellahin at the centre of both political and artistic preoccupations. Another landmark among the literary representations of peasant life in Egypt is *Maze of Justice* by Tawfiq al-Hakim (1898–1987). This book is a biting satire on the folly of trying to apply a legal system which is quite inappropriate to the peasant way of life. By the time that it was published in 1937, it was clear that the romantic idyll was no longer a credible vision for literature or for life.

Egyptian Earth was the artistic expression of a new ideological phase. It highlights the ultimate bankruptcy of the systems which had governed Egypt until 1952, and looks forward to new departures. In its heroic idealization of peasant solidarity in the face of government oppression and corruption, its vision is in some senses just as romantic as Haykal's had been back in 1913. But although its ideological commitment is clear, we are also in the presence of a considerable work of art which makes significant advances beyond the literary representations of the fellahin prior to the 1950s. The literature of Haykal's and al-Hakim's generation tends to observe the peasant condition from the perspective of the cultured city-dweller. With the generation of al-Sharqawi and Yusuf Idris, the world is viewed from the perspective of the peasants themselves: we see life through the eyes of Abdul Hadi and feel via his emotions and those of the whole range of other rural characters. The book is rich with the colourful variety of peasant speech and song, and the reader can savour the sensitive portrayal of the timeless features of Egyptian rural life: the profound visceral attachment to the land, its produce and its animals; the volatile temperaments of the villagers that explode into surprisingly violent anger and which equally surprisingly subside into warm and genuine reconciliation; the colourful and active roles played by the women of the community within the limits of the accepted structures that define honour and shame; the beauty and mystery of the peasant girl Waseefa, who inspires the sexual fantasies of several of the male characters.

The Revolution of 1952 was proclaimed in the name of Abdul Hadi and his fellow villagers, but although the plot of *Egyptian Earth* is actually set in the 1930s, during the

Sidky dictatorship, there is perhaps an unspoken fear in the author's mind that the new regime may repeat the mistakes of its predecessors. When the Free Officers abolished the 1923 Constitution and disbanded all political parties, al-Sharqawi may have suspected that one set of exploitative bureaucrats was merely being replaced by another, with equally scant interest in allowing the peasants to take charge of their own destinies. *Egyptian Earth* remains al-Sharqawi's outstanding contribution to modern Egyptian literature. Through its translations into numerous languages and its highly popular film version by Youssef Chahine, it is arguably the most widely known work of modern Arabic fiction both inside and beyond the Near and Middle East.

Robin Ostle
St John's College, Oxford

EGYPTIAN EARTH

PART ONE

THAT WAS the summer I finished primary school. When I went home to my village, I heard a lot about Waseefa – whom I could not remember.

Usually the boys in the village would question me about Cairo. They would ask me to say a few sentences in English, or joke in English, or open an English book to show what the letters looked like. But this year they were all talking about Waseefa. We were loitering outside Sheikh Yusif's shop; he was the grocer, and his shop was on the main road from the village to the river.

I asked the boys who this Waseefa was.

One of them, adjusting his skullcap of grey wool, murmured:

'You mean, you've forgotten Waseefa, you mean Cairo's made you forget her?'

The boys smiled, and still I could not remember her. One boy raised his eyebrows. 'So you don't remember Waseefa who used to jump with us into the canal, all day long, four, or was it five years ago?'

And another boy, leaning on his little mulberry stick just as the older men lean on their staffs, broke in: 'She's come to the boil; she came back from the town last winter.' Then he turned to me, scratching his back, 'You really mean you don't remember her, my friend? Waseefa – your wife!' And the boys burst out laughing, and I joined in the laughter, suddenly remembering all that had taken place between Waseefa and myself.

The year before I went away to school we used to bathe in the small canal near the village, all of us together, boys and girls. We used to roll in the dust and cover our faces and heads with mud, to pretend we were demons. Then we jumped into the canal and plunged into the muddy water, our shouts mingling with the cries of ducks and geese which welcomed us with flapping wings.

One day we all met by the small canal as usual, just before the time for noon prayers. Before we undressed, Waseefa challenged us:

'For a change, let's swim in the river.'

She knew a place which was not too deep, where we could stay within our depths. For in those days we were too small to swim in the river, though we longed to do so, like the bigger boys who could even cross it.

She alone could climb the mulberry tree and shake it, so that we could eat the fruit; she alone could make necklaces from berries; and she alone climbed Abdul Hadi's frighteningly high sycamore, to come down with a handful of fruit, still green, for us to play with, or to eat. She would answer back any men who shouted at us when we played;

if necessary she would insult them too. Therefore as soon as Waseefa proposed swimming in the river, we at once ran after her, enthusiastic to splash the water, and to dive into it like the bigger boys.

Near a deserted waterwheel we took off our clothes. It was easy to see that Waseefa was older than us, for her body already resembled that of a grown woman. None of the rest was more than eight, so we always examined Waseefa's body with interest. She was nearly twelve, her waist was already well defined, her hips too; the lines of her body were well formed, and we boys enjoyed touching her breasts and her back.

We piled our clothes in a heap under a tree. We then went into the water, our pride warring with our fear. Just at that moment some women came down to the river to fill their pitchers. One of them spied us. The hem of her black dress in her teeth, she rushed up and grabbed Waseefa by the thigh, screaming:

'Get out, you shameless slut! Pushing yourself like this among the boys ...'

Waseefa answered with her usual defiance:

'Slut yourself! Are you my mother or father? Be off with you. No one beats me, I am the daughter of the Chief Guard.'

At that moment another woman threw a handful of mud at her.

'What shame! You are not a baby, you almost are a woman, but already you act worse than Kadra.' Waseefa shouted back:

'What business is it of yours, you hypocrite? You have a good time yourself on feast-days!'

We were astonished by Waseefa's courage, and we stood defiantly in the water. But a third woman threatened to take our clothes to our families and leave us there naked. This got us out of the water in a hurry.

'Let's go,' Waseefa suggested, 'to the waterwheel which belongs to your cousin, Abdul Hadi. We can play in the shade of his sycamore.'

We all agreed. Waseefa got there first and leant against the trunk of the tree that shaded the waterwheel. Nearby there was a place for prayer, surrounded by a low fence. We all sat down in a group, near Waseefa, waiting expectantly to see what game she would think up. Some way off Abdul Hadi was bent over his hoe. Waseefa looked at Abdul Hadi, and under her breath said, 'Thank God, he's still at work.' She then asked the boys where Kadra was. One of them said she was with the other children, picking insects off Mahmoud Bey's cotton. Waseefa sighed, and looked at us all, and we waited to hear what game we would play – for she knew many. But this time she made no suggestion. Instead, she began to tell us about what she had seen, the day before, at her sister's wedding.

Her sister had married a man who had moved to the town and now wore a tarboosh, as well as a jacket over his gallabya. She told how, after her sister and the midwife had gone into the bedroom, she and Kadra had slipped in unnoticed. With the others she had waited for the groom. He came at last, wearing a silk gallabya, his brilliant red tarboosh was pushed forwards on to his forehead. But he was not carrying the white handkerchief which grooms should carry. And when he saw that the room was occupied, not only by his bride, but her mother, the midwife and several little girls, he drove them all out in a rage, insisting that he be left alone with his wife-to-be. Thereupon the midwife rushed out, beating her face and asking the Chief Guard if this kind of wedding was the new fashion in the cities. Muhammad Abu Suweilim rushed angrily inside and slapped the groom on his face and ordered him to use a handkerchief with his daughter, just as all grooms did with reputable girls of the village. In every way let him follow tradition!

So after a while the midwife went inside again and the groom turned the white handkerchief round his finger and again the two little girls slipped into the room.

We listened, all ears, to what Waseefa told us, and our hearts thumped, and we edged closer to her. She enjoyed her recital. Her eyes glittered and her lips parted. We nudged each other and anxiously entreated her to go on and tell us the whole story of her sister, the groom and the white handkerchief.

So Waseefa told us all, from the moment her sister screamed out, to the moment when shouts of joy greeted the white handkerchief, now stained with blood, which the groom threw to the people waiting outside. The men carried other handkerchiefs on the tips of their staffs, and went through the lanes of the village shouting, 'He's a good fellow!' while in their wake the women danced and clapped their hands above their heads and chanted excitedly:

'Tell her father, if he's hungry, to eat's all right!
His noble daughter's honoured us tonight!'

5

Waseefa left out not a single detail.

When she finished, we were silent. Some of us then began to hunt for a shady place under the tree.

Waseefa suddenly looked at the prayer-place.

'What about playing at weddings now?'

She chose the players. She herself would be the bride; she needed a girl to play the midwife, it was a pity that Kadra was away picking the worms from the cotton, and could not be with us; a smaller girl had to make do. For the groom, she chose me, because of my city connections, all my brothers being away at school in Cairo, where I would soon join them. For the bedroom Waseefa chose the prayer-place. First she went in, then the midwife, and last of all, myself. The other children stayed outside, the girls making the traditional cries of joy, while the boys took little sticks and waited.

But the game did not reach its climax, though I, as groom, was ready. For at that moment Sheikh Shinawi arrived. The Sheikh was the village *mufti*, the preacher at the mosque, the teacher of the children, the adviser of the old. A tall, stout man with a bull neck and a large stomach, he was a man who enjoyed fiestas and every opportunity for eating. We children believed that if he wanted, he could swallow a cow whole. He was popular, someone to joke with, though nearly everyone had been beaten by him in school. Now, from behind our 'bedroom' wall, the children's songs suddenly hushed, and their frightened shouts mingled with the sound of running feet. 'Look out! Sheikh Shinawi ... What a disaster ... Run off before he gets you ...' And at the same time we heard the authoritative voice of the Sheikh himself. It reminded us of

6

the way he intoned the Koran when we had written a passage on our slates at school. We heard his voice (he was now on the bank by the sycamore tree) telling the children to be off, to keep away from the place of prayer, and not defile it.

The children's voices receded. We heard the click of the Sheikh's beads and his voice intoning some verses of the Koran. He blew his nose, spat in the direction of the children, took off his shoes, and stepped into the place of prayer.

We were taken utterly by surprise, Waseefa, the midwife and myself; we crouched against the wall of mud and reeds, trying to conceal ourselves in the folds of the mats. But in vain. The Sheikh saw us, in astonishment. He stared at us, his face gone pale. I peeped at him, and saw him step backwards, murmuring something I could not hear. He stared at Waseefa's half-naked body, then exclaimed:

'I take refuge in God from this filth and sin. I take refuge in God from Satan the Accursed. Oh, God! Oh, God! Are they human or are they devils? "Say, I take refuge in the Lord of Daybreak from the Evil which He hath created."'

My throat was dry, I huddled closer to Waseefa, and the midwife huddled close to me. Waseefa burst out, 'It's not my fault, by the Prophet! Forgive me, it was his idea, not mine, that we should play at marriages.'

The Sheikh was no longer afraid. His voice rang out.

'So it's you, you pigs, you filthy creatures ... Even in the place of prayer. By God, I'll throw you in the river.'

We were terribly afraid. The Sheikh could do whatever he liked, could carry out any threat, justifying any action by some saying of the Prophet. Desperately I clung to Waseefa, and

7

she clung to me, in equal terror, and the little midwife threw herself on top of us. We were all undressed, in readiness for our game. The Sheikh fell on us with his huge hands. 'Still at it, in front of me? In front of me, you lie on top of one another, you blasphemers? Be off with you, be off!' He wrung his hands. 'I don't know what has become of this village. From top to bottom, it's all filthy. Abdul Hadi, come here! Abdul Hadi!'

Abdul Hadi was hoeing near the waterwheel, but hearing the Sheikh's cry, he ran up. Our terror increased as the Sheikh continued:

'Why these children don't sleep in the noon time ... They go to the river at the height of the sun ... Aren't you afraid of the river-jinn? I wish to God she would carry you off – it would be better for you than to grow up in evil!'

Our mothers had told us about the river-jinn, the evil spirit that crept from the river at noon to carry off in her scarlet fingers whatever children she could find. If she found a small boy walking alone she would entice him with her fingers, 'Come and eat dates, little boy!' But when he followed her, she would drag him down into the depths and he would never be seen again. But these stories were not the cause of our fear: what frightened us was the Sheikh, glaring down at Waseefa's body. 'A black year for you, my girl! Though you are almost ready for marriage.' Looking at me, where I lay huddled against Waseefa, he cried out, 'Get out, all of you, leave this holy place which you are defiling.' To Waseefa, 'Who is your father?'

'The Chief Guard,' she said, weeping.

'Muhammad Abu Suweilim? So light can beget darkness.'

Abdul Hadi wiped the sweat from his brow.

'What's all the fuss?'

Before the Sheikh could answer, Abdul Hadi recognized me. 'It's you, by God,' and he sucked in his breath.

The Sheikh told the whole story to Abdul Hadi. His words filled me with shame and horror, but Abdul Hadi burst out laughing and pulled my hair. 'A chicken, and already you're cocksure!' But the Sheikh was not amused, and he scolded Abdul Hadi. For the first time we heard terrible words from the Sheikh's lips: fornication, and worse, adultery, 'the destroyer of homes'.

Abdul Hadi picked up a stick from the ground and beat Waseefa with it. 'The boy's but a child, he's too small to know what shame is, but you, you slut, you are ready for marriage ... Is this shameful game the only one you know?'

While Waseefa was crying under his blows, the little midwife made her escape and Abdul Hadi picked up a lump of earth and threw it at her back. 'Wait, a fever take you!' But the girl did not wait, and Waseefa and I ran after her. When she was at a safe distance, Waseefa turned and shouted back: 'May you be whipped one day, Abdul Hadi, and you too Sheikh Shinawi!'

But as for me, I could not forget the angry Sheikh, with his purple cheeks and his denunciations of fornication, adultery, and broken homes. It all seemed so causeless. We had been so happy at our game; the children had sung, we had laughed, there was nothing in our actions that deserved such heavy words, nothing in particular that deserved 'the fire'. My father

9

had told me: 'Don't lie: because those who lie are burned in the fire.' And from that moment I had never lied, although I had seen many liars burn others with the fire of their lies. But no one had so far told me that children's games could also lead to fire.

But that evening, when Sheikh Shinawi visited us, he whispered for a while in my father's ear, then burst out in a loud request for a fiesta, in honour of God. My father then called me to him, and gave me a beating. Although he did not tell me, I knew the reason. And I never played that game again, for I now knew that it, like lying, could burn me with fire. I did not ask my father why this should be so; instead I would ask Waseefa. But I could not find her. She no more came to the canal just before noon, and no more sat on her doorstep in the evening, beating out rhythms on an upturned tray, while we children joined in the choruses of her songs. I heard that in the evening her parents whipped her and forbade her to play with us anymore, and her father told Abdul Hadi to heighten the fence round the prayer-place, and to make a door which could be locked to keep children out. And the year after that, I went away to Cairo, to live with my older brothers, and to get ready for school. When I returned to my village the following summer, it was to learn that Waseefa had left to live with her sister in the chief town of the province. Her sister's husband worked as odd-job-man in the agricultural school.

Four years passed ... five ... and I had finished primary school, and come back for the summer holidays, loaded with books, and also with dreams of secondary school, of wearing long trousers and a jacket with an inside pocket, a tie which would flutter in the wind, and Oxford shoes. I begged my mother, kissing her hand, to intercede with my father to give me a monthly allowance, instead of pocket money, now that I had passed the exams of my first school. And I began to dream of little silver coins jingling in my pocket, and of a watch on my wrist. But this my mother refused; it would distract someone of my age from his studies. 'A watch, like long hair, is the privilege of secondary school boys.' And yet I still dreamt of a watch, as well as of studying French, and would sometimes glance at my wrist as if it carried a watch.

But most of all I dreamt of taking part in demonstrations. For I had heard so much from my brothers about what they did in the university to protest against the dismissal of Taha Hussein. For at that time the name of Taha Hussein, our most famous writer, aroused immense admiration among all students.

These dreams drove out Waseefa. The children spoke her name to me, but I wanted to tell them about Cairo, where I had seen things utterly new to me.

For at that time Cairo was in a state of continual unrest. From what my brothers said amongst themselves, as well as from the newspapers, I knew that a man called Sidky ruled Egypt with fire and iron, having first suspended the Constitution in the interests of the English. And I had seen him unleash English soldiers with red faces on the streets of Cairo, to bolster up his authority. At that time I was in the Muhammadiyah Primary School, and every day I heard machine-gun fire. On my way home after school, the whole city would vibrate with firing, and nevertheless every morning the workers were on strike once more, and the students were demonstrating.

The Khedivial Secondary School used to pour on to the streets every morning, shouting: Long Live The Constitution! Freedom! Independence! Down with Sidky and his English masters! One morning in March they invaded our school, much to the distress of the headmaster. But we joined the bigger boys, delighted to be asked. We were part of a vast procession, surging through the streets of Helmia Gedida, shouting the same slogans, united, enthusiastic, our hearts and our voices one, our blood afire, while from their balconies women watched us approvingly, and even girls normally hidden behind shutters appeared in their windows to applaud. But suddenly we ran into a line of pink-faced English soldiers, their guns towards us. Screams from the balconies. One of us shouted, 'Complete Independence Or Immediate Death!' Women implored us to go back. We went back. But we now found ourselves confronting Egyptian soldiers, brown-faced, like the men in my village, calling to each other by the same names borne by the men at home. But they were holding truncheons, which crashed against the earth, against our heads.

All this I told to my friends, all that I remembered of Cairo, my dreams, the demonstrations, my long trousers, the English, Sidky, my watch. From time to time they listened, but they reverted to Waseefa. Yet they knew Sidky's name. One of them asked me 'This Sidky, tell me, just how big is he really? If he and Abdul Hadi fought, say with sticks, who would win?'

Before I could reply, someone else said that Sidky was a fabulous creature who could outfight a hundred Abdul Hadis – but at some other game than sticks. He fed on bread made of pure wheat. He never touched maize bread, such as we ate. He drank iced water from a tap. Sheikh Hassouna, the headmaster in the next village's school, had been transferred to a remote part of Egypt because of his support for the Constitution. Another boy whispered in my ear that the Chief Guard, Waseefa's father, Abu Suweilim, had been dismissed for the same reason. The village had boycotted the Election in which Sidky had tried to impose his new 'People's Party' on the country. Not one villager had bothered to vote. The local magistrate had told Abu Suweilim to drive the electors to the polls. But Abu Suweilim had seen them registering the votes of dead people, and he refused. Yet another boy led me out of earshot of Sheikh Yusif's shop, to tell me that even Sheikh Yusif had lost half of his one acre after the Constitution was suspended. In fact, the boys told me so many things, that I realized that although they had never taken part in a demonstration, they nevertheless knew far more about the Constitution – and with the bitterness of experience – than I did myself.

And I had a new respect for Sheikh Hassouna, the schoolmaster, and a new pity for Abu Suweilim, the father of Waseefa, my childhood friend. I learnt that he was now working his half acre all alone, and that Waseefa had come back so as to help him. Now that he was unemployed, he could not afford to pay someone to assist him. Waseefa's return made the whole village think of little else. For one thing, she alone of all the village women not only wore a brightly coloured dress, instead of the customary black, but also wore it quite openly, regardless of public opinion, which was divided: some people saying her father could not afford a new black dress, others said that having deprived her of her life in the town, he did not want to deprive her also of her coloured dress. But all agreed on one thing: that the new Waseefa was most beautiful, with an elegant, citified accent. Yet when Muhammad Effendi, our schoolmaster, with a monthly stipend of as much as four pounds, asked for her hand, Abu Suweilim refused him, saying he did not want his daughter to marry someone from the village. Abdul Hadi, rumour said, had made a point of visiting his old friend, Waseefa's brother-in-law, and of saying the Opening Prayer of the Koran in his company. Yet another rumour spoke of a cousin of Waseefa's, Abdu, who had approached Waseefa's mother – but as he had left Cairo without a job, he too was rejected. With all these rumours, my head was in a whirl about Waseefa.

One evening my friends and I were loitering in the broad roadway near Sheikh Yusif's, gossiping about everything. Suddenly an old she-donkey trotted by, ridden by a young man in a striped gallabya, somewhat grubby, letting his legs hang down on one side of the animal.

'That's him ... that's him ... Abdu, her cousin ... spent all his life in Cairo from the time his father went to work there as a groom ... when the old man died he came back, said he wanted to help Abu Suweilim ... not a thing does he know about farming ... look how he sits sidesaddle, as if he was inspecting his huge estate!'

And we watched the donkey till it disappeared down one of the village lanes.

At this moment a long line of girls came in sight, carrying their water-jars from the river. All of them wore the usual long black dress, except for one; her voice too stood out from the voices and the laughter of the others. Taller than the others, she carried her jar full of water on her head, as did the others, but at a yet more attractive angle. She wore a transparent black veil over a bright red kerchief which covered most of her hair.

'That's Waseefa, that's her,' said one of the boys. 'Don't you remember her?'

The women came nearer. I heard Waseefa's voice, 'Shush! Kadra, we're almost in the village, be polite ... And the procession came near, and I marvelled that my village of low, dusty houses had given birth to someone as lovely as Waseefa. Her neck was full and fair, her body strong, her breasts pronounced. In every way she stood out from the other girls, from the blue glass bracelets she wore on her wrist, to the slippers on her feet. Not that she was beautiful, so much as attractive, with a complexion the colour of honey and cheeks brilliant with life.

Her thick black hair fell in braids from her red kerchief onto her breast; her nose was small and shapely; and with all these details of physical beauty went an elegance which marked her out from the other girls.

'Waseefa!' I shouted out, as the girls passed. The boys were astonished, as no one had ever got away with speaking in public to Waseefa before. A boy whispered that surely she would empty her water over my head as a punishment. But I stood up and introduced myself to her and complimented her on the way she had grown up. Whereupon she (who was taller than I was) glanced down at me, while I looked up at her, from her head allowing my eyes to descend the length of her whole body. At once Kadra recognized me.

'You've come, you've come! How's Cairo? Praise God you are safe and well!'

And Waseefa smiled and welcomed me with the same warmth.

'By God, what sweetness! It's you! How are you? What a time it's been ...'

And her smile lit up her whole face, and her eyes sparkled, and from the way she smiled, and the way her cheeks dimpled, I recognized she too had been away to the cities.

'Have you brought me something nice from Cairo?'

I could not answer; I had never given her a thought.

I heard many stories about Waseefa in that first week of my holidays. One concerned Alwani, a Beduin boy born in the village. One evening Alwani, who was guarding a plantation of watermelons, saw Waseefa going alone to the river, just as the first glooms of darkness were covering the house, fields and water. At sight of her, he clapped his hands and shouted out joyfully: 'Welcome! Welcome! Stay a moment ... There was no one else in sight, the farmers had driven their animals home. This emboldened Alwani, who selected a plump melon, saying, 'I work for the masters, I obey them utterly. Take this melon. Even the Prophet accepted a present. Take this extra sweet melon, it will refresh your heart in this heat.'

Waseefa angrily replied, 'Blight on your heart, you Beduin scoundrel!'

But her anger only made Alwani more delighted. 'Ah! But from you I accept anything. I like such tirades. A lover's beating is sweeter than raisins.'

Offering the melon, he stood in her way; Waseefa rejected the melon with one hand, with the other still holding her pitcher. She was furious.

'Who do you think you are, you good-for-nothing Beduin? You urchin? So proud of working for the masters, and yet stealing their melons!'

This only brought laughs from Alwani. 'Just this one, please!'

Waseefa's fury mounted. 'I care nothing for you or your masters, and I curse your thieving. Let me pass!'

But Alwani still stood his ground, still offering her the melon. 'I take all your insults, only please accept my present. And remember, I am an Arab sheikh, Waseefa. Accept my present, girl!'

The word 'girl' enraged Waseefa. 'May you bite off your tongue! Girl, you say: pestilence take your girl and your parents! You exhaust me, you make my life bitter, you boy from the desert! Girl, you dared call me girl, did you, I am your mistress, and the mistress of your masters. I know your reputation. You used to perch in the branches of Abdul Hadi's sycamore, peeping at us when we went swimming. By the Prophet, if my father, or Abdul Hadi, or Muhammad Effendi, or anyone passing had seen you, they would have snapped your neck for you!'

'A pretty speech, by the same Prophet, a pretty speech! Continue. Say more, I like it, only continue.' And at the same time he held out the melon till it touched her breast, saying at the same time. 'It's perfect, my mistress, take it, if only to make peace, in the Arab fashion.'

Suddenly Waseefa put her jar on the ground. 'Good, give it to me.' And she took the melon and threw it with all her force in Alwani's face, and having done this, continued to the river, to the place, not far from Abdul Hadi's sycamore, where the women went for water, a place screened from the bank by a thick growth of bushes.

This story spread round the village, and none of the youths who heard it dared be familiar with Waseefa. The rebuff to Alwani was the greater, since he was already popular with more than one woman in the village, and he was respected by men too. Like his father who had drifted to the village before him, he was brave, a good shot, an expert at the stick-game so popular in the villages, and was employed by the landowners to guard their orange-groves or plantations of melons. He possessed a very old gun which he had inherited from his father; besides this gun, and a stout heart, he had inherited nothing else. But these two possessions won for him a deep respect from Beduin marauders and the good-for-nothings of the village. Now the story of his encounter with Waseefa became so well known that even among the children of the village the phrase 'like Alwani's watermelon' became proverbial. It, and her father's insistence that she should never marry someone from the village, protected Waseefa from the suitors who would otherwise have importuned her. Only

Abdul Hadi refused to give up hope. As he said to Sheikh Yusif, 'Her father neither says yes nor no. I shall be patient. After all, he can't expect to marry her to the Sultan, can he?' And he thought again of his old friend, her brother-in-law. As for Sheikh Yusif, he said in front of the mosque, just before they went in to pray, 'Really Muhammad Abu Suweilim is not acting properly. If you wanted, I would drive my daughter to your house by force. Really I would!'

Abdul Hadi placed great hopes on his friend, who had been at school with him, and indeed grown up with him. He liked the same songs, the same games, and now that he was married, and living in the town, Abdul Hadi would write to him regularly, sending him the texts of any new songs that had appeared. Waseefa liked Abdul Hadi, as he was the only person who could reconcile her sister with her husband when a quarrel broke out between them. And she knew perfectly well that he wanted to marry her, but she could not decide what she felt. She had set her mind on marrying someone who wore a tarboosh, like her sister's husband; at the same time she was always happy when she saw Abdul Hadi sitting amongst the men of the village, listening to her singing at a wedding. For Waseefa had not outgrown her love of singing, of dancing, of the stick-game, which had been her childhood loves; she still liked to put on a black veil and attend the ceremonies when it was permissible for a respectable young woman to dance, very modestly, in front of the men.

'He spread his handkerchief,' she would sing, and the men would answer, 'on the stretch of sand!' and she would go on:

'There on the sand she comes to him!

Oh, you, hiding behind the wall,
Who are you? Guest or groom?'
And in another voice would reply:
'Guest I am, I hold a sword!
With which oppressors will be gored!'

And all the men would repeat, 'Oppressors gored! Oppressors gored!'

I had always loved the songs of the village girls, and Abdul Hadi remembered this. One afternoon he called in at our house and asked me to go with him to a big wedding to be held that night. He was wearing a flowing gallabya of blue cashmere. In his hand he held the stout staff with which he had made himself famous in our village and the next.

Night fell and the village band played at the head of the wedding procession. I walked with Abdul Hadi; there were the joy-cries of women, various songs; I was proud to be with him. Suddenly the band stopped walking in a large open space, the men formed a circle, and Abdul Hadi began to cross sticks with a man famous for the game from the next village. He struck the earth with his stick, then twirled it round his head; the other champion did exactly the same. Abdul Hadi then went through a series of elaborate movements, raising the stick, stooping to the earth, turning round – and each movement was then copied by the other. At last Abdul Hadi struck at the stick of his opponent and all the onlookers shouted out: 'Long live your prowess, Abdul Hadi! Congratulations ... Bravo!' But Abdul Hadi did not use his advantage to strike his opponent. Instead, he embraced him, much to the other's surprise, who could not refuse such chivalry. And then the band struck up again, and we moved on. And once again Abdul Hadi took his stick and repeated the same pantomime as before, and each time the joy-cries of the women acclaimed him. And at the tail end of the procession the little boys imitated Abdul Hadi with mulberry canes.

Later that night Abdul Hadi came to fetch me, and we went to hear Waseefa sing. In one hand he held his tall stick, in the other my hand. We went down a long lane and came to a house with benches outside on which sat a large number of men. Many women and girls were seated nearby on the earth. We sat on the last bench, near the girls. Waseefa was seated in a place of honour. Abdul Hadi told me that the groom was Waseefa's cousin, and that he worked in Cairo. A small drum was placed in front of her. As we arrived, Kadra was dancing, to the embarrassment of some of the younger girls, who looked very shy. Then it was Waseefa's turn to sing. She held her head on one side, her face was dreamy, absorbed in her song, and she smiled vaguely in the direction of Abdul Hadi and myself.

Waseefa sang from her heart, absorbed, rapt, as though she would sing forever, a kerchief round her neck, holding a small drum on which to beat the rhythm. Even when they took the drum from her, to heat its membrane over a fire, she did not stop singing. I remember two lines of her song:

'Whenever I ask when you'll come, you ruin me: For you are sweetness itself, and beauty.'

The way she sang was more melancholy than joyful; such sadness thrilled me. But I heard Abdul Hadi say under his breath: 'I ruin you – why? You ruin the village! If you don't believe me, ask your father!' When at last she stopped, she got up, combed her hair, wiped her face with the hem of her dress, and left the floor to Kadra, who began to sing lascivious songs with a sexual voice:

'On the large bed you flatter me, my darling, to what end? To what end?'

Waseefa sat down near us, wiping her forehead with her hand.

'Well, did you like my song?' she asked me. 'Here in the village we know nothing of your Cairo tunes.'

My heart burned in my breast, and I whispered to her:

'You've not asked me what present I've brought you from Cairo. I've brought you a bottle of perfume.' Abdul Hadi was talking to someone behind us, and did not hear.

In a low, excited whisper she replied, 'Truly you've brought me a present? Perfume! Where is it?'

'Come to me by Abdul Hadi's waterwheel. I'll give it you there.'

'Good, I'll come. First I'll change into a black dress. But we must come back quickly to hear the songs.'

She left first, then I followed, taking care to slip away without being noticed by Abdul Hadi. I walked in excitement through the dark, narrow lanes of the village and then to the road which led to the river, to the waterwheel, the prayer-place and the sycamore, all so vivid in my memory.

I walked down the dusty road towards the river. It was night, and I was alone. The air held the heat of summer, and the road seemed long and deserted, with no moon above, and not a breeze from the surrounding fields. Only the stars glittered above my head like the eyes of demons. The dusty road ended, I was on the river bank, where here and there a few bushes grew. And into my head came the fairy stories I had heard, in particular of the night-fairy who would come out of the river and sit by the bank in the shape of a tall, pale peasant-woman with a pitcher to fill. But if anyone whom she asked for help in filling her pitcher came near, she would take him into the depths of the river, and he would never be seen again. I shivered remembering this tale, though I knew no one who had perished in this way. And I remembered those who had been killed by the river, in my childhood, and before I was born: this was the time, surely, when their ghosts would walk? And my thoughts then left the village tales, and instead I thought of mummies and Frankenstein, such as I had seen on the screen in Cairo cinemas. I nearly cried out with terror at being alone, only I feared my voice more, and just then I reached Abdul Hadi's sycamore. It, too, looked ghostly, with its mysterious leaves. And amidst the shadows I saw the pale cheek of Waseefa, vague in the gloom, but shining. And I was astonished that she was not afraid, and felt ashamed of myself, and the drumming of my heart. This was the first time I had ever been with Waseefa alone. Even when we had played together as children, we had never been alone. There had always been other children with us, for our elders, in particular Sheikh Shinawi, had impressed on us that Satan always interfered when a boy and a girl were alone together, and that we must always play together in a group. Even when we had played at being married, we had not been alone.

And now I was a boy of twelve, not a child of eight, and I knew all the secrets of what happened between boys and girls. And here I was alone, for the first time, with a girl more beautiful than a thousand. A girl I knew, in every detail of her body, from our childhood explorations, just as she had known every detail of my body too.

Waseefa spoke with a confident simplicity. 'Why are you staring at me? Are you afraid? Come and sit near me.'

Night had spread its flat blue darkness over everything, over the prayer-place, the sycamore, the waterwheel, the river, the fields, a flat, unchanging colour. The river was silent, so were the fields. Only an occasional fish would leap out of the water, only from the fields a half-heard croaking, and from the distant village the muted barking of dogs.

I picked up the hem of my gallabya and came and sat near her, on a spreading branch of the tree. She put her cheek close to mine, I felt her breath on my face, and she whispered in a husky murmur, 'Do you remember our last meeting here, in the place of prayer?'

I pretended to laugh, and she laughed too, recalling how Sheikh Shinawi had stepped into the prayer-place just as we had reached the decisive moment. She recalled all this without embarrassment, talking quietly and easily, in a voice that I again noticed had picked up traces of a city accent. And I said nothing in reply. Lightly she touched my arm and suggested that we should leave the river-bank, which was rather public, and go to the prayer-place instead. I was intoxicated. We left the river, on which we could see a few lights glittering, far off, on the dark water. Into my head flooded all the love stories which I had read, despite the efforts of my brothers to prevent me doing so, in the Cairo magazines. They jostled with the love films I remembered from the cinemas, and even with the phrases I had read in the Arabic sub-titles under the foreign films. These too I had seen in defiance of my brothers, who at the time were boycotting all foreign imports, including American films. The distant lights grew nearer ... And crowded with these images of films and stories, I thought that I should take Waseefa in my arms, and that we should exchange fiery words at least till dawn. But when it came to the point, I merely put my arm round her waist. Good, I consoled myself, it is now up to her. She must say, 'My world!' Just as someone in the magazine stories would do, someone as ripe for love as she was, someone as beautiful as an Indian princess. Now my thoughts were on medieval knights and their ladies. So I squeezed her waist and managed to get out, in a voice that surprised myself with its husky lowness, 'Darling, I love you!' To which Waseefa sat up abruptly. 'What's that? Speak up, can't you? What do you want?' So with great effort I managed to say the same thing again, a little louder. I now expected a great love scene. She would roll her eyes in ecstasy, she would murmur of her love through her trembling, kissable lips, she would heave and pant, she would whisper, 'Darling! Darling!' again and again, and together we would be lost in a surge of adoration until dawn came.

But nothing was as I had imagined. Instead, she blew her nose, wiped her forehead and cheeks with the back of her hand, and said:

'You are saying all this rubbish to me?'

And she pretended that what I had been saying must have been in English, a language of which she knew not a word. This reduced me to silence. She stood up, walked to the river and spat, with her back to me, and called me to join her. Sitting on the waterwheel, she began to sing:

'In front of the house of him I love
A tree, some shade, a song, a breeze
If my father frightens you,
Know my father loves you too
If my uncle frightens you,
My uncle does not care a fig
If you don't make me cross the stream,
I'll take off my clothes myself and swim.'

Her voice suddenly changed, interrupting my pleasure.

'Where's the bottle of perfume?'

I did not know how to answer. Instead, I stared across at the pale lights which moved so silently on the water. I felt my throat constricted, I was in an agony of embarrassment, and only with great difficulty could I at last declare that I had not, in fact, brought her the scent, but instead had with me two shillings, the price of such a bottle, which she could easily buy for herself when next she visited her sister in the town. Waseefa seized the coin from my hands almost as though it might escape. Holding it in her hands, she did a little dance, her eyes vivid with delight. In the dark, she stumbled by the waterwheel, and I jumped to save her, which only made us both tumble on the ground, by the well. She kissed me, laughing. We stood up, and I dusted my gallabya, while she held up the coin and exclaimed:

'How wonderful, a florin, a whole florin for myself!'

She leant against the fence of the prayer-place, and carefully undid her dress and hid the coin inside between her breasts, which I saw gleaming whitely against the dark material of her clothes. And then she took me by the hand and pointed to the fence.

'You remember the last time we played in the prayer-place? And how little we were then? Now the first time we play together, as grown-ups, will be in the prayer-place too ...'

I said that the fence had got bigger since we last played here.

'And we, too, have got bigger,' she replied. And after a moment's silence she laughed, 'This time Sheikh Shinawi won't be able to interfere.' And she danced round the fence with a new look in her eyes which excited me and made me feel that I was really a man, even if my official age was only twelve. And then she danced as though in defiance of Sheikh Shinawi, mocking him not only with words, but with the posture of her young yet ripening body, pushing out her breasts as though to mock his teaching, and that of all the Sheikhs in all the world.

But I had still no weapon with which to defy the world. And the very name of Sheikh Shinawi reminded me of fire, of adultery, the destroyer of homes, and his image led to that of my father: perhaps he would send someone to the wedding, to see where I was. I would not be found. I imagined him bursting in between Waseefa and myself, and his rage.

'Waseefa,' I said, 'listen ... I must go now.'

'What are you frightened of? I should be more afraid than you. You are at least a boy ... no one in the village would come to the river at night. They're all at the wedding. The night is pitch. Don't be frightened, my dear ... even the boy Alwani, who spends every night by the river, standing guard over the melons, even he's skipped off to the wedding. There's nothing to be frightened of at all.'

Her defiant courage made me burn with desire to kiss her and embrace her, from her warm plump lips to her breast that I had seen when she had hidden the coin. She began, however, asking me about the girls in Cairo: what were they like, and what did I do with them? I answered not a word, for not a word could I tell her on this subject. 'Those city girls ... how do they dress? How do they eat? How do they behave with men? Is it true they bathe in scent? Do they spend a florin every day? Here in our village no one, not even the Sheikh al-Balad, possesses a florin for himself.' To all these questions I could not give a proper answer. I had heard from my older brothers that the whole world was in a state of crisis, that in America they threw wheat and coffee into the sea, while in China millions were dying of starvation. From my father, too, I had heard how here in Egypt cotton was sold dirt cheap, how farmers were enslaved to moneylenders, how the government gaoled people who could not pay the tax.

In school, I had seen for myself how many of the boys came to class with gaping shoes; they would push their socks down, to hide the holes; they would walk carefully so as not to show the patches in their trousers. My own father, each new school year, would have one of my older brothers' suits repaired for me. None of us, except a very few, had known what it was to wear new clothes. I told Waseefa all about this, and about the gloom that was written on so many faces in Cairo, the stooped shoulders; I told her of the women whose faces were veiled but whose tattered dresses were not enough to conceal their thighs. My words depressed her, and she heaved a long sad sigh. And I thought, as she sighed, as she heaved her plump breast in sympathetic sadness, of how I had obtained the florin ... With what difficulty. Whenever I asked my mother for money, she would say: 'What do you need with money? You eat and drink and sleep at home, what more do you want?' To get more needed arguments which filled the house with noise. How strange that I had given away, and so easily, with so little thought, a coin that had been so difficult to win! I had just handed it over, without a moment's thought. And yet I had been so happy to do this, I did not regret it at all. I went a little way from Waseefa, stood by the river, and watched the pale lights gleaming away across the water. The sounds of men and women talking came from the boat; it was a sailing-ship, and Waseefa stood and looked for it with me.

'That boat, will it go to Cairo?' she asked.

'I wish it could carry me off to some faraway place,' I said, 'this very night.'

She sighed, there was a moment's pause, then she embraced my body with force, and said: 'In Cairo, don't the girls do this?'

Instead of being pleased, I was suddenly angry with myself. I should never have given the two shillings to Waseefa. It was as if I was trying to buy these moments of pleasure from her; I was as bad as those men who seduced poor girls in the magazine stories. I was bitterly ashamed.

If I had not promised the bottle of perfume, she would not have come to the sycamore so late at night; if I had not given her the florin, she would not have embraced me now. Waseefa guessed none of what I was feeling. 'Don't be so timid!' she said, laughing at my solemn face. 'Come on!' And she pulled me by force through the gate of the prayer-place, and tumbled me on to the ground. But I felt corroded by shame and repentance, I could only think of sin and of seduction, and Waseefa became aware of this, and stopped embracing me, and drew away, her own face suddenly as miserable as mine.

'Gracious, you are still only a child. Why lead me to the river at night under false pretenses? Little brother, of little use!'

I tried to explain to her about sin, and shame, and repentance, but in vain. Despite all my words, she burst out:

'By the Prophet, I can't understand a word you're saying. Perhaps it's because I am ignorant, I don't understand the language ofeffendis.'

She rushed out of the place and stood alone by the river. Then turned to me with a new note in her voice.

'But listen, this is important. By all you hold dear, don't speak a word of this to anyone. Not a word, I beg of you. This village is full of scandalmongers. If you told them … Please, please, I've never done this before, never …'

And very tenderly she kissed my head and put her arms around my shoulder, saying how loyal we must both be to each other. And I felt overwhelmed with pity for her, and wished that somehow I could be rich and could give her all she needed. Suddenly as we stood in silence by the bank, we heard the sound of a solitary flute, very piercing, not far off, seeming to come from behind us. She trembled and for a moment panicked; then we discovered that it came from the boat, and not from land. Her mood changed from fear to excitement in a moment. She rushed down to the edge of the water and wanted to begin exchanging badinage with the people in the boat; this was a custom in the villages, and people would shout really obscene things to passing boats, and their crews would shout back, respecting nothing. But I restrained her, and the boat passed quietly, and we heard a rough male voice singing on the deck.

'A galleon full of beauties,' it sang, 'in the eastern port:
You who love fair girls are killed without retort …
You who love dark girls … unripe, no fruit …'

The rough song restored me to delight, and the words gave me of a sudden the feeling that I was really a man, and could accomplish anything. And I kissed Waseefa firmly on her cheek. And she gently smiled, and at the same time the song grew further and further off, until it was lost in the darkness of night. Waseefa turned to me sadly and said:

'If only we could spend our whole life in singing and dancing, eating and drinking, if only we could live without worrying all our life. For a moment she was silent, then kicking off her slippers she dangled her feet in the water. They made quiet little ripples below.

'If only I could wake up one morning at home and find beside my bed a pitcher full of florins.'

Then she stood up, drying her feet on the hem of her dress, and she gave me one last kiss. She had to go. Her father was at work on a distant field, by the big canal, and she must take him his supper. I was alarmed at the thought of her going all alone to the canal, but she brushed aside such fears; even though her father was no longer Chief Guard, there was no one in the village who would dare to treat her disrespectfully. What about Alwani, I asked? He would certainly be back by his watermelons by this time. To this she retorted that she feared no one at all in the village. She had lived in the town, she had learnt many things there; she knew that neither Alwani, nor the Sheikh who employed him, nor yet the Magistrate himself counted for anything. Everyone went in fear of the official above him. The Magistrate who was omnipotent in the village, was subservient to the governor of the province, and he had been seen kissing the hand of the Minister of the Interior, when that official had visited the school where her sister's husband worked.

As for Alwani, the last time he had come to their house, she had been washing her father's clothes. Alwani had stood staring at her, and Waseefa had picked up the washing tray and hit him over the head with it, and he had gone off in silence. 'But you know he wants to marry you?' This made her laugh. If Alwani wanted, let him come and work as a labourer for her father, or as a shepherd; if he wanted to get married, let him take one of the migrant girls who went from farm to farm, working by the day. Such were worthy of him! They sold their labour, having nothing else to offer, not owning even a scrap of soil for themselves. 'Those who have no soil, have nothing, not even honour!' This was the reason they flirted with Alwani, poor wretched girls who lived for eating only, moving from place to place, offering themselves to men like Alwani, who regarded them as of no more value than a cob of corn they might pinch from their employers' land.

I understood nothing of Waseefa's outbursts, or of the bitterness which underlay her words. But as we moved off into the night (I was walking a few yards ahead of her, as she had asked me, so that we should not be seen together) I heard her say to herself, in her saddest voice:

'Ah, my poor Kadra! Every fiesta, and you're worth no more than a piece of corn!'

So ended our meeting, and all that night I could not sleep for thinking of Waseefa, wishing that I was able to help her, or that I was old enough to get married.

To get married ... The very idea would put the world against me; my father, my mother, my whole family. I was not yet a man, I was only twelve.

The next morning I wished I had spent the whole night with her under the sycamore. I repeated over and over again what she had said to me, and what I had said to her; and new things came into my mind which I should have said to her, but did not. Just as I was on the point of going to her house, my father told me to put on my shoes: he was going to take me to the neighbouring town to see the oculist.

Every summer I suffered from the oculist, but it was impossible to refuse. The oculist was a grim-faced, harsh voiced person in dark glasses. He used to discuss the Constitution with my father, the elections, the crisis, and what the English were up to. I knew my father enjoyed these discussions and shared most of the oculist's opinions. So that morning my father and I rode to the town in a horse-drawn cab, and the oculist prescribed for me a pair of dark glasses like his own, which my father bought me. He then left me in a cafe kept by an Armenian, where I passed the time eating baklawa and reading the newspapers, till my father collected me and we rode home together.

Sitting beside my father, I felt ashamed to let my thoughts dwell on Waseefa. I turned them instead to my dreams of school, of my new jacket and long trousers. I suddenly asked my father for a new suit. This request shook him. Like every other father at that time, he found such a request difficult to grant. Like other fathers, he tried to keep his financial difficulties secret, to save his face in the eyes of the world. He never had much cash himself.

After a while he said that perhaps God would make it possible for us, only later in the summer, before term started, not now, in the first week of the holidays.

The cab left the main road and took the path that ran

from the town to our village, along the river bank. Suddenly we saw four women on the road, one of them in a coloured dress. My eyes were still smarting from the drops, and I took off my glasses to see better.

'Put them on again,' my father said crossly, 'and keep them on, except at night.'

I was terrified lest he should notice that I was interested in Waseefa. Our cab reached the girls, and three of them turned their backs to us, but the fourth, Waseefa, who had spied me in the cab, smiled to us as we passed. I was on the point of jumping down into the road, but then the cab reached our house. I stood, turning to look for Waseefa.

'Stop dawdling, boy. The sun is hot, go up and rest your eyes.'

From my bedroom window I saw Waseefa pass with her pitcher. I wanted to leap down in front of her, and ask her to see me again by the sycamore. But it was too late. I then thought she might return to the river for more water. But she did not. I had to wait until after sunset, when standing by the door of our house, I saw her pass with some other girls. They all smiled at me, and I whispered urgently to Waseefa. 'Meet me like yesterday, after supper.'

Immediately we had eaten, I left the house and this time I was not frightened of the road. My head was filled with the things I should have said and done the previous night. I wanted to make up for lost opportunity.

I reached the sycamore. There was no one there.

I searched the prayer-place and the waterwheel. No one.

Angrily I turned back to the village, looking over my shoulder continually in case Waseefa should be behind.

Suddenly I saw a woman wearing a black dress. Waseefa, without a doubt! I rushed back to the river. But the woman crossed into a field, and then vanished in the darkness. The field was full of melons, the melons guarded by Alwani. I was filled with rage. She had lied to me when she had told me about Alwani. She was having a love affair with him, and was making him promise not to tell anyone, just as she had made me.

I was filled with a rage that was all the worse for being impotent. I ran home sweating, and in front of my house found Abdul Hadi waiting. He whispered that my father had been hunting for me throughout the whole village; if I went in quickly it would be for the best, and he would guarantee that he would take my part. 'But quickly,' he repeated, for he wanted to go to his waterwheel. On the nights that his wheel was turning, he would go and watch by it all night, singing interminable ballads about love and heroes, while the water raised by the wheel would pour through a little canal under the bank, and then pass in a circle round his field, flowing in little runnels dug by his hoe, until all the earth was moist. Sometimes I would spend the whole day, till dusk, sitting with Abdul Hadi by his wheel, listening to his songs. But my family never allowed me to spend the nights with him. It was felt somehow improper that I, a boy being educated in Cairo, should do such a thing; this feeling was shared by Abdul Hadi.

This night the wheel was not turning, but my thoughts were so confused I did not ask him where he was going. I was thinking of the blow I had suffered in seeing Waseefa go into the melon-field; I was thinking of my angry father and his thin cane; I was planning how I could slip into the house and put on some more clothes under my gallabya before I met him.

'What were you doing, down by the river, just now?'

Abdul Hadi's face had been expressionless, but a sly smile was now playing on his lips.

My anger fought with my tears. 'You want to marry Waseefa? Well, go down to the river and see who she's with.'

Abdul Hadi picked up his long staff and burst out in a fury: his oaths and his thumping stick resounded as he ran off. He had forgotten his promise to intercede with my father! With a heavy heart I went indoors and put on all the clothes I possessed, till my body looked like a pumpkin under my gallabya. When he saw me, my father fought down his smile and said in real anger that never again must I leave the house after supper without his permission.

When I was in bed, my father's anger and also his smile were with me all the night, and also the figure of the woman vanishing in the dark into the fields. Was it Waseefa? Was it someone else? Who could tell?

PART TWO

I WAS TWELVE and I had thought myself a man, ready not only for the struggles with authority which the demonstrations involved, but also for love. But I was still a child, and my summer was a child's summer: largely spent indoors, reading, studying my books, playing with other children. I wore my dark glasses. I obeyed my father.

But men like Abdul Hadi, who were not too young, had a different summer. It went on beyond the threshold of my father's house, but I built from what I saw and heard a picture more vivid than anything I read in my school books. Abdul Hadi and Waseefa were more real to me than the Caliphs and generals of history, their events more meaningful.

That night, for example, Abdul Hadi rushed off into the night, his stick throwing up dust like drops of darkness. He arrived at Alwani's field and peered narrowly through his eyes in the hopes of discerning something from the darkness that merged with the darkness of the earth. But he could see nothing at all, and no sound could be heard but the sound of his own angry breath. He whirled his stick in the air, then held it under his chin while he rolled up his sleeves. Then he held it behind his head in his two hands, and so advanced into the field, ready to fight. He came to the place where Alwani used to sit, and to sleep. There was nothing there, only a melon rind, which he kicked away, and a jar of cold water, from which he drank greedily, making an aggressive noise with his lips – and a cheap cup for tea, and a black kettle. Suddenly he saw a woollen rug, which Alwani used as a blanket against the dews of dawn ... it was heaped up. ... In a new rage Abdul Hadi picked up the rug in one hand, his stick ready in the other. But there was nothing under it, except the black earth. Relieved, he put his stick back on his shoulders and continued to stride through the furrows of the field, kicking at every melon which he saw.

Searching the riverbank, he shouted provocatively into the night: 'Come here, Alwani! Come here, you Beduin boy!'

And suddenly Abdul Hadi remembered the truth: he had seen Alwani that very evening outside Sheikh Yusif's shop. Alwani, the poor Beduin, who owned nothing, who had no relations in the village, whose only possession was his gun, whose only skill was at the stick-game and at guarding fields, used to buy his sugar, tea, and tobacco, every evening at Sheikh Yusif's, and at the same time he would join the group sitting there, for a chat, before the village went to bed, and he would go off alone to watch in the fields. He had also seen Alwani with Kadra, in the evening, while Kadra was waiting for an ox to drop its dung, which she would mould into a fuel-pat, and Abdul Hadi remembered the obscenities which Kadra had uttered about the ox ... Kadra, a girl who danced at every wedding, a girl who would openly discuss sexual relations, on whatever occasion, and who would sell herself cheaply on a feast day, or a harvest celebration.

Abdul Hadi sighed with relief. Alwani and Kadra were of the same kind, both should consort together. Both lived in the village without property or family. Kadra's relations had cast her out when she went to work for a rich young bachelor, who had an estate of thirty acres. Mahmoud Bey had got rid of her after two years' service, when her looks had still been fresh, her breasts still firm. And now, she had come back to work in the fields, or to do odd jobs in houses where the women did not go out.

Singing a mournful song, Abdul Hadi came to his wheel, and the place where the women filled their jars. Here he had heard the dirty songs of Kadra, seen her obscene gestures which shocked the other girls. As when Muhammad Effendi had passed by, the schoolmaster, in his striped gallabya with its foreign-style collar, his shiny shoes, his elegant flywhisk, his long white cap.

By the river there was a deserted windmill. It had belonged to Mahmoud Bey, had been burnt down, and was no longer used for anything ... except for Kadra's assignations.

Suddenly a horrible thought. What if Waseefa was using the windmill with someone? What if her friend Kadra had brought her here, had introduced her to someone ... to Muhammad Effendi? And feverishly he began to search every corner of the place, down to the holes where the snakes lay. But without result, there was no one there.

Back he went to his wheel, and in the immense solitude of night he felt an urgent need to talk to someone.

The earth itself seemed to him a symbol of strength, of that which will endure forever, and of honour! In all the night there was nothing to see. And yet he knew it all, he knew every inch of it, every detail. This land was his own life and his own history. When a boy Abdul Hadi had been given a little hoe, the same tool that his father had carried before him. And when he had grown up, and his father had died, the hoe had grown too. He knew the history of this land, of its crops, of its beasts, since the time he had first tethered a buffalo. That had been when he was eight ... he remembered hammering the wedge into the earth. Not one detail connected with this land would he ever forget, and after him his son would inherit his memories with the land itself. The land never let you down. His father had planted *berseem*, had changed to cotton, then to beans, or perhaps sugar cane, and always the land was generous, if you were generous to the land. If you were faithful to the land, if you tended it and cared for it, it would care for you. An acre ... a separate acre: it gave him a special standing in the village. Not only in the village: when he visited the town, he could sit with his uncle in the Armenian cafi, with the Omda, with all the notables. An acre ... How many people in the village owned as much? Even the Omda did not own more. Of course, to be an Omda he had to have ten acres, but his family had arranged this, with fraudulent title deeds, so that he could assume office. No, Abdul Hadi was one of ten who owned an acre, or more, in the village. But how good it would be if his brother, the employee in the city, would give him his acre too. That would make two. But that was not important. Let his brother take the income from his land, he had a wife and children to support. Abdul Hadi had his feet deep in the earth ... that was better than living as an effendi in the city!

Abdul Hadi crouched on the earth for a moment. He had a great desire to talk to someone. If only Waseefa was sitting by him as his wife, or she working at the wheel with a great ox, he irrigating the land a little way off, both of them singing as the water trembled over the earth. He threw away his cigarette. He felt love for everything, for Waseefa, for Alwani, for the village, and he began singing in a rough melancholy voice;

'Wretched, perplexed, with drooping wing, the dove,
'Settled one day, unflying, by his love'

As his voice resounded across the spaces of the dark, the only other noise was the creaking waterwheel on the other side of the river. Suddenly a cheerful voice broke the night.

'Hullo, there! Don't stop, Abdul Hadi! Give us a romantic song, a song from your romantic heart!'

Abdul Hadi stood up.

'Welcome, welcome, noble Sheikh of the Arabs!'

And striding from the bank he came to the melon field and saw a small fire burning, a kettle bubbling away in its heart. And Alwani, affecting a Beduin accent, stood up to greet his guest.

'Welcome to you, noblest of the youth! Welcome, prince! Accept my tea!'

And the two of them crouched down by the fire. In a courtly gesture he made as though to spread the rug for Abdul Hadi.

'Repose upon it, noblest of the Arabs! By Allah, I am honoured.'

'Come off it,' Abdul Hadi laughed, 'are we city gentlemen with pot bellies that we should need a carpet? Do we smoke ready-made cigarettes? Have we perhaps turned into Beys of a sudden?'

And both of them sat on the bare earth, laughing uproariously at the joke.

Alwani poured the boiling tea, after it had stewed for many minutes, in a thin jet into Abdul Hadi's cup, and after a sip Abdul Hadi said: 'This is real Arab tea, excellent! Thank you.' But despite his pleasure in the tea, his thoughts seemed preoccupied, and Alwani, who had meanwhile dropped his high-flowing Beduin speech, said: 'The water-wheel's working?'

'No,' Abdul Hadi replied, briefly.

Then suddenly he turned to Alwani and said: 'Where were you this evening?'

'First the wedding, then buying tea from Sheikh Yusif.'

The mention of Sheikh Yusif launched Alwani into a long complaint about the grocer, how ruthless he was, and how unwilling to extend credit, despite the roaring trade he was doing in the village. Alwani had to plead to get his provisions; that evening Sheikh Yusif had at first refused to give him anything. Finally, he had thrown a packet of tea at his head, saying it was the last time he would get anything without paying for it.

'Don't worry, things will improve,' said Abdul Hadi, absent-mindedly.

'Improve, how can they? And when? If when I'm paid I owe it all, and more, to Sheikh Yusif?'

Abdul Hadi had forgotten the tea. Filling his cup,

Alwani asked him casually if he could perhaps lend him four shillings.

'Four shillings! Can you even get the smell of four shillings from me? I am broke, utterly broke, it's useless asking me.'

Alwani sucked through his lips pessimistically.

'It's a black year for all of us. Did you hear that even the Bey had his farm confiscated from him?'

'You're a year out of date,' replied Abdul Hadi. 'That was last year. Now there's a new Ministry, the Bey's friends are in office, and don't forget, he's the nephew of the Pasha. They are the government.'

'But your brother lives in Cairo, Abdul Hadi. That puts him in the government too.'

Abdul Hadi smiled, was silent a moment, then said, 'My boy, this government is theirs only, the decisions are theirs only. The Pasha belongs to the People's Party, and this party has ruined all Egypt. My brother in the government, you say? Oh no, think again.'

Alwani began describing his better days, days when he had been in the employment of Mahmoud Bey. At that time Mahmoud Bey had raised sheep on his estate and had employed Alwani to take them to market. This had given him many opportunities to fill his purse. There were always very small lambs which he could say had died on the road, or had been mislaid, and he could sell these on his own account and profit to the extent of a shilling or two. But after one of his visits to Cairo, the Bey had returned in sudden need of cash, and had sold all his flocks. This had put Alwani out of a job. After much entreaty, he had been allowed to stay on, guarding the orange groves. Here, too, he had had opportunities. The village women used to come and offer him money for windfalls. But this profitable business was spoilt for him by Kadra. At that time she was working in Mahmoud Bey's house, and had ideas above her station. One day she came when Alwani was up one of the trees, and asked him for a particularly succulent orange. Alwani had refused, saying that not even the Bey could eat from this tree; and yet she wanted to gobble up the whole orchard, piece by piece. In a rage, Kadra had picked the orange she wanted for herself. Alwani had come down, thrown mud at her, and hit her. Kadra had rushed off to the Bey and told him everything. The Bey had then begun to spy on Alwani, until one day he caught him red-handed, selling windfalls to the village women. He had beaten him, kicked him, and taken away his purse with all that it contained. 'Did you ever hear such tyranny, Abdul Hadi?'

Abdul Hadi answered with only half of his attention.

'Things will get better one day, Alwani. Your God will help you … Our God will help us.'

His thoughts were on Waseefa. What if she had gone to the Bey, that dandified creature in his flowing gallabya of valuable cashmere?

Though why should she do such a thing?

Mahmoud Bey used to ride on a splendid horse, proud, nimble, beautifully groomed, along the one road that led to the town, and there on the river bank he had been known to pick up village girls. But would he dare to do such a thing with the daughter of Muhammad Abu Suweilim, who had been Chief Guard? And would Waseefa herself stoop to such a thing? His thoughts were confused, and while Alwani sipped his tea, Abdul Hadi asked him point-blank if Mahmoud Bey had been anywhere near that night. Alwani clicked his teeth to say 'No'. Had anyone else been along the bank by the river? Again, 'No'. Abdul Hadi got up to go. Alwani objected that his guest had not drunk the three cups which were part of the regulation of Beduin hospitality. But Abdul Hadi was too worried to perform the etiquette, and with a half-smile he took his leave. But just as he was about to go, Alwani froze: he had heard the sounds of people, some distance off.

'Have you brought your revolver?' he whispered, getting out his shotgun. At the same time he clutched under the rug for some rocks. 'Load it, and let's get down to the bank and hide there.'

'Why on earth …?'

'There are men coming towards the village, up to no good.'

Abdul Hadi raised his voice. 'Men? What men? Men coming to do what? In the middle of the night? What have they to do with the village?'

The noise came nearer, the sounds became words and phrases, in an accent different from that of the village, and then two men appeared riding bicycles.

'The men of the night come to us on steel donkeys,

speaking a foreign accent. They are probably from London!'

Both men laughed, and Alwani put down his gun as two strangers came into full view. One of them was dressed in a western suit and a tarboosh, the other in a silk gallabya, white jacket and woolen cap. They stopped right in front of Alwani and Abdul Hadi; the one in the gallabya alighted first, holding his bicycle with one hand, with the other taking hold of the bicycle ridden by the man in the tarboosh. The latter shouted down to them:

'Salaam Alekum!'

Abdul Hadi and Alwani scrambled up the bank, and Alwani greeted the men with his Beduin voice: 'Welcome, oh Arabs! Welcome! Let us offer you tea, let us prepare you a feast! Let us sacrifice a sheep! Welcome, oh Arabs!'

The man in the gallabya cut him short.

'Listen to me, both of you. Which of you is working his waterwheel?'

'They're from the 'rigation,' Alwani whispered; then in a loud voice, 'No one here's turning his waterwheel.' Abdul Hadi was familiar with the faces of the men from the provincial Irrigation Department, from the chief engineer down to the ordinary workmen. But this engineer's face was new to him, the one he knew never rode a bicycle. But he recognized the face of the man in the gallabya. This fellow would come back to the village, after the engineer and his assistant had stopped a wheel turning, and start it up again, for a bribe of four shillings. But this year no one in the village could afford such a sum. Abdul Hadi said to the workman, 'Can't you look for yourselves, and see if any wheel is working?'

47

This made the engineer angry. 'We know you fellahin, and the tricks and deceits for which you are famous. We want a straight answer.'

Alwani dropped his Beduin accent, and in a normal voice, but with many servile expressions of respect, such as calling the Engineer "Chief Engineer", swore by his life and his honour and by God, that he and Abdul Hadi had simply been sitting by the river.

'Then who,' asked the man in the gallabya, 'was that girl we saw, about an hour back, disappearing into the fields? Who was she? Whose wheel is she working?'

'A girl? ... a girl working a waterwheel? ...

And where was the animal? Are you crazy?'

'Hold your tongue,' said the engineer. But Abdul Hadi was murmuring to himself ... 'A girl ... Where's she now?'

The engineer, not hearing what he said, continued: 'You want us, I suppose, to sit up all night watching your waterwheels? Then break them ...'

Angrily Abdul Hadi replied, 'Break them? Why should you break them, even if you find them working? We still have five days to go, five days in which we can use them for irrigation as and how we like. Or are you leading up to a four-shilling piece?'

Abdul Hadi's tone enraged the engineer, who turned angrily to the workman in the gallabya, asking him what this meant. The workman foolishly replied that it had been customary to accept such a sum, for turning a blind eye, but that in the present circumstances this should be raised to at least ten shillings a wheel. The new engineer warned him that he would be punished when they got back to the Irrigation Department.

Alwani let out a triumphant guffaw. 'Hurray! The government's divided against itself.'

But Abdul Hadi seriously challenged the engineer, who ground his teeth with irritation at this discussion in which he was being involved. 'The situation is this: instead often days, you now have five days a month. The official order was sent to the Omda several days ago.' 'The Omda? I don't care what order the Omda has had, or not had. I intend to work my wheel the day after tomorrow, and if anyone tries to stop me, I'll throw him down the well.'

The workman said soothingly: 'We all know that you are an honest, straightforward man ... someone who understands. This is a Government order: irrigation cut to five days instead of ten for the foreseeable future. Outside these five days, no use of waterwheels or canals. These are the regulations, so stop making such a fuss.'

'Oh, no, sir! I won't make a fuss, I'll just let my maize die of drought. So will the others who've not yet watered their dry land.'

Alwani broke in appeasingly: 'Abdul Hadi, these are Government orders, the matter's finished.' But Abdul Hadi's only reply was to thwack the earth with his stick and to shout with all his force: 'You call this a Government? A Government which steals half our water – and for whose benefit, Alwani? You know, as well as I do, for the Pasha, the Pasha who's recently bought a stretch of new land, land not fit for dogs to eat off, and he wants to improve it by taking our water.

Wonderful, wonderful, this Government of ours! Stop the wheels, shut the canals. I can see blood will be flowing before water …' And shaking his stick he rushed along the road to the village, the Effendi and the workman making way for him as he passed. His stick could be heard pounding the earth, his voice shouting imprecations against the Government, and he vanished into the darkness. 'And tomorrow or the day after I shall work my wheel, as I like, when I like.'

In silence the two Government officials rode off towards the town.

No sooner had they gone than a female figure, draped in black, emerged from the undergrowth by the river, pushing aside the tall rushes. 'Curse you, you men from the town,' she murmured, 'curse you for my poor suffering feet, and Waseefa, what a job you gave me, all for a boy who barely comes to your waist. Is that what a city education does for a man, makes him so attractive? Just as well she didn't come herself, like last night, or these men would have seen her, certainly …' Alwani's eyes were fixed on the road which the two men had taken. When they were at a safe distance, he burst out, 'Government! My respects to you, Government,' and he spat contemptuously. 'You dismiss us from our posts, you imprison us in your gaols … Filthy Government …'

Alwani turned, hearing a woman's laugh, and saw a figure dancing coquettishly in front of him, at the same time imitating satirically the vowels of the engineer: 'Yes! No! How! Now! May you rot, you men from the city, with your tongues as twisted as a harlot's …'

'Shush, Kadra, shush, don't let the world know you've

come to me.' Then flirtatiously, in the rude words by which the village people express intimacy, he whispered: 'Come to me … may you have your hide well beaten … Come to me … let me slaughter you! I have a melon …'

Delighted, Kadra sang out: 'Of course I've come to you, Sheikh of the Arabs!' And she danced in front of him, wiping her sun-coarsened face with her hand, letting her loose breasts jump inside her dress. But suddenly she slowed her dance, and said with a note of caution: 'But not if you treat me as you treated my cousin …'

'It wasn't my fault,' Alwani protested. 'And since she went to the town, I hear she's had a huge success. I promised her a bushel of maize, but somehow I never got round to getting it. Otherwise she would have had it, certainly.' He dropped the tones of apology. 'Come to me, or I'll cut your throat! Come and choose which melon you like the best.'

With his bare feet, Alwani kicked away the stones that lay round his gun. He picked up the gun, looked at it disgustedly: 'I've not cleaned the barrel since before Ramadhan, I've been so busy.'

He took Kadra's hand, and they sat down on the earth side by side. 'Strange how pretty you are,' he said, 'and as sweet as sugar, but you need to be beaten, beaten in your heart.' And he spread the rug for Kadra. But she pushed him, hitting his chest with the palms of her hands. 'Not such a hurry,' she said, 'first the melon!' He overpowered her. 'If we stay together till morning, everything is ours!' Kadra laughed. 'If only it could be … Ah, well …' And she pulled the blanket on top of them.

Back at home, Abdul Hadi thought no more of Waseefa.

He rolled cigarette after cigarette till he had finished his packet of tobacco. The waterwheel … the canal … the water cut by half … the young maize pushing its frail green shoots through the caked earth, the loveliest sight of the year, the earth yellow with spring ... all this condemned to die of drought. At the orders of the Government, he, Abdul Hadi, known to everyone as a skillful farmer, would allow his maize to die of thirst? No, never! Come what might, he would work his wheel the day after tomorrow, in the evening; he would plant and irrigate as he wished.

Next morning the sun rose over the village streets, filled as usual with animals on their way to the fields; and the women herding them knew every detail of what had passed between Abdul Hadi and the engineers. So did the men. Kadra told everyone, only omitting the reasons which had taken her to the river so late at night.

Abu Suweilim had also had a brush with the engineers. They had threatened dire punishments if he did not shut off his canal, and to avoid trouble, and to disprove their allegations that he was a troublemaker, always against the Government, he had complied with their orders, and blocked the waterflow; but early in the morning, before sunrise, he had gone back and opened the canal again. Other people had had similar experiences.

Abdul Hadi did as he promised. He went to his field and started the waterwheel. He waded bare-foot through the mud, opening the runnels to the flowing water; while to guard the wheel, and encourage the blindfold cow if she stood still, he left a small boy, hired for tuppence-halfpenny.

In the late evening the engineers arrived and found the wheel working. They wrote Abdul Hadi's name down on their list, as they had previously written down the name of Abu Suweilim. And the little boy ran terrified to the village, telling everyone he met that the Government had smashed all the waterwheels by the river.

Abu Suweilim's house was crowded with women and girls, while the men sat outside the front-door, by the threshold. And the boys of the village, equally curious, infiltrated like cats among the grown-ups, asking the same questions, till they were shooed off by the men. One of the boys, less afraid than the others, asked Abu Suweilim why the men had written his name down.

Abu Suweilim sat in silence, but Sheikh Yusif turned to the boy in rage and shouted: 'Your curiosity will get you into trouble ... Who are you? Who's your father? Mannerless brat!'

'I am Shaaban's nephew.'

'Hell take you! Go back to your sums. Stop poking your nose into grown-ups' business – mind your own, if you have any – you plague me,' and turning to the others he said: 'He is a pest. Comes to my shop. Asks the price of tobacco. I say, "five corn cobs". "No," he says, "four." "Right, four," I agree. He says: "three." Is this a village? Is this education?'

At this point, Abu Suweilim, till then silent, broke in to say, with a quiet calm voice that reflected both his anxiety, and his consciousness of his former status as Chief Guard, that it was true, the Government men had come in connection with water, not with elections, or taxes.

Hearing his words, some of the boys whispered that Abu

Suweilim would spend this night in prison, as his name had been written on the black list.

Confused conversation, confused ideas, all day, from the time in the morning when Abu Suweilim had returned from his fields, and nobody had gone home to eat. Abu Suweilim himself had not eaten all day. And now the sun set over the flat roofs of the village. Constant talk, constant thoughts; one moment an outburst of rage, the next a return to calm; and all the time, as they thought of a solution to the problem, Abu Suweilim clapped one hand against the other in perplexity. 'Cut half our water off. Five days instead of ten? Why? Why? And how can we irrigate our fields?'

As they were talking, Abdul Hadi suddenly arrived, barefoot, without his gallabya, which he had left at the wheel, in his undershirt, his feet still covered with the mud of his field. With the usual greetings, he sat down in a place vacated for him. Inside the house the women crowded round, repeating the name of Abdul Hadi, and with a louder voice Kadra could be heard telling the story of his encounter with the engineers.

Abu Suweilim turned to Abdul Hadi. 'What news do you bring? Tell us! What has happened now? They'll take the water from us, will they? We know for whose benefit! What a black day this has been. First they take away my position as Chief Guard, and we are silent. Then they send Sheikh Hassouna to the other end of Egypt, and we say nothing. And now they will let our crops die of thirst, and what do we do? Have we become so impotent that they can do with us whatever they like? Are we men, or members of a harem?'

Not a word did Abdul Hadi say in reply. But his nostrils flared with rage, and he rubbed the thick hair on his bare chest, matted with mud from the fields, and one boy whispered to another: 'Look! Abdul Hadi has one lion's hair on his chest, he's looking for it, to rub ...' This interruption angered one of the men, who picked up a little stick and chased the boys off with it, cursing loudly. Whereupon Sheikh Shinawi raised his voice to suggest that everyone present invoke the name of the Prophet.

Waseefa inside the house tried to peep at Abdul Hadi, but she could see nothing; all the men had their backs to the house, and all she could see was the little boys who had been chased away, trying to worm their way back. Sheikh Shinawi asked everyone to join him in the Chapter of the Koran called *Ya-Seen,* as a way of invoking God's vengeance on the men from the Irrigation Department. At this Abdul Hadi could keep silent no longer. He asked with ironical politeness that the reverend Sheikh should either think of something better or keep his mouth shut and let others do the thinking. The Sheikh trembled with rage.

'Ah! You can sink so low, Abdul Hadi? You can blaspheme so openly? I've long known that you never bend your knees in prayer. So be it! Let the rest of us remember the evening prayer, let the rest of us go to the mosque.'

'The evening prayer won't run away. Can't we thrash out this problem first? Where do you think the evening's going to run to?'

'May the spirit of God strike you down, you and your blasphemies!' And he turned to the men sitting down. 'Come on, you and you – time for prayer. God may then give you abundance.'

And some of the youths who worked as labourers in the fields got up – labour was not in demand at that moment, and they had nothing to lose in going to the mosque; possibly the Sheikh would find them a job. The only ones left behind were Abu Suweilim, Abdul Hadi, Sheikh Yusif and Muhammad Effendi. There were also some little girls, singing and dancing in front of the corn mill that stood near Abu Suweilim's house.

The sight of the little girls at play reminded Abdul Hadi that Waseefa, too, had once played in the same way in the same place and before her, another generation had done the same thing. Her big sister, now married and living away in the town. And after Waseefa, a new generation would sing the same sad, yet beautiful songs, would play in the same way, would make the same traditional movements in their dancing and would beat out the same rhythms on an upturned tray.

Sheikh Yusif was trying to speak, but his words were drowned by the noise of the little girls, and he shouted to them angrily:

'Do I leave my shop just to hear you, you little gypsies? Has our village become a place for dancing-girls?' And he chased them off into the distance.

'Could I have a drink of cold water?' Abdul Hadi asked.

Inside the house he found Waseefa, and shouted to her: 'Give me a drink! Don't you have a jug of cool water?' And lowering his voice he said tenderly:

'Passing your way, in thirst, you let me drink:
Disastrous jug! One free you threw in clink!'

Changing his tone, Abdul Hadi asked why she had been to the river by night. This sudden question terrified Waseefa, she began to deny everything. Abdul Hadi went on to describe the engineers. This came as a relief to Waseefa, who could say truthfully that the girl by the river was not her, but Kadra.

And seeing that she had no more to fear, she began to upbraid Abdul Hadi for asking her these questions: he had no rights over her, she was not his daughter, nor his sister. She did so in a loud voice, and Abdul Hadi tried to calm her, tried to get her to whisper, in case someone outside would hear what they were saying.

Waseefa tapped Abdul Hadi on the chest, as a token of apology. But their talk had been heard. From outside Abu Suweilim bellowed, 'Where on earth have you gone to, Abdul Hadi?' Abdul Hadi replied with a defensive shout: 'Am I not to drink, then? Is that what you mean, Uncle?' His uncle replied, 'Drink if you want to ... the time you've taken you could water a whole field.' Abdul Hadi picked up the water-jug and drank loudly from it, then returned to the threshold, smacking his lips. Abu Suweilim looked at him suspiciously. Flicking his fly-whisk Muhammad Effendi said, 'You've certainly kept us waiting.'

'Kept you waiting? From what – catching the train? An hour I've sat here and this is your first utterance, that I've kept you waiting. Can't you think of a solution without me – is that it ?'

Muhammad Effendi replied as though the whole matter bored him.

'So you solve our problems for us, do you? You who create them for us!'

'No god but God!' Abdul Hadi burst out. 'You're just a boy, Muhammad Effendi.'

'Just a boy! You dare to call me boy!' And Muhammad Effendi got to his feet, clutching his flywhisk. 'Boy yourself, Abdul Hadi, or rather, sixty boys rolled into one!'

Only the intervention of Sheikh Yusif and Abu Suweilim prevented the two men from starting a fight, so angry were they both. Abu Suweilim urged both of them to calm down, to sit down, to forget the angry words that had passed between them. And Sheikh Yusif pointed out that everyone who had ever been born, himself included, had been a boy once, so there was no particular sting in the word 'boy' to justify such a quarrel. Little by little the two men allowed themselves to be calmed down, if not reconciled, and each finally mumbled a half-meant apology to the other.

Just as they had re-settled themselves by the threshold, Sheikh Shinawi came back, followed by those who had joined him in the mosque. They returned to their places, and once again voices were raised in discussion of the disaster that had befallen the village. One man suggested going to the Omda.

'What crazy idea is that?' asked Sheikh Yusif. 'Did it come to you as inspiration in the mosque? God blight any such idea. Who is this Omda that you talk about? What good have we had out of this Omda since he took over our village?'

'All our difficulties are due to that idiot,' Abu Suweilim said emphatically.

These open attacks on the Omda alarmed some of the villagers, and Sheikh Shinawi, though he said nothing, showed by a shaking of his head what he really thought.

'We don't depend on the Omda,' Abdul Hadi said. 'Omda! You can have him.'

At this moment Alwani arrived, and going up to Sheikh Yusif he whispered something in his ear.

'The shop's closed! Wait till after the night prayers, then I'll see what I think about you. You can't get your tea and sugar by snatching it.'

Aggrieved, Alwani crouched on the ground, facing the threshold, his hands on his knees, near a group of workmen similarly squatting.

'People today have nothing but a tongue left: no heart, no generosity, no kindness.'

Returning to the Omda, Abu Suweilim said that he never consulted the people in the village. He had known all about the Government's decision to cut the water by half, and yet he had told no one in the village. He should have had the mosque drum beaten, should have announced the decision to everyone, as he had done on similar occasions before. But he had not even told Sheikh Shinawi. It had been deliberate. He wanted to surprise the village while the people were acting illegally, though in ignorance, and he wanted to have certain people – chosen by himself – caught and punished.

Sheikh Yusif added that this same Omda had supported the Government in the elections when everyone else had decided to boycott them. He had registered people's names just as he wished, and he had deceived many people by slyly insinuating that the new Constitution of the People's Party would be of benefit to them. Whereas in fact it had harmed the village in every way.

There was a moment's silence.

Suddenly Muhammad Effendi slapped his lap with his flywhisk. He had found the right solution! He prepared himself to announce it by clearing his throat, spitting on the ground in the direction of one of the seated workmen, and wiping his mouth with his immaculate handkerchief. What they must do was to write a petition to the Minister of Public Works. Mahmoud Bey was a friend of his, he could deliver it. Perhaps he might even secure an interview with the Prime Minister himself, Ismail Sidky Pasha.

Abu Suweilim immediately disapproved: experience proved that the Government could be moved by fear, never by shame. And when Muhammad Effendi tried to expound his idea, Abu Suweilim broke in irritably:

'Let the Government say what they like. Let them cut the water by half. But let us do what we want, let us continue to irrigate as we did before.'

This gave Muhammad Effendi the chance to show the advantages of his project. By all means let the village go on irrigating as before. At the same time the petition could do no harm, and it might do good, if its determined words frightened the Government into cancelling their new policy.

There was a general shaking of heads in agreement, and no one was more enthusiastic than Abdul Hadi. His face was suddenly transfixed with joy. 'Up, Muhammad Effendi, up and write it now! You write it, we'll put our seals or thumbmarks to it. And don't forget to insert a few of those words you educated people use in school ... I don't know, words like *whensoever, heretofore, inasmuch as*. And two or three phrases from the newspapers. That'll impress them.'

This was an opportunity for Alwani: 'Excellent, Abdul Hadi. But my uncle Sheikh Yusif knows all these words that so delight you. And more besides, many more! You write the petition, uncle! And we will make a collection, we will collect four or five shillings, to be a fee for your endeavours. You write the petition!'

Abdul Hadi only smiled at this new bribery by Alwani. 'Noble sheikh of the Arabs! Come out of your maize grove, come out and relax. Sheikh Yusif's not in need of money. And Muhammad Effendi will write the petition as a public service.'

'Why shouldn't Sheikh Shinawi write it?' Abu Suweilim asked. 'He could insert some powerful verses from the Koran. They might even convert the Government.'

Abdul Hadi said wickedly: 'Ah, yes, he would put in about Hell and the Judgment and Eternal Punishment. The Government would carry on their policy as before, and say, Why not ask your angels to send extra water from Heaven?'

Abdul Hadi's words threw the Sheikh into a rage, but Abdul Hadi stopped his tirade by making a promise: if the Petition succeeded, and if the water was restored to the village, then he would make a fiesta in honour of God, and would personally kill a goat in Sheikh Shinawi's honour. At the mention of the goat, the Sheikh's rage evaporated, but not his wits. 'Make it a sheep, make it a fat sheep, Abdul Hadi, my friend, and may God reward you! And make your promise secure by reciting with me the Opening Prayer.' And Abdul Hadi covered his face with the palms of his hands and recited the first verses of the Koran. All those present joined in as well.

'Now I shall go and write the Petition,' said Muhammad Effendi. 'I shall make it a mixture of entreaty and warning, and I shall embellish it with some of the mannerisms of Manfaluti.'

The mention of this name puzzled and impressed most of those present, including Abdul Hadi. 'Who is Manfaluti?' they whispered, and what are mannerisms?

Muhammad Effendi, the admirer of the essayist Manfaluti, was a small, thin man with a quiet voice. Weedy, with a scraggy neck, he shaved regularly and trimmed his moustache in a way followed by no one else in the village. Occasionally he would read a newspaper, and quote from it articles which caught his fancy. His gallabya was always spotless, its stripes sharply contrasting, and his yellow shoes were shiny. He wore his square white cap on the back of his head, so as to show his carefully combed hair, which he alone of all the villagers wore long. Another peculiarity: he would buy the strongest-smelling scents from the neighbouring town. He even carried a little bottle in his pocket wherever he went.

Turning over in his mind the phrases he would use, he saw that the staring faces of those around him were all in accord with his idea.

Abdul Hadi said: 'Sheikh Yusif, you go and fetch the pen and ink.'

Muhammad Effendi had already gone off for the paper. And while Sheikh Yusif went to his shop, Abu Suweilim went indoors and brought out his lamp Number Ten, which he only used on very important occasions. And he held this lamp over the head of Muhammad Effendi who had returned and had sat down on the large bench covered with reed matting. The men stood around in admiration. Muhammad Effendi read aloud each word as he wrote it, holding the paper across his knees, and dipping for ink in the pot held out by one of the men. And when he had finished, he read the whole thing right through, slowly, word by word, with great pride, explaining as he went any words which seemed difficult to his audience. And when all was done, and all explained, Sheikh Shinawi got up and fetched a little dust from the ground and sprinkled this over the wet ink.

And now that it was done, all those present signed it, either by pressing their thumbs on special ink which Sheikh Yusif had brought with him, or by using their seals: all this in an atmosphere of festivity and excitement, with Sheikh Shinawi uttering prayers that the affair should be blessed, and imprecations against Satan, lest he try to harm the village.

Only one last difficulty arose. Muhammad Effendi wanted to show the Petition to the Omda. Abu Suweilim, bitterly distrustful of the Omda's tricks, opposed any such idea. But Muhammad Effendi could not be dissuaded: he would show the Petition, as a matter of form, to the Omda, and then, first thing in the morning, he would present it to Mahmoud Bey. As the men rose to go, Kadra's voice broke out in a song of victory: the men of the village were lions, their sword was made of gold!

A week passed after the writing of the Petition. The village waited.

On Friday, after the noon prayers, Sheikh Shinawi picked up from the floor of the mosque the old, yellowed book from which he read a sermon every week, and put it in his pocket. He stood by the niche which points to Mecca and asked the people to wait. Then with a stately pace, smoothing his robust belly as he went and murmuring prayers beneath his breath, he climbed to the bench reserved for the reader of the Koran and stood in full view of the worshippers, resplendent in his Friday gallabya. Some of the men scratched their feet, while others looked up at the Sheikh expectantly.

'God sendeth down rain from Heaven to revive the earth when it dieth of thirst.'

The farmers were silent.

'Yet now we have waited a long time for water to refresh and revive our thirst-ridden land, but nothing has happened, neither a new decision from the Government, nor yet a miracle from Heaven.

'The reason for this is that God punisheth the wicked, and sendeth a curse on those who disobey his commandments, as he sent in times past on Aad and Thamud.'

The worshippers listened to each unctuous syllable as it rolled from the Sheikh's tongue, their thoughts on the thirsty earth. One could bear it no longer, and whispered to his neighbour that all this had nothing to do with Aad and Thamud; it was simply a question that the water had been cut off, and everyone knew it was the work of the Government, not of God.

And a young fellow at the far end of the mosque burst out:

'What nonsense is this? You mean that our God will send

you rain to water your land in summer? You mean that it was God who sent us this drought? Why should he punish us? Are we the only wicked village?'

Very angry, the Sheikh groped the air, as if for his cane, but he had left it outside. He cursed the young man as a blasphemer, an apostate, one possessed by Satan. His very presence in the holy place was a defilement. Let him get out, let him be thrown out, immediately, by the god-fearing farmers. But no one moved except the young man himself, who stood up in a good humour.

'Blessings on your holy place! I took time off from Mahmoud Bey's orchard to come to prayer, and I shall now go back there.'

But his departure did not quieten the Sheikh. Instead, he prayed that such impiety might be rewarded with Hell, and began to recite those verses from the Koran and those sayings of the Prophet that dealt with punishment and Hell. Strangely, he did not recite them in the classical language in which they are written, but translated them into the colloquial Arabic of the village, so that they seemed very near and very familiar, these stories of Moses and Pharaoh, of Aad and Thamud, as though they had taken place recently in a nearby village. And Abdul Hadi listened to all his outpourings in silence, not altogether at ease; he was not somebody who prayed regularly, every day, but only once a week in the mosque.

Abdul Hadi heard the same sermon, the same repetitions of threatening verses, that evening, after the last prayers, at the doorstep of Abu Suweilim. And once again he did not answer back, but listened politely. For while it was true that he was obsessed with the question of the water, he was also troubled by a new preoccupation. He had begun to notice that Kadra was always in Abu Suweilim's house. A girl without land, without relations, without honour, a girl with no morals and no control over her tongue, she was visiting Waseefa too often. Her voice could be heard, laughing and joking with Waseefa, by the men sitting outside. This was not good. Kadra had helped Muhammad Effendi, Abdul Hadi knew, to meet certain other girls, and even some respectable women. This was dangerous. Waseefa had shown her interest in Muhammad Effendi by her eagerness to serve the coffee herself. When he was not there, she let Kadra bring it, or handed it to her father on a tray, for him to serve.

But all the while the voice of Sheikh Shinawi, talking about Hell and punishment, reverberated behind Abdul Hadi's thoughts, and he was forced to pay attention, and in his own mind to answer back. So the lack of water was a divine punishment, because the village was irreligious? The village's punishment was the Pasha's reward. Yet did the Pasha pray? The Sheikh said that he gave alms, and the village did not. But what alms did the village have to give? At least the village said its prayers. And Abdul Hadi thought of other villages, far off, of which he had heard, where the landlords owned everything, where the farmers were hired serfs, owning nothing at all. Yet those landlords did not pray nor give a farthing in alms, and the wrath of God had not struck them. Their canals continued to flow merrily with water, their trees were bowed down with fruit. Such landlords would drink alcohol in the holy month of Ramadhan, they would seduce any young girl that took their fancy. Yet they were not struck down by the wrath of God, nor was their water cut off by the Government.

Perhaps if the Sheikh himself owned some land, perhaps if he had mixed his sweat with the earth, and perhaps if he had seen the tender maize shoots wilting like dying children, perhaps then he would have understood, and stayed silent. Even if he owned the merest vegetable patch, and had dug this with his hoe, and had sown it with seeds, perhaps then he would not have equated the action of the Government with the wrath of God. But the Sheikh was not a farmer. He was, with his preaching, more like a man who had something to sell, and provided he could sell it, let the earth perish with thirst! People with land sat in the full glare of the sun ... people like the Sheikh and Kadra were in the shade.

Such were Abdul Hadi's thoughts as the Sheikh continued to rant about hell fire, prayer, reward, punishment, curses, alms and destruction.

That evening Waseefa did not serve the coffee herself, but handed it on a tray to her father. With a quick elegant gesture Muhammad Effendi took the tray from her and himself distributed the coffee to the guests. His self-assurance brought a smile, but not a gentle one, to Abdul Hadi's lips, who with ill-concealed malice asked him what had happened to the Petition.

There was a moment's pause, then Muhammad Effendi replied that, as he had heard from the Omda, Mahmoud Bey had taken exception to the way in which the first Petition had been written, and was intending to write a new one himself.

Raising his voice, Abdul Hadi said that what he wanted to know about was the new Petition. 'We all know about the first one, Muhammad Effendi, we all know that Mahmoud Bey said farmers should never address the Government so impertinently, that he enquired what donkey had written the Petition.'

Abdul Hadi's loud voice reached inside the house, where Waseefa was sitting with Kadra on a large brick. Abdul Hadi was delighted to see his words embarrassing Muhammad Effendi. He now continued to mock Muhammad Effendi with a laugh that held no warmth.

'Of course everyone in the village knows about Mahmoud Bey calling you a donkey. The Omda has broadcast the story to the world. The whole of it ... And I know everything, yes, everything ... I understand every part of you and your actions, muddy them up though you may.'

And lowering his voice to a whisper, Abdul Hadi said, as if to himself: 'Four whole pounds ... every month ... four pounds with which to strut as lord of the earth ... and he just a donkey ...'

Before Abdul Hadi finished his muttering, and before Muhammad Effendi could reply, Sheikh Shinawi returned to his iteration of hell and punishment and destruction.

'What, are you boring us again with all this talk?' Abdul Hadi turned on the Sheikh. 'It was God who did this to us, was it? Not the engineers, not the Government? Why don't you go and look at the Pasha's land, all along the highway? If you did, you would see it awash with water, the river simply turned on to the earth, not needing pumps like ours. That is God's doing, Sheikh? No, no, you hold your tongue a little. Your words tear our beards. You talk without thinking. Because you're like one of those mules who just live off the earth, pasturing wherever they wish, without stall or home.'

The familiar attack produced the familiar reply of Apostate, Infidel, Hellhound, but was interrupted quickly by Abu Suweilim.

'Enough of this quarrelling. This Mahmoud Bey has neither taken the Petition to Cairo, nor written another one himself. The Omda has ruined us with his double-faced dealings. And yet I warned you. Now Sheikh Yusif is skulking in his shop, so embarrassed is he to show his face, remembering what he said about the Omda. And you, too, Muhammad Effendi – I warned you about the tricks of the Omda, and you both said that he was harmless. You've seen the result. He is indeed the trickiest of tricksters. I would not be surprised if he even invented the phrase he attributes to Mahmoud Bey, calling you a donkey. It is quite possible he put those words into the Bey's mouth, just to give them currency in the village.'

The idea that the Omda should have invented such words against him outraged Muhammad Effendi, and fumblingly he began to throw the blame onto Mahmoud Bey's lack of education.

'You see,' he said, 'I wrote the Petition in classical Arabic, at which Mahmoud Bey is weak. I wrote it in the manner of Manfaluti. One of my sentences, to which he took particular exception, said that if the water was cut to five days, then the "swains would couch on loam, Heaven their only quiet". He simply could not understand this style.'

Abdul Hadi broke in with a triumphant smile: 'Tell me, Muhammad Effendi, this "loam" you speak of ... is it just earth? I begin to think that Mahmoud Bey had some reason in what he said, about the Petition, about everything.' And referring to the rumour that Mahmoud Bey had asked the Omda whether these fellahin slept, normally, on beds or on the earth, he tauntingly enquired whether Muhammad Effendi's father, the lamented Radwan, had slept on a brass bed.

Abdul Hadi's raillery made Abu Suweilim and even Sheikh Shinawi laugh, despite themselves, and the Sheikh joined in the joke, using phrases from the Koran to ridicule the preposterous suggestion that the people of the village slept on beds. 'Of course we recline on rugs, as if we were already in Paradise, and not in this village.'

As for Muhammad Effendi, all his embarrassment was because he feared that Waseefa might be able to hear, and he tried to reduce the sounds of the conversation, but every word was heard by Waseefa, standing just inside the house. With divided heart she heard Muhammad Effendi mocked. She heard Abdul Hadi's boast that he knew everything; this made her afraid. Had Kadra told him something? When she whispered this question to Kadra, the other girl violently denied having given anything away. Let her tongue be torn out by its roots if Muhammad Effendi's name so much as came to its tip! No, no, to cause trouble between people, to set people against each other, this was worse than murder! And there were tears of sincerity in Kadra's eyes.

Yet this same Kadra would give herself to the youths of the

village, and so cheaply, sometimes for as little as a cucumber, on a hot summer's day. She had often introduced other girls to Muhammad Effendi, even to Abdul Hadi. This was why she knew how vital it was to keep the secrets of Muhammad Effendi, and the other young men who were her friends. Kadra knew everything about the relations between men and women, she recognized that Waseefa was attracted by Muhammad Effendi and that Muhammad Effendi desired Waseefa, and she took Waseefa aside and whispered to her strange new information about men and women, information which brought a blush of shame to Waseefa's cheeks, but which at the same time stirred fires deep within her being, fires of sexuality which she might repress with shame but which only burned the fiercer. All this Abdul Hadi would guess, and of how Muhammad Effendi, rejected as a suitor by Waseefa's father, would get Kadra to arrange a meeting with Waseefa, offering her a bribe to do this, even a small sum for the attempt. If he could not have Waseefa as a wife, he would try to have her as his mistress, in a rendezvous arranged by Kadra.

And meanwhile the villagers went on irrigating their land, whenever the backs of the engineers were turned; to the rage of the Omda, who, styling himself the 'Government's representative', wrote down their names, or telephoned to the local police station to have the offenders put in gaol. Yet the men laughed in the face of the 'Government's representative', in spite of his threats. They had a deep distrust of the Government.

On a previous occasion it had taken land from villagers in

twenty villages to build a highway linking the Pasha's estate with the main Cairo road; while the natural thing to have done (and which would not have taken a pocket-handkerchief of land from one farmer) would have been to repair the old road that ran by the river bank. The villagers remembered all this, and how, at that time, the Pasha laid the foundations of a splendid new Palace at the end of this new road. And then suddenly the Government in which he had influence fell from power. Work was discontinued on both the Palace and on the road. The Pasha's word no longer carried weight in Cairo, and his nephew, Mahmoud Bey, could no longer give orders to the local police. But this new Government did not last since the English did not wish it to last.

And back came the Pasha's friends, this time disguised as the 'People's Party'. They rigged the elections, with the help of the Omda, and although everyone in the village boycotted the voting, the village suddenly found itself with a new deputy – none other than the Pasha. The new Government claimed that it represented Egypt, just as the People's Party represented the people.

All these events were known to the men of the village, and they reverted to them constantly: the dismissal of the Chief Guard, the transfer of Hassouna, the schoolmaster, Muhammad Effendi's uncle, to the other end of Egypt. And meanwhile the Omda's voice rose louder, while Mahmoud Bey insulted, kicked and struck, right and left, whoever annoyed him. In a neighbouring village he did worse. He was passed by some villagers on donkeys, who without dismounting, as was usual, shouted 'Permission!' Mahmoud Bey instead of giving the normal reply, 'Permission granted!' had sent them all to the police station. There they were severely beaten, made to drink horse piss, and tormented until each of them would shout, in his extremity of pain, 'I am a woman'.

Against this background of violence, the villagers now learnt that the Pasha had started once more on his new Palace. They looked at the future with grim forebodings: he would want to complete the new road, and this would need land. Their land.

Mahmoud Bey's tearing up of the Petition was a new cause for Sheikh Yusif to mope inside his shop, to chase away the little boys who loitered in front, or leant against the trunk of the sycamore swelling stoutly from its age-old dust.

At the same time, the tearing of the Petition gave him some pleasure. Sheikh Yusif had been pleased to hear the writer of the Petition described as a donkey, for in his own mind he was convinced he could have written it far better himself. After all, he had been a listener for years at Al-Azhar Mosque, while Muhammad Effendi, educated in the neighbouring town, had only seen Cairo, mother of cities, but once, while his father had never set foot in it at all.

Sheikh Yusif had felt a certain repugnance for Muhammad Effendi, ever since the day he had let drop the suggestion that he should marry his daughter to him, and Muhammad Effendi had shown no enthusiasm for the project. He had a business reason for disliking him too. Owing money in the town, Sheikh Yusif had borrowed a few pounds from Muhammad Effendi. Instead of relying on a promise to pay, he had insisted on taking some of Sheikh Yusif's land as surety, and when Sheikh Yusif had been unable to repay his debt, he had taken the land and worked it.

So much for Sheikh Yusif's pleasure. He had more cause for pain. The village boys were whispering that Abu Suweilim had been quite right to warn against the Omda, and that Sheikh Yusif, Muhammad Effendi and Sheikh Shinawi were to blame for presenting the Petition first to the Omda and then to Mahmoud Bey. For why on earth should Mahmoud Bey have sympathized with a Petition against the interests of his powerful uncle?

What the villagers said was right, and for fear of being made to look foolish in front of everyone, Sheikh Yusif kept to his shop and no more joined the evening gatherings outside Abu Suweilim's house.

Then one evening he had a visitor: Abdul Hadi, who asked him outright why he was isolating himself from the rest of the village. Sheikh Yusif paused for a moment. (Alwani was hovering near the shop, on his usual quest.) He found it very difficult to speak, so embarrassed was he to admit that Abu Suweilim was right. But at last he managed to do so, admitting that Abu Suweilim had been right: the Omda was Mahmoud Bey's man, and Mahmoud Bey would never go against the interests of his uncle.

'Only just discovered this, Sheikh Yusif?' Abdul Hadi burst in passionately. 'Of course the Omda is the stooge of Mahmoud Bey, of course! And look how Mahmoud Bey has acted since the new Government came in, driving so arrogantly, nose in the air, a real two-hundred-acre drive, not a thirty acre drive. Oh by no means!'

By the time Abdul Hadi had finished, Sheikh Yusif had seen a way of escape from his sense of guilt.

'And we just followed behind this Muhammad Effendi, the donkey! Damn those who walk on four legs – or four guineas! Though I happen to know that since Sidky came to power, he earns only two. The same with all the Effendis and employees ... damn them! All their salaries cut. Those who took fifteen now take twelve, even though they've got their precious university degrees in their pockets.' Envy underlay his words as he went on. 'Muhammad Effendi ... where did he pick up his knowledge? Not from his poor father, I can assure you. A man that lived off sour milk and maize bread, while his splendid son buys the most expensive cakes I have. If I had completed my studies at the Azhar, why, man, I'd be an inspector at the very least, or a headmaster, like all those who sat beside me, and who are now important men. Muhammad Effendi, indeed! Tell him to go and get some cheap girl he can have for two pence.'

The hovering Alwani seized this opportunity (noting the thin smile on the old man's lips) to burst in with: 'Wise and wonderful words, Sheikh Yusif, on my oath! What a tragedy that you did not compose the Petition!' Sheikh Yusif stopped him with a laugh.

'Speech is one thing, payment is another, and no sugar or tea for you till you pay what you owe me.'

With a laugh, Abdul Hadi rapped a piastre on the counter between himself and Sheikh Yusif, and slapping Alwani on the back, he said: 'Give the Sheikh of the Arabs whatever he wants.'

Sheikh Yusif unlocked his drawer and gave Alwani, his face gleaming with pleasure, his tea and sugar.

Alwani then told them how he had been taken by his master, the Sheikh al-Balad, round the whole village, and how they had passed the waterwheels that were working against orders. The Sheikh al-Balad had sworn at the villagers, threatening them with gaol. After their tour, he had abruptly asked Alwani to go, alone, and discreetly open the canal closed by the engineers and let the water on to Mahmoud Bey's land, just enough to freshen it, and then to shut the canal again. 'After that,' Alwani said, his voice rising with excitement, 'you should have seen how the old man trembled when he asked me, very secretly, to do the same thing for his land too ... and the Omda's.'

Sheikh Yusif gasped in astonishment. Silent a moment, he pushed back his turban to scratch his short, greying hair; then pushed his turban back into place, and turned to glare at a man standing behind himself and Abdul Hadi.

'What are you standing there for, in your uniform, what do you want, boy? Speak out, Abdul Aati!'

One of the village guards was standing at attention, in his official black tarboosh and dark gallabya, his gun slung across his back, his feet bare. Staring straight ahead of him, he ordered the two men to report to the Omda's Residence at once on important business. Abdul Hadi tried to brush him off nonchalantly, but the man stood his ground, asking them to do what he said, and go to the Omda's. What did the Omda want? The guard claimed to know nothing: everyone must go to the Residence, taking with him his seal. That was all. He stood at attention in front of the shop as though nailed there.

'Seals? ... Seals, Abdul Aati? Some people in this village can write better than the Omda. What does his Excellency want with our seals?'

In fact, the guard knew little.

The Irrigation Engineers had paid a midnight visit and found traces of water in the villagers' fields, and other signs that the canal had been opened. The first thing in the morning the Omda had received two abusive telephone calls, one from the Magistrate, the other from the Lieutenant of Police.

The Omda was furious, but Praise God, no one had overheard the insulting conversation.

The Omda's complexion was pale yellow, his body was small and punily built, and his voice was low. A short, trim beard of snowy white lent a certain dignity to the wrinkles of his face, and a smile never left his lips, even when inwardly he was most angry. He had been educated at the Azhar years before Sheikh Yusif, and in Cairo he had had dreams, like other students, and like them, he had left the dreams behind in that immense city and had returned to his village, there to intrigue for petty power.

No sooner had this Omda congratulated himself that no one had heard the Lieutenant's insults, than the telephone rang again, this time to warn him that if the Government's orders were defied, he would be held responsible, unless he gave a detailed list of all offenders to the police. In a fury, the Omda decided to go at once to Mahmoud Bey and lodge a complaint against the Lieutenant. So off he rode to the Estate, his favourite guard, Abdul Aati, walking behind him;

77

and when he came back he brought with him a document in his pocket and a sense of satisfaction in his heart.

For the Omda was one of those men who always know how to get by, whatever the situation. His recipe for success was to bow to those in power, and to do whatever they wanted. His only aim was to please the powerful. He did not care at all if their aims might spell ruin to the village. Even if they requested him to hand over all the people, women and men alike, to be machine-gunned, he would probably oblige, with his usual smile. He had been instrumental in having many villagers beaten up at the police station, and he had, of course, been party to Abu Suweilim's dismissal from his post as Chief Guard, just as he had been the chief agent of the People's Party in the elections. Similarly, when the previous Government had been in power, he had curried favour with the brilliant lawyer who had then represented the neighbouring town, even though this Government had been elected fairly, without pressure being put on the voters. He would serve any Government, whatever its colour.

In truth, when he had first heard of the new irrigation decrees, the Omda had sent Abdul Aati to tell all the villagers about them. But Abdul Aati had not done so. He had turned the matter over in his head, and come to two conclusions: either the Omda had become senile and deranged, or he was worn out by the demands of his wife, a plump, whiteish young woman, half a century younger than her husband.

As soon as he got back from Mahmoud Bey's, the Omda ordered out the guards: they must put on their uniforms and line up in the wide yard in front of his staircase. The guards, obeying, lit the large lanterns and sprinkled the dusty ground of the yard with water, and waited for the Omda to finish supper. At last he came out in the robes he wore to meet the authorities: a long kaftan over his undervest, and a shawl worthy of a Shah round his neck. He stood on the steps, Abdul Aati behind him, surveying the guards in their high black tarbooshes, their guns slung across their shoulders. They greeted him by stamping their bare feet in a most military manner on the watered dust.

The Omda started by cursing them for allowing the people to defy the new regulations. After each phrase, each insult, Abdul Aati repeated his master's words, one by one, from behind, in the same tone of voice.

'Are you my deputy?' turning on Abdul Aati the Omda shouted in a rage: 'Come out from behind me, get into line, at once! Are you the Omda, or am I?'

To the concealed laughter of his fellows, Abdul Aati slipped into the middle of the line. The laughter still further enraged the Omda who, redoubling his curses, began a diatribe against the villagers; to use water outside the regulation periods was the equivalent of theft! Putting all the emphasis he could into his low quiet voice he said that in future any illegal use of water would be treated as the equivalent of pilfering.

This statement was greeted with incredulous murmurs from the line of guards.

'Right,' the Omda said, drawing out each word to give it emphasis, 'you are all of you sacked!'

This only doubled their laughter, and one of them, trying

to choke down his laugh, said: 'But we ourselves watered your land, Omda! Don't the laws apply to people like yourself, people in authority? Was that pilfering, too?'

And before the furious Omda could answer, another broke in, puzzled and angry: 'How can it be pilfering to take water? Is there a wall we can make a hole in, to steal in and take the water?'

The Omda came down the steps and shrieked: 'Gypsy village! May a wall fall on all your heads! Oh God, oh God! Don't you understand anything, you there? And you, and you! The water belongs to the Government, and the Government only, and the Government can do with the water what it likes. Understand?'

But it was impossible to persuade the guards. To them, water was something that belonged of nature to plants; plants had the right to drink, and to drink till they were satisfied. It was as simple as that. To the guards, the water was the same as the sun and the air. It was Abdul Aati who put their thoughts into words, by asking if the sun too was the property of the Government, and could be rationed. This question, coming from his favourite, made the Omda more angry than ever; but it amused the guards who stamped their feet on the earth, sending up sprays of mud which made the Omda cough. At this moment the Omda's plump young wife could be seen looking out of the window; then with a smile her white face turned back into the darkness.

The Omda was aggrieved with Abdul Aati as never before.

'You of all people, whom I made my special attendant, you whom I allowed into my house and to see my women – you to attack the Government in public like this. What has become of you, Abdul Aati?'

But Abdul Aati would not allow himself to be stopped. 'You told us that irrigation was the same as pilfering, you asked if we understood, and we didn't. Is the sun owned by the Government? What about the rain, is that theirs too?' The Omda tried to silence him, but in vain. 'The rain that the Reverend Sheikh tells us God sends down from Heaven, is that the Government's?'

The Omda finally lost his temper. 'You interrupt me, would you? You cut in while I'm talking, you drown my voice with yours? You criticize the Government in public? It's time for you to learn a lesson, my boy. Lie down! Lie down! But first fetch my stick from indoors.'

Abdul Aati went indoors and came out carrying a long tough cane, reinforced with wire. He took off his gun and laid it on the stairs. But he did not lie down, instead he stood protestingly in the middle of the yard.

'This ground's damp. The Government's uniform will get muddy. Or do you want me to strip for you?'

What was implied by this last remark made the others roar with laughter.

'Lie wherever you like, boy! But lie down.'

Abdul Aati went to the top of the stairs and lay down on the small platform outside the door. The Omda thereupon began to beat him severely on the back, while the watching guards trembled with pity. Only Abdul Aati showed no reaction at all. When it was over, he stood upright among the other guards, while the Omda exclaimed that it was like scratching his back, to give him a beating ... he showed so little reaction.

Suddenly the Omda remembered the paper in his pocket. He gingerly looked at it. Changing his tone, he ordered the guards to disperse throughout the village, and to bring back all the men, and with them their seals, not omitting one. Let them also muster all the benches they could lay hands on, so as to prepare for the whole village to assemble.

The Omda went indoors.

As for the Guards, they exchanged looks, laughs, astonishment, but did as they were told and went to collect seals and benches from all the houses. They brought one bench from Muhammad Effendi's, another from Sheikh Shinawi, a third from another house. But no one thought of asking Abu Suweilim, or Abdul Hadi, or Sheikh Yusif, to lend a bench. Only Abdul Aati went so far as to try and persuade the two last to come to the Omda's house. Having failed to do this, he went off to fetch Sheikh Shinawi.

The Omda told the Sheikh that Mahmoud Bey had written a new Petition, a thousand times better than the old one, and that he wanted every man in the village to put his seal to it, or his signature, and when this was done, he would take it back to Mahmoud Bey. He would collect signatures from the other villages affected by the new decrees and finally Mahmoud Bey would himself take the Petition to the Cabinet in Cairo. The whole matter needed speed; so that the decrees could be changed before the new rota began.

Sheikh Shinawi signed the white paper without asking anything; and after him, several others who knew how to write. Below these signatures the villagers affixed their seals. The Sheikh cursed anyone who asked to have the Petition read aloud. And when a number of signatures had been added to the Petition, the Sheikh got up and left the Omda's house, and went from one end of the village to another, driving everyone he met, with curses or exhortations, to take his seal to the Residence to endorse the new Petition. He reached Abu Suweilim's house last. There was no one sitting at the threshold, there was no light from the sitting room inside. So pausing at the half-open door he shouted: 'Anyone at home, in the name of God?'

Hearing no answer, he stepped into the darkness of the house. Waseefa appeared from a door in one corner. On her head she carried a small tin lamp, which gave a yellow light mixed with smoke. She politely asked the Sheikh to come and sit down in the sitting-room, while she prepared him coffee. Where was her father? The same question had just been asked her by Abdul Hadi. Perhaps her father was now at Abdul Hadi's house, or at the shop of Sheikh Yusif?

'No,' said the Sheikh, 'the shop was shut, and the house was far, and no lights were shining.'

'Then I will go and fetch my father,' said Waseefa, adjusting the lamp on her head, and at the same time inviting the old man to rest in the sitting-room, where she lit the large lamp in its glass container. But the Sheikh found it hot indoors. 'A night indeed, a night in very truth,' he murmured. He would prefer to wait on the threshold, in the open air. And Waseefa walked into the night alone, filled with vague fears, the pale-yellow lamp agleam upon her head.

The sound of Waseefa's slippers on the village earth was the only sound in the empty night. On her head, high above her upright body, gleamed the tin lamp. No sound but the barking of dogs, no guard in sight. A few boys passed her; they were on their way home from the Omda's, having signed the Petition. They whispered that perhaps it was true, she was engaged to Abdul Hadi after all, and was on her way to his house. Or she was on her way to an assignation with Muhammad Effendi in the old graveyard. But a third protested that this was impossible.

The narrow lane between the low, mud houses ended; in front of her a broad road bent towards the fields. Out of the shelter of the houses, she went more slowly. A breeze from the open country brought relief to the hot night, at the same time blowing out her lamp. But a brilliant moon lit up the landscape, and Waseefa laughed at herself for having bothered with a light.

From near Abdul Hadi's house she heard a murmur of voices. His house was built by the maize fields that stretched as far as the graveyards, old and new. Seated on a pile of dust, covered with a rush mat, were Abdul Hadi, Sheikh Yusif and her father. The three men were eating, Abdul Hadi plying her father with morsels. She heard Abdul Hadi's rough laugh as he chewed onions and she heard the crackle of breaking loaves. There was a delicious aroma of old cheese steeped in whey. Abdul Hadi's mother was an expert at the preparation of this kind of cheese; if only the old woman would teach Waseefa the secret of how to make it!

Her father was gazing out across the flat expanse of fields, indigo in the bright light of the moon; date palms, dark tombs. Abu Suweilim shook his head at the wide earth through which the first shoots of cotton and maize were shivering.

'They'll make these shoots die of thirst, will they? Young shoots, needing water? And what of this new Petition, brought from Mahmoud Bey, being signed, sealed and thumb-marked by all the village?'

At this moment Waseefa reached the door of the house.

She went further and stood by the edge of the heap of dust.

'Good evening!'

Her sudden, silent arrival took them by surprise. Her father was astonished that she had left home so late at night, after the last prayers. She told him she had come because Sheikh Shinawi was waiting for him at home. Abdul Hadi lifted his hand from the food; he ground his molars together slowly, broke no more bread, as he wanted to hear every word. Her voice, merging with the sad night scenery of fields and gloomy trees on the horizon, aroused in him a mixture of emotions, the strongest of which was the desire to see Waseefa go into his house and never come out again, for her to live with him for ever and ever. 'Please join us, Waseefa. Eat with us, please!'

'No thank you, Abdul Hadi.'

What greater happiness could a man have than to own his land, and to have indoors a woman like Waseefa ... Waseefa herself, no other woman would do!

But Abu Suweilim made to go home, to receive Sheikh Shinawi. Abdul Hadi, refusing to let him leave, told Waseefa to go inside and rest, while he would go back and meet Sheikh Shinawi. After a moment's hesitation, Abu Suweilim told Waseefa to go indoors to greet Abdul Hadi's mother, and then it would be time to go home.

Sheikh Yusif broke into the conversation, asking where Muhammad Effendi was hiding.

The question astonished Abdul Hadi; but Abu Suweilim replied calmly, without a doubt he would be at the Omda's Residence.

No, he wasn't there, Sheikh Yusif said, for the guards were looking for him everywhere.

Rage coloured Abdul Hadi's cheeks. Waseefa came out from visiting his mother. Was it possible that she had been meeting Muhammad Effendi? Was it possible that his dry, horny hand had been at play on this fair, honourable flesh? He wished suddenly that any man who touched a woman would leave an ugly scar, visible to other men. Why hadn't God arranged something like this? Instead of arranging to deprive the villagers of their water?

Waseefa stood in front of them now, waiting for her father to get up to go. Abu Suweilim prepared to take his leave, and behind Waseefa the moon shed its light on the quiet fields.

Aggressively Abdul Hadi asked Waseefa about Muhammad Effendi.

When he pressed his questions further, as if to place doubts on her statement that she had been at home, Abu Suweilim himself brought the topic to an end: his daughter had said that she had been at home; there was no need to speak further. And followed by Waseefa, he left for home.

Morning came. The Petition was still at the Residence, awaiting seals and signatures.

On his way from the fields, Abdul Hadi ran into some young men who told him that despite Mahmoud Bey's urging to have the Petition signed by everybody the night before, there were still many names lacking. The Bey was furious, and Sheikh Shinawi was energetically patrolling the village, gathering those who had delayed taking their seals to the Omda's. The guards were doing the same thing to those in the fields. Abdul Hadi came on a group being cursed by the Sheikh: they were persisting in asking what the new Petition was about.

'Won't you read them its contents first?' he asked disapprovingly.

'I take refuge in God from you, you child, Abdul Hadi! Always objecting. As for the rest of you, be off and sign!'

Abdul Hadi went to Abu Suweilim's house, while the Sheikh continued to stand in the road, brandishing his stick, waylaying anyone who tried to make off to the fields. He even ordered them to round up the seals belonging to women landowners in the village: their names, too, must be on the petition.

'Whoever loves God and His Prophet will go to the Residence to sign. Others are blasphemers, apostates.'

As for Abu Suweilim, Abdul Hadi found him sitting on the platform by the door, alone, thinking. Before joining him, Abdul Hadi asked Waseefa to give him a drink. She was filling a pitcher from the large stone jar in the middle of the house.

'Strange, Abdul Hadi,' she whispered to herself, 'always so thirsty, do you want always to drink from my hands?'

But she gave him a pitcher, and while he held it to his lips, her father shouted, asking if he had heard any news of the Petition: something he would never sign unless he read it first. Did anyone in the village know anything of its contents? Handing back the pitcher, Abdul Hadi said:

'True, not one person's seen what's in it.'

And putting heavy sarcasm into his voice, for the sake of Waseefa:

'But surely it'll be better than the one written by the donkey.'

Abu Suweilim could not get over his distrust of the Omda.

'Listen, Abdul Hadi, Mahmoud Bey's going to Cairo. Why don't you go with him? Your brother, Mustafa Effendi, he's there, he'll keep an eye on the matter. I have no faith in petitions to Governments.'

'But I'm all alone here, uncle. Who can I leave my land to? This month in particular, that's worth all the rest of the year put together.'

'At least let's know what's written in the Petition. Where was Muhammad Effendi hiding himself last night? Waseefa, my girl, you run and see if you can find Muhammad Effendi.'

Waseefa, standing at the door, was embarrassed by Abdul Hadi's critical glance. And as she turned to go, Abdul Hadi angrily asked Abu Suweilim why he sent his daughter to Muhammad Effendi.

The morning sun was reaching its height over the village.

Abdul Hadi shouted to Waseefa, 'Don't you bother, I'll go myself.'

She came back, half pleased, half disappointed. And just as Abdul Hadi stood up to go, he saw a boy on a donkey some way off. He shouted to him, but the boy did not hear. Another boy passed, his donkey loaded with manure, and Abdul Hadi pulled him to a halt and told him to go to the Omda's to fetch Muhammad Effendi. The boy rode off quickly. Abdul Hadi returned to his place, looking at no one. The boy was soon back: the Omda himself was looking for Muhammad Effendi, the guards could not find him anywhere.

'Where's he hiding himself, Abu Suweilim?'

Abdul Hadi glimpsed the body of Waseefa, nervous inside the house.

A fat duck waddled out of the house, followed by a goose which pecked at Abdul Hadi's foot. Abu Suweilim kicked it away, calling his daughter to remove both birds. But Abdul Hadi got up and shooed them inside. He was in two minds whether to ask Waseefa outright if she had had a meeting with Muhammad Effendi the night before.

'Come and sit down!' Abu Suweilim called out to him. 'What on earth's the matter with you, Abdul Hadi, to make you so unsettled? Well, go yourself, and find out what's in the Petition.'

'It's easy for you to be at ease, you who only know half the story ...'

In front of Sheikh Yusif's shop, Abdul Hadi saw Alwani leaning on the counter. The old grocer was scolding a small girl who was trying to beat him down on the price of washing blue.

Having defeated the girl, Sheikh Yusif shouted to Abdul Hadi: the Omda had not waited for every signature, but had sent the Petition – unread by anyone in the village – to Mahmoud Bey.

Before Abdul Hadi could say anything, Alwani broke in with fulsome praise of Sheikh Yusif, who had been proved right. 'No one here appreciates your worth or your capacities, Sheikh Yusif.'

This compliment by no means pleased the old man.

'Enough, boy! Hold your tongue, you Beduin. No one knows my worth, you say? No one appreciates my capacities? Let me tell you: I am well known and well appreciated. The men I studied with at the Azhar. I studied more than any of them. They are all judges, inspectors, teachers. Why, the very least of them is an Omda!'

In vain Alwani tried to explain what he had really meant.

'Where's Muhammad Effendi hiding himself,' Sheikh Yusif asked Abdul Hadi, ignoring Alwani. 'His brother, Diab called here, looking for him: the guards want him too.'

'Hiding? If only he could be hidden from the village before he destroys it!'

Sheikh Yusif greeted Abdul Hadi's malice with prolonged laughter. And seeing his amusement (for Sheikh Yusif was not a man to laugh often) Alwani joined in obstreperously. Sheikh Yusif could not forgive Muhammad Effendi: the one man in the village who earned four pounds a month, yet who spent nothing. He worked alongside his brother, and from their land took enough to live on, so he could save his whole salary, pound by pound. In addition to this, he still worked half of Sheikh Yusif's land as well. Sheikh Yusif was hoarding his profits, penny by penny, to ransom his land from Muhammad Effendi, having lost half of it already to the Government, in lieu of tax. The confiscation of his land had filled his heart with rancour, but also with pride, that his gesture in refusing to pay tax, along with that of thousands of other farmers, had shaken this pro-English regime that had brought disaster to Egypt. As to the land taken by Muhammad Effendi, Sheikh Yusif was determined to get it back. But Muhammad Effendi constantly tried to persuade him to sell it to him outright. Sheikh Yusif never put his grievance into words, but Abdul Hadi's mocking laughter filled him with delight, as well as the feeling that one day he might escape from his nightmare.

'He's certainly a cold fish, that one! His father died on a diet of whey and rough bread, he gobbles sweets and buys up land. Yes, it would be a good thing if he vanished from the village before he ruins it. A real cold fish!'

Laughing no longer, he lowered his voice to say:

'And besides, he wants to rob me on a larger scale. My friend, he wants to marry my daughter, so he can take over all my land. He pesters me daily ... the donkey!'

Yet all this was a lie, as Sheikh Yusif knew perfectly well. It was he who had broached the subject of marriage, and Muhammad Effendi had given no response at all. But Sheikh Yusif was pleased that Abdul Hadi swallowed the story.

Alwani leaned towards Sheikh Yusif and whispered:

'Would you like me to beat him up for you?'

Sheikh Yusif was horrified at this suggestion: that Alwani, or some other worthless ruffian like him, should think of beating up someone of standing and influence, like himself!

'Be off, you Beduin, thief, highwayman! Beat him up? beat him up, how? I take refuge in God. May he protect us all from such Beduin roguery. Come inside, Abdul Hadi, it's cooler inside the shop; outside it's heating up,' and despite Abdul Hadi's desire to go to his fields, the old man pulled him inside, leaving Alwani in the sun. Abdul Hadi felt pity for Alwani's dejection.

'A *mahrouqa*, Sheikh of the Arabs,' he said, using the Beduin word for a cigarette. But the Arab boy waved it aside, pleading with Abdul Hadi to explain to Sheikh Yusif that he really wasn't a robber, but an Arab Sheikh, and a descendant of the Imam Ali.

'Ah, so you're a descendant of Ali, are you? A Sherif? May your worthless heart be cut in bits.'

Taking heart from Abdul Hadi's laughter, Alwani tried again. 'By the Prophet, O Sheikh Yusif, I have but one desire – to serve you. Whoever you love, I love; whoever you hate, I hate too. An excellent cigarette. Give me some tobacco, too, for Abdul Hadi's sake. And may God double your acres!'

With a smile, Sheikh Yusif handed him his tobacco, then carefully recorded the purchase in his long account book.

'You're a fox, Alwani.'

Putting the tobacco in his pocket and laughing happily, Alwani went off to his melon-field. Abdul Hadi was eager to go too, but the old man wanted to unburden himself to someone. The cotton pods swelling on the short young stems were already lost. And with economic ruin, the market for girls was finished too. Who would marry his daughter in such a crisis?

As he walked away towards Abu Suweilim's house, the hot sun on the back of his neck, Abdul Hadi turned over cotton and girls in his mind, a deep melancholy settling on his soul.

On arrival at Abu Suweilim's house, he found Muhammad Effendi sitting there at the threshold, and worst of all, Waseefa herself pouring coffee. This was the first time that Abdul Hadi had seen such a thing. Normally she stood, her body behind the door, holding out a tray. Never had she poured coffee at the threshold to a man, other than her father. Abdul Hadi's curt greeting confused Waseefa, so that she spilt some of the coffee on Muhammad Effendi's gallabya.

He laughed softly. 'Good luck! May you get a new dress from God!'

Muhammad Effendi was out to annoy him at any price! Abdul Hadi refused to sit down in the shade, but stood in the glaring sun. But Abu Suweilim compelled him to sit down between himself and Muhammad Effendi. The schoolmaster's neatly combed hair, shaved face and elegant scent disgusted Abdul Hadi. Abdul Hadi asked in a dry voice:

'Where were you yesterday night, Muhammad Effendi? The whole world was looking for you.'

Muhammad Effendi trembled with silent rage; Abdul Hadi felt that his own heartbeats must be audible to the others. Abu Suweilim suddenly looked up from his coffee.

'You know where we finally unearthed him? At the barber's! We sent that devil of a girl, Kadra, to look for him, and she went underground and came up with Muhammad Effendi.'

'Kadra?'

He looked at Muhammad Effendi's newly shaven chin, redolent of scent. Abdul Hadi shook his head. What was his connection with Kadra? Had she arranged a meeting with Waseefa? Had Waseefa's nocturnal walk been to meet him? He was filled with distress. If only he could leave this world, to be quit of its anxieties ... even to go and live in the town, to see Waseefa's sister, and to discuss with her and her husband the whole problem. But to leave the world was impossible, and to leave his land at this time of year was not possible, either; there was so much to be done with the cotton and the maize. Perhaps he would go indoors and beat Waseefa until she told the truth, until she repented of what she had done.

But what had she done?

For in truth he did not know if Kadra had introduced her to Muhammad Effendi, or if the schoolmaster had been with some other girl.

Abu Suweilim broke into his sighs, his nervous leg-twitchings, by remarking that Muhammad Effendi was going to accompany Mahmoud Bey, when he took the Petition to Cairo.

Abdul Hadi hid his spite under a false smile.

'How can Muhammad Effendi journey with the Bey, when the Bey called him a donkey, Si Muhammad?'

Muhammad Effendi exploded in wounded rage.

'What's your purpose in always bringing up this story? Are you trying to make me ridiculous, Abdul Hadi? Is that your purpose?'

And with a sudden fury both men began flinging Kadra,

and each other's manliness, to and fro, till Abu Suweilim shouted to them to make an end of this nonsense. He pulled them back into their seats, scolding Abdul Hadi, in particular, for his rudeness.

'Are you cocks, to fight like this?'

'He's acting like a cock throughout the village! He is the one who wrote the Petition like a don –'

Abu Suweilim shouted to him to be quiet.

'Enough of this, embrace each other, and let bygones be bygones.'

Reluctantly Abdul Hadi rose to make it up with Muhammad Effendi. The old man's distress had moved Abdul Hadi, and he leant towards Muhammad Effendi apologetically, asking his forgiveness. Muhammad Effendi forgave him, and at the moment of doing so felt a sudden rush of affection for him.

The climbing sun now probed the shade, too; the noon heat was everywhere.

Muhammad Effendi said he must go to Mahmoud Bey's house at dawn, to fix the time for their journey.

Abdul Hadi said in a warm voice: 'Go and come back safely, Muhammad Effendi!'

In all three, as they went their separate ways, there was, their quarrel resolved, a feeling of tenderness, of faith, and of new confidence in each other.

Muhammad Effendi was on his way to Mahmoud Bey's estate before sunrise. He took the short cut between the fields and the canal. On his way he passed a scraggy cow, then a bony ox, pulling the plough, behind them a man, then a woman, scattering seed, a prayer in their hearts. Pity seized Muhammad Effendi at the thought that these seeds might die in the ground, unless the government changed its decrees: the seeds would die before they sent up their beautiful green shoots, loaded with ears. But perhaps the Petition he would be taking would allow the seeds to sprout, to grow, to flower and bring to harvest.

But he must hurry if he was to reach the Bey's house in time. In his haste, he stumbled in the narrow way, almost falling headlong into the fields of growing maize.

As soon as he reached the big house, he was received by Mahmoud Bey. Without waiting for any questions from Muhammad Effendi, the Bey said that he had received so many signatures that it would be possible for them to take the noon train from the local town, and deliver the Petition immediately to the Prime Minister.

Muhammad Effendi's heart leapt with pride at the thought of meeting the Prime Minister. Would they really meet him?

Certainly the Petition would reach the Prime Minister, Mahmoud Bey answered. And then, after a moment's silence, he asked Muhammad Effendi to arrange certain fees for his travelling and his services. What he was doing was only done to serve the villagers. Each village should contribute something; Muhammad Effendi's village should make a contribution of ten pounds. As he spoke, his voice mingled a certain embarrassment with his usual authority.

Muhammad Effendi did not reply, but in his mind he turned over how he could pay. After a short while, he took his leave. The two men would meet at the station. And this time Muhammad Effendi ran the whole way back to the village. Quite out of breath, he came to his brother, Diab, at work on the cotton by the canal field.

'Quickly, Diab, fetch the she-ass, join me at the house!'

On his hurried way home, Muhammad Effendi saw in his mind's eye visions of the Cairo he had not visited for two years. He pictured the elderly Prime Minister, who could deal death to thousands, eating sandwiches quietly in his office.

Meanwhile Diab left his hoes, ran to the top of the field, and pushed into the stable where on summer nights he would sleep, guarding the animals. He untied the pretty little donkey with her glistening white coat, and led her by the nose into the sun. Diab took great pains to do anything that seemed important to his brother. This donkey was very precious to Muhammad Effendi, who himself bought her beans from the town, and himself would give her a weekly bath with soap, in the river. Yet Diab had still not entirely forgotten a sense of guilt associated with this donkey. For some years before he had tried to have that kind of relationship with her which is not uncommon between adolescents and various birds and small beasts. Muhammad Effendi had surprised him in the act, had cuffed and kicked him, angrily shouting that this was no cheap, dung-carrying mule, but a highly precious, delicate beast. In any case, Diab could no longer try anything of that kind, now he had grown up. Kadra solved his sexual problems for him, and when he took her to the stable, he did not give a thought to birds and small animals.

Arriving at his house, Diab found his brother shut in the

room he had had specially built on the roof, removed from the quarters of Diab and his mother. As Muhammad Effendi had built this room after becoming a schoolmaster, their mother called it 'the Effendi's study'.

Muhammad Effendi shouted from behind his locked door:

'Tether the donkey, Diab, and run to Abu Suweilim's. Tell him I'm going to Cairo today. In fact, this very moment.'

Diab spread a strip of felt on the donkey's back and over that laid a velvet saddle. In her mouth he placed the bit and attached the leather harness. 'Now you stay put. Don't jump about,' he murmured. While he went off to Abu Suweilim's, his mother chased the cock to kill it.

Up on the roof, in his locked room, Muhammad Effendi had finished dressing. He took a flask of scent from a drawer and poured it on his hands, then on his head. He adjusted his tarboosh to what he took to be an elegant angle. This done, he opened a wooden cupboard let into the wall, and from under a pile of papers, a woollen cap, and a large book, he brought out a heavy leather purse and from it extracted a banknote.

'Enough, this one pound.'

Then he pulled out a ten-pound note, contemplating it at length. Then he undid his foreign-style shirt, and slipped the note into the pocket of his striped *beledi* waistcoat.

'And that, sir, is for Mahmoud Bey, though how we'll ever get the village to cough up ...'

He then put two pounds, not one, in his wallet, and the wallet in the inside pocket of his jacket.

'And that money's for you, sir!'

He replaced the purse, locked the cupboard, and put the key in his trouser pocket. Before leaving the room, he gave a last satisfied pat to his jacket, made a last adjustment to his tarboosh, and then went down the staircase made of mud. His mother was slaughtering a cock. Still on the last steps, he told her that the time was getting late. Mahmoud Bey would be waiting.

'Can't you wait,' she asked, 'so I can prepare this cock for your uncle, Sheikh Hassouna? And a few cakes as well?'

He laughed: time was getting on, and Mahmoud Bey would be waiting for him to take the train. He kissed his mother's hand.

'Go in safety, my son. Our Lord prosper your purposes and bring you safely back.'

And while he untied the bridle and stood waiting for Diab to come back, she told him to be sure to call on his uncle in Shubra, and perhaps stay with him. If he had the chance, he might hint for one of Sheikh Hassouna's daughters in marriage. Before he could reply, as he stood there waiting, holding the bridle, a neighbour passed. Could he buy her something from the town, if that was where he was going? Crossly he snapped back:

'I'm going to Cairo.'

The woman seemed astonished. In that case, let him wait at least till she had prepared some food for her son, a cabdriver in the capital.

Muhammad Effendi had a sudden vision of himself carting packages and parcels from one end of Cairo to another, from Gizeh to Shubra and Bulak, if he listened to the requests of all those who had sons working in the city. And what would Mahmoud Bey, famous for his quick temper, say if Muhammad Effendi sat down beside him with a pile of openwork parcels? What would he say if Muhammad Effendi arrived in his cafe loaded with such encumbrances?

'I'm not going to visit Our Lady Zaynab! I'm not on pilgrimage. I'm going to meet the authorities about the irrigation.'

At this moment Diab came back. He had not managed to find Abu Suweilim: Waseefa did not know where he had gone, but she sent her prayers for Muhammad Effendi's safe return.

Muhammad Effendi glanced at his watch with an elegant gesture.

'It's twelve minutes past ten. The Bey will be waiting in front of the ticket-office.'

And to the shouted good wishes of his mother and all the neighbours he strode off, Diab holding the donkey's bridle. Some women shouted to him to say a prayer for them in the mosque of Lady Zaynab or the Imam Shafei.

Muhammad Effendi made a detour to say good-bye to Sheikh Yusif. Jokingly the shopkeeper detained him a moment longer:

'Take care of yourself in Cairo. I know what I'm talking about. It's a hard, dangerous city. Don't pick anything up there, Muhammad Effendi, come back alone!'

Muhammad Effendi laughed at this veiled reference to women, and still laughing he wounded Sheikh Yusif. 'Why should I come back alone? Perhaps I'll pick up a husband for your daughter, Sheikh Yusif!'

Three men standing by the shop smiled, and as Muhammad Effendi left, Sheikh Yusif muttered, 'Strange! Was he teasing me? Does His Excellency really think I would like him as a son-in-law? By God, even if she was twenty-five, I would never agree to such a marriage.'

The bystanders all knew that it was the old man's dream that someday Muhammad Effendi should marry his daughter; a pallid, unattractive creature whom sickness had dried up before her time.

'She's been perfectly brought up, as you all know. I've concealed her since she was twelve. I begot her in the heyday of my youth, when my blood was strong and hot, when I used to eat pounds of meat every day!'

All the women in his household were enclosed, wearing a veil over their faces if they so much as set foot outside the house.

'You're right, she's a real gentleman's daughter, Sheikh Yusif.'

The compliment soothed the old man.

'Not so? And you think I'd marry her to your Mr Muhammad Effendi?'

He rubbed his dry face with a withered hand, shaking his head the while, his eyes staring at the faces in front of him, to see if they were joking.

'A noble ass, a velvet saddle, a royal ride! All for you, boy, all for you, donkey – as Mahmoud Bey called you –now off on a mission to the Authorities! How splendid. A mission to do what? Ah, I forgot: the Petition, the Petition which nobody in this wretched village has bothered to read. What did they sign, I wonder? Perhaps not a petition at all, but a promissory note.'

While the men talked politics, Muhammad Effendi had reached the outskirts of the village. In the narrow lane to the river bank, he paused by a large stone, and used this to mount the donkey, and stretch his feet into the stirrups.

The donkey ran off prancingly, Diab running behind. A feeling of sadness filled Muhammad Effendi as the village receded behind him. He was desolate to be leaving home. He turned in the saddle asking his brother, barefoot in the dust, to make her slow down. A little incident then gave him pleasure. They passed a girl carrying an empty pitcher. Hastily, she turned her back to them and retreated into a field, putting down her pitcher and modestly averting her gaze from the two men.

'Who is that, Diab?'

'One of Sheikh Shinawi's daughters.'

'Excellently brought up!'

She had feared to greet Muhammad Effendi carrying an empty pitcher, for that would have been a most discouraging omen to someone setting out on an important journey.

Diab sighed with relief. Like all the villagers, he was extremely superstitious, a prey to many fears of the unknown; his character was optimistic one moment, pessimistic the next, for no concrete reason. He was sure that the Sheikh's daughter, just like her father, knew the secrets of things.

On to the main road to the town the donkey carried Muhammad Effendi, his legs flapping against her sides, his hand waving in greeting to right and left. Then to Diab's relief they reached the last limits of the village land: but five other villages lay before them on their way. Diab's feet sank into the dust of the road, his breath came in gasps, and his eyes were stung by the dust raised by the donkey's hooves. The schoolmaster's thoughts were aroused by the little river flowing gently with muddy waves.

'A strong flood.'

'They'd take it from us? The Devil take them.'

And Diab, whose feet were broiled as if by hot ash, was pleased when ahead of them an avenue of trees offered shady patches where the dust was cool and soft. What a pity the Government did not plant more trees, did not repair the dusty road, instead of cutting off the water.

'Why don't we marry you to Sheikh Shinawi's daughter, Diab? When we've sold the cotton.'

After a moment's silence Diab blurted out:

'Cotton! And if we don't sell the cotton? No marrying? We've no cash, is that it?'

His brother stayed silent.

'And when I do marry,' Diab ran faster as the ass increased her speed, 'I've got no choice but that girl? She's got nothing, I don't want to marry a preacher's daughter.'

'You'd prefer the Sultan's, would you? Don't get ideas above your station. And what's wrong with the preacher's daughter?'

Now Diab said nothing.

'Or would you prefer Kadra? Shall we marry you to her?'

Diab pursed his lips.

'That one!'

Once again he was silent.

The donkey continued to trot. Here and there, on the river, boats moved, loaded with jugs and jars. A breathing silence filled the world, with the heat burning the road and the fields and the scattered trees, empty of birds.

After they had passed three villages the scene changed. Men were directing the water into small canals.

'By God,' exclaimed Diab angrily, 'here the wheels are turning, the land is drinking. Has our village blasphemed or something, that its fields should be left thirsty?'

Muhammad Effendi shook his head in silence, drumming his heels against the flanks of the ass, who continued to trot and trot. And as the sun rose higher, the summer heat grew more intense and Diab's feet felt scorched.

'What about Abu Suweilim?' said Diab suddenly.

'Well, what about him?'

'Wouldn't he be a better relation than Sheikh Shinawi? His daughter, she would be someone ... sweet as a mouthful of butter. Won't you betroth me to her? Now, or must we wait for the cotton? A year ago I paid my forfeit for not joining the army. No point in putting off marriage once you're grown. Why don't you arrange my marriage with Waseefa, Muhammad Effendi? And remember, the land we took from Sheikh Yusif is next to Abu Suweilim's. I think it's meant that we should plough the whole lot together.'

Diab's face shone with delight at the prospect. But his brother was amazed.

'You ... marry Waseefa?'

Diab, his eyes on the ground, was happy.

'Yes, me ... cream ... like the top of the milk ...'

The hooves of the ass were now rattling on paved road; they were at the edge of the town; and the heat of the asphalt was intolerable to bare feet. It was ovenhot. Diab could no longer repress his fatigue, any more than he could keep back the sweat which poured from his forehead, face and body. If only, he murmured to himself, he had brought his shoes!

And now the ass had to thread her way between crowded cabs, perplexed by the horns of cars, the bells of other vehicles, the cracking of whips. Once she nearly threw Muhammad Effendi. As for Diab, his eyes took in the rows of houses on each side, while his nostrils dilated to the odour of wheat bread and beans steeped in oil. He became dizzy with looking at all the things exposed for sale.

His brother cut into his contemplation by looking at his watch.

'I've time to do the last part on foot. You ride the donkey home.' And choosing a discreet part of the road, he dismounted.

'Goodbye, Diab, and look after the donkey and my study. Keep the door locked all the time. You're not a boy any longer, but a man of twenty. I'll be back in two or three days. Greet everyone in the village, one by one, and in particular Abdul Hadi and Muhammad Abu Suweilim. And take care of your mother, Diab. Don't annoy her or squabble with her while I'm gone.'

Diab kissed his hand, and Muhammad Effendi walked off alone, smoothing his suit as he went.

Diab walked the donkey till the pavements turned to fields, when with a sigh of pleasure he mounted the comfortable velvet saddle. But a spiritual pain seized him as he looked back to the town, trying in vain to pick out his brother among the tall houses and the crowded traffic of carts, cars and cabs. He felt suddenly very lonely, and sad too because he had got no clear reply from his brother about Waseefa. Nevertheless, he sat proudly as the donkey trotted away from the town. His mind was engrossed with a vision of Waseefa, tall, fair, plump like cream, her face lovely as jasmine, her father's land marching with his own and Muhammad Effendi's.

They took the wide road by the river, the same that an hour ago had burnt his feet. Now he was astride as noble a mount as the Arab steeds famed in legend. On and on the donkey ran, past village after village, and high in the heavens the sun flamed over everything and everyone; no work was being done, people lazed in the shade of trees; they returned Diab's greeting as he passed, but with less respect than they had shown to his effendi brother. Despite his pride in the ass, Diab felt lonely, and his mind turned, despite itself, to the fearful noontime fairy he had been told of as a child, and to keep up his spirits he tried to whistle a song, but it would not go right, and he fell into a silence which felt like death.

Reaching the village, Diab pulled the donkey to a halt, to survey for a moment the surface of the river, gleaming iridescent under the disc of the sun, so that looking at it his eyes felt a physical hurt from the glare. He let go the bridle, kicking the donkey's side, and they were in the village lanes.

Suddenly, in the narrow way, he saw a girl: no ordinary village girl, from her dancing walk, from the angle at which she held her pitcher with a plump hand, and from the brightly coloured dress, which only one girl in the whole village wore.

'Waseefa,' he muttered to himself. 'My destiny!' On her arms glass bracelets glittered.

Like a horseman, he gripped the donkey with his legs; like a chivalrous knight, he thrust out his chest, prodding the donkey with his bare heels, pinching her coat under the saddle. The astonished animal reared, raised her head, let out a loud bray, and charged ahead far faster than before, raising a storm of dust.

With an agile gesture, the girl flung the contents of her pitcher at the beast and its rider. With a mocking laugh she shouted:

'What's the matter with you? It *is* you, Diab, and not some knight ... all this pomp and noise!'

Crestfallen, Diab recognized Kadra.

'What tricks are you playing, dressed up like this?' With mockery, with obscene oaths, she caught hold of the bridle and pulled the donkey to a stop. She had wanted to wash her dress that day; she had tried to borrow a dress to wear, while she filled her pitcher for the Omda's wife, and not one girl or woman could be found to lend her one, except Waseefa.

And while Diab tried to unprise her fingers from the bridle, she asked him in the same insolent tones:

'And what did you bring me from town? A corn-loaf at least, or some pepper cakes? You *have* brought me something?'

He broke her grip, freed the bridle and urged the donkey away.

'Something? Why? May poverty take you!'

He laughed, alone. Kadra suddenly collapsed into a staring

sadness, and in a gentle voice, full of bitterness, asked:

'Diab, why do you say that? Aren't I poor enough already?'

'If you want a couple of cucumbers, meet me tonight at the stable.'

She shouted her bitter reply.

'Ah, you want something from *me*, do you?'

Trying to hide his embarrassment with a dry laugh, he kicked the donkey. But still with obscene language she held him back, leaning towards him to whisper that if he wanted something, he'd better bring some marrows as well as cucumbers. Her dry breasts shook.

Fortunately it was so hot, there was no one about. Behind open doors Diab saw old women lying on the ground, yawning, or hunting for lice in other women's hair. Sheikh Yusif's shop was shut. Every threshold glared in the heat. Diab reached home, and while he was tethering the donkey, his mother asked anxiously if Muhammad Effendi had caught the train all right.

'Yes, he caught it!'

He took off the saddle and began to wipe down the donkey, not looking at his mother. Again she asked him if his brother had really caught the train, in front of his eyes.

'Didn't I tell you he caught it the first time?'

His mother was satisfied.

'May God guard you from the evils hidden in the Unknown.'

His mother's words made him shiver, and he felt renewed longing for his brother.

He piled beans in front of the donkey – more than usual; and with the hem of his gallabya wiped the sweat from his face. He then asked his mother for his dinner. He ate it sitting on the big platform at the entrance to the house, in silence, the only sound the cracking of maize loaves and the grinding of his teeth. And after eating, he wiped his mouth with the back of his hand, belched, and drove the donkey into the field.

Diab was no longer a boy, yet, during his whole life, Diab had never done anything except at the bidding, and under the direction, of his brother, Muhammad Effendi. He was the one who could solve any problem, who could haggle at the market over prices, or tell him when to plant beans instead of clover or clover instead of wheat, who knew the different kinds of manure. To Diab, Muhammad Effendi was everything in life: ability, the power that came from money and wealth that was the product of knowledge. He was the future and all that gives pride to the spirit of a man.

That evening Diab waited by the canal, in his hands a cucumber and some small marrows. In his boredom, he chewed on a cucumber. If Kadra did not come, he'd have to get back to the village. This was the time of day when Kadra scraped a living, by getting in behind the beasts returning from the fields and catching their dung to make sun-dried circles to be burned in ovens.

The sun sank and Diab threw away the vegetables. He shut the stable door and went home to keep his mother company.

On his way he saw that the cucumbers and marrows were throttling the young cotton shoots with their small pods. Was it time to hoe them up? Alas, the only person who could answer this question was Muhammad Effendi, and Diab had forgotten to ask him before he left.

Next day Diab worked in the field. At noon, just as his thoughts turned to home and food, he saw Kadra arriving with his dinner, sent by his mother. The two of them ate together in the stable, and Kadra stayed with him till evening, and when she left him, she carried on her head a load of cucumbers and marrows. Eating happily, she called back to Diab that he must be satisfied with her visits: for the stars themselves were nearer to him than Waseefa. Diab smiled in silence, and lay down on the roof of the stable, under the shade of a tree.

But when she had gone, he felt very much alone. Again he thought of his absent brother. What should he do on the farm? Should he uproot the cucumbers, or leave them? If his brother did not come back in time for the new irrigation period, should he start on the field near the river, or the one by the canal?

Melancholy possessed Diab as the day declined, and as he lay there on the stable roof. He could stand it no longer. He walked to the village and stood in front of Sheikh Yusif's shop. This was something his brother had forbidden him to do. This was the first time he had disobeyed Muhammad Effendi. His brother had also told him never to smoke or drink tea, or do other wasteful things.

He saw Alwani at the shop, on his nightly descent for supplies. Sheikh Yusif was shaking his head, stimulating the fears of those who had signed the Petition. The Omda, he was saying, had handed it to Mahmoud Bey, read by nobody.

One man said that he had never wanted to sign it, only his wife had insisted.

Another had been overruled by Sheikh Shinawi.

A third said that the blue fairy herself could not have wheedled his seal from him, yet somehow he had yielded and signed.

Diab was just about to make his contribution when Abdul Hadi arrived.

He was not in a cheerful humour. Diab asked him what weighed on him. Abdul Hadi took Diab's arm and led him aside. Abu Suweilim had just heard Kadra talking to Waseefa in the most disgusting language. Diab's name had come into her obscenities. Abu Suweilim had beaten both girls, and had banished Kadra for ever from his house.

Diab was deeply embarrassed. He tried to clear his throat, preparatory to saying something in reply, but Abdul Hadi had drifted back to the shop. Was it correct, he was asking, that the irrigation period started in three day's time?

'No, alas, in two.'

'Two days only?' exclaimed Diab. 'Will Muhammad Effendi be back in two days?'

Abdul Hadi shouted:

'You think the Government will change its policy in two days? That it will read the Petition and change its policy at once?'

One of the bystanders said, 'What business is it of the Government's? We know our business. Let them mind theirs.'

Sheikh Yusif took off his grubby white turban and rearranged the red Moroccan fez which he wore underneath, with its blue tassel. It was quite impossible, he said, that Mahmoud Bey and Muhammad Effendi should present their petition in two days.

Diab pondered a moment, then asked what this Cairo was. Why shouldn't Muhammad Effendi contact the Government, given two whole days? Didn't the Government have an official Residence, just like the Omda's?

Disregarding him, Abdul Hadi suggested that the thing to do was to get all the waterwheels working at once, and perhaps break the embankment, so that water could flood over all the ground at once. One of the bystanders suggested that the canal should be cut too.

Replacing his turban, Sheikh Yusif glanced at Diab.

'You asked me about Cairo?'

He shook his head sadly. Cairo was no longer supportable. Cairo had been itself in the days when Sheikh Yusif had been a student at the Azhar. In those days it had been select. Nowadays anyone with a pound or two in his pocket could go and live there. (Abdul Hadi smiled, seeing that Diab had missed the point of the old man's sarcasm.) The best summing up was in the verse of the poet:

'Not everyone who wears the turban embellishes it;

Not everyone who rides a horse is a horseman;

Not everyone who calls you by your first name is a friend.'

With flattering rapture Alwani exclaimed:

'My brothers, he knows everything! He even knows the poetry of the Arabs. He's as clever and knowing as a monkey!'

'A monkey bite you, you thief from a stable of thieves!' Sheikh Yusif was enraged. 'Get away from my shop! May you be monkeyfied!'

No words of apology or explanation would relax the frown on the old grocer's face and Alwani retired to the sycamore across the way from the shop. Diab meanwhile asked Sheikh Yusif if he thought it was possible a letter would reach him from his brother tomorrow.

Quite impossible! Letters from Cairo took three days at least.

'A letter from Muhammad Effendi must arrive tomorrow!' Diab shouted. *Must* arrive, if he was to know which field to water first, or to tell his hand from his head.

Next day the sun had not scorched the dew from the trees, before Diab was standing by the large post box fixed to the wall of the Residence. After an hour's wait, he squatted on the ground to play a game of draughts with Abdul Aati. Suddenly he saw the postman. Abdul Aati, the guard responsible for taking the letters, got up, casting a glance back at his counters, the red ones; he was winning, and Diab, whose black pieces had been nearly all taken, was relieved that the post had come at this moment, as he was proud of his reputation as a draughts-player. A group of children had been following every move; now they clustered round the Box.

The postman, riding an elderly blue-black donkey, wore a dusty khaki uniform, and, to protect his neck against the sun, a large handkerchief under his frayed tarboosh. He carried a huge, tattered bag. He shut his patched umbrella and handed the bag to Abdul Aati, who held it open while slowly and methodically the postman delved within for envelopes and packages.

'Any letters from Muhammad Effendi?'

Indignantly, the postman glanced up at Diab, then went

back to his delving. His dry, wrinkled face, his flat, shapeless nose, his mouth downturned under a thick grey moustache, all composed the picture of a man, with knobbly chin and clouded eyes, who had suffered from life, a man weeping without tears. A townsman, he felt no sympathy with the villagers, hence his grim face and his bored expression.

'Sir, Your Excellency, Mister Postman: haven't you something from Muhammad Effendi?'

Stifling his anger, the postman replied through clenched teeth:

'I haven't x-ray eyes to see inside the letters.'

'All right, but ...'

The postman read the addresses on the envelopes. The boys took some of the letters, after Abdul Aati had made sure of the addresses; the rest were left to his custody. The postman opened his umbrella, got on his donkey and rode off.

Diab was desolate.

On a sudden impulse he ran after the postman, seized hold of the donkey, and shouted:

'You haven't said if there's a letter from Muhammad Effendi or not. Read the envelopes in your bag properly. Mine will have on it, "to his brother Diab, with greetings".'

Angrily the postman retorted that there was no envelope addressed to Diab, and as for knowing what was inside the letters, he was a postman, not a soothsayer.

'God ransom me from this work! Thirty years, and not a penny saved.'

Diab shouted after him.

'Why so cross? Don't shout at me like that. Don't get so

irritable. There's no letter – why didn't you say so earlier? Plague take you, insolent townsman!'

In the evening, when Diab went to the shop, he was greeted with a line of song:

'I sent him letters ... but no answer came!'

Sheikh Yusif laughed loud and long; so did the other loiterers. Only Diab saw nothing funny.

'Why are you suddenly so witty, Sheikh Yusif? Would you laugh at me like this if my brother was here?'

Sheikh Yusif now mixed taunts against Muhammad Effendi with those against Diab.

Next morning, with the same impatience, Diab played draughts, waiting for the post. This time the postman hit at him with his furled umbrella.

'Pest on you village people, and your letters! Your years of letters!'

When Sheikh Yusif taunted him again that evening, Diab burst into a lengthy speech.

'What's wrong with you, Sheikh Yusif? Why are you so angry with me and my brother? The whole village envies us ... why? Slandering, gossiping, backbiting village! I know what you've got against us: we work harder than you do. Our land is more productive – and why? Your land was going to ruin, we redeemed it, with our sweat, our hoes, our skill. What do you know of farming? You know how to taunt. By the life of the Prophet, that's all you're good for, Sheikh Yusif, you and this whole malicious village.'

As he spoke, he punctuated his eloquence with frantic finger-proddings that threatened to put out one of Sheikh

Yusif's eyes. The old grocer's yellow face paled, his breath came hot and suddenly he leant over and slapped the boy on his face. The sting of the slap resounded. Diab touched his cheek: the silence of tension. Diab's self-control was almost gone.

'So, Sheikh Yusif, you strike one of God's creatures? You who boast of having studied at Al-Azhar? A man like yourself, made by our Lord? No matter, Sheikh Yusif. You are an old man, like my father.' A moment's further silence, then his parting shot: 'May God forgive you!'

This phrase reduced the old man to a quivering mass of nerves. He felt about to collapse. Some men took Diab apart and soothed him, others tried to soothe Sheikh Yusif, but the old man shut up his shop and stumped off to see Abu Suweilim.

He found Abu Suweilim sitting in the moonlight with Abdul Hadi. There was a gentle stillness in the night. Abdul Hadi was as near the door as he could get, turning at every chance of seeing Waseefa. It hurt him that she no longer poured them coffee now that Muhammad Effendi had gone. Looking at the serene dark skies of night he muttered under his breath:

'I made friends with my friend and I found him befriended
And the friend of two never sticks to one ...'

Abu Suweilim smiled.

'You are right, Abdul Hadi, my boy. The friend of two never sticks to one.'

Abdul Hadi murmured:

'And the friend who oppressed me is at odds with me.'

Abu Suweilim interrupted him with a laugh:

'You're turning to love songs, are you? Is your heart turning to love? Has it come to this? The tyranny of the Government, and your thoughts turn to love?'

Abdul Hadi laughed, looking towards Sheikh Yusif. But the old man could not manage a smile. He wanted to unburden himself about his clash with Diab. Abdul Hadi's first reaction was to laugh, but then he said:

'Poor thing! That boy's a pathetic creature, Sheikh Yusif, no brains at all.'

Their silence was broken by the clicking of Sheikh Shinawi's beads. When he saw Abdul Hadi, he scolded him for not coming to evening prayer, even though the mosque was right next to his house.

'You mean, that mosque was put up for my benefit only, Sheikh? I'm not the only one. Why not blame Sheikh Yusif and Abu Suweilim, too?'

Cornered, Sheikh Shinawi laughed.

'You're certainly a sly one, Abdul Hadi.'

The others laughed.

Abdul Hadi got up to go. He wanted to sleep early. He would be getting up first thing in the morning to work his waterwheel; the new period started tomorrow.

Sheikh Yusif suggested they should all follow Abdul Hadi's example.

The fields by the canal, Abu Suweilim said, would never get their share of water in five days.

'Don't worry,' said Abdul Hadi, 'things will be put right.'

'Put right, how?' asked Sheikh Shinawi, standing up to go. 'If not by prayer? Come to mosque at dawn. Say a couple of prayers, so that your Lord will bless you and your land.'

As he walked away, Abdul Hadi said under his breath:

'Water first, and prayer afterwards, that's the better system.'

The Sheikh said: 'That boy Abdul Hadi will never reach Paradise. His life and his tongue are too uncontrolled.'

'You're very hard on him,' said Abu Suweilim, turning to look up, 'predicting misery for him in the afterlife, as well as here.'

Abdul Hadi went indoors to bed, and dreamt of Paradise – of Paradise in this world, not the next.

Dawn still hiding behind the horizon, a pale light over everything, and the voice of Sheikh Shinawi from the minaret, disjointed, tired from sleep, and sad. In the fields the small green shoots heavy with dew trembled, while gentle breezes caressed the earth. The air was beautiful and still, the sky, the river, the trees, all a new creation seen for the first time. And well before sunrise Abdul Hadi was standing barefoot in the canal which brought the water from the river bank, digging at it with his hoe, lifting up lumps of heavy mud, to make a channel for the water going to his field. His cow was turning his waterwheel, at its side a small boy rubbing his eyes. And not far off was another man similarly bent over his hoe, digging a route for water – Diab. And all along the bank men were spread out, half-naked, bent over the water, preparing a way for it to reach their thirsty fields. But Alwani, who had spent the long night guarding the one melon-field by the river, was getting ready to sleep.

Abdul Hadi noticed that the water had become sluggish. He raised his head, his body still bent: the wheel was turning. He stood upright, expanded his chest, put his muddy hands upon his hips and contemplated the world. The last murks of night had left the sky. Chattering and crying the birds had left their trees, the beautiful white birds with elongated beaks. They flew in whirling flocks to alight on the earth and to play in the water, pecking and picking without fear.

Abdul Hadi strode to the waterwheel. To latecomers whom he passed on his way, he shouted, 'Hurry! The sun is up, it'll soon be scorching!'

'A miserly flow you've got.'

'I'm on my way to see what's up.'

As he reached the river, he was singing to himself:

'The Judge of Love above the mountain high Demands who's left his love ... it's I, it's I!'

Unknown to himself, his voice was loud and clear, and from far off a voice answered him, 'Poor Abdul Hadi, may your separation soon be over!'

Abdul Hadi reached the river. The sun had by now dried the dew from the trees, and the river flowed stilly, silently. Its surface caught the varied colours of the sky. A solitary boat moved. By both banks the nets of fishermen knocked against the water. The morning mist had dissolved in the heat of the day. Along the bank, voices and shouts resounded, noises of activity, united with the melancholy groans of the straining waterwheels. From his position by the wheel, Abdul Hadi could see, far off, another man bending in the water from the large canal over the iron screw; evidently the water was flowing normally in the large canal. This was encouraging. He leant over his wheel, carefully examining each of the receptacles which lifted the water from the well; all were in good condition. The little canal, too, which brought the river water into the bank and under the waterwheel was also clear, and pouring strongly into the small canal that led to his field. Abdul Hadi traced the flow of water alongside his neighbour's fields, till suddenly it diminished and became a mere trickle, crawling like a drunkard. The wall of the canal had been broken in a number of places; the water was flowing through these holes into the fields which Diab was working with his hoe. He was furious that Diab had dared to steal his water in this way, taking the water raised by Abdul Hadi's own wheel before he had taken what he needed himself. Did Diab want to do with him what the Pasha had done with the village? For the Pasha's land, too, was alongside the river, which gave him the right, he considered, to take half the village's water for himself. But a Pasha was ... a Pasha. Behind him, in the neighbouring town, stood the ranks of those capable of sending men to prison. If anyone thought of beating this Pasha, he himself would be beaten, and the beating would not cease till it had left him dead. Why was Diab stealing his water, like the Pasha? Without permission?

He received no polite answer from Diab.

'God opens, God knows. ... Be off with you, Abdul Hadi!'

And he returned to his hoe, beating the earth with it, his feet in water. Abdul Hadi ordered him to go himself and repair the gaps which he had made, and then get off to the village, and leave people to the jobs they understood. Shaking his fists, Diab began to speak to Abdul Hadi as he had spoken to Sheikh Yusif: the whole village was envious of himself and his brother, Muhammad Effendi.

So Abdul Hadi went to the bank and himself dragged up in his hands a large lump of mud; with this he blocked the hole in the canal through which the water was flowing towards Diab's field. His heart now at rest, he returned to his work.

And now the threads of water which flowed to Diab and his neighbour were cut off. His neighbour, working bare-chested and up to his thighs in water, noticed the sudden lack, and turned his head to Diab, clicking his tongue in irritation.

'What's this bully Abdul Hadi up to this time? Who does he think he is? The Government, to throw his weight about in this manner? The next thing, he'll break the waterwheels.'

Bracing his body, shouldering his hoe, Diab shouted out that he himself was going to reopen the canal, and whoever this annoyed could go and drink from the sea, or from a pond! And without another word, he ran to the bank and hacked a gap so that once again all the water began to flow towards his own field, and that of his neighbour. And in a voice which endeavoured to conceal his anxiety he shouted out:

'Listen, Abdul Hadi. I have one day of the waterwheel, and so has my neighbour Massoud. You say it's your waterwheel, do you? We have a day's use of it, so has Massoud, and the eastern sector they have two days. I'm taking my day now. You take your animal off, for here comes Massoud's wife with his beast.'

It was indeed true that the villagers had made this arrangement concerning Abdul Hadi's waterwheel; a famous carpenter who lived on the other bank had built it, and people had shares in it according to the amount they contributed to the cost. But these shares had been arranged when the period for irrigation was ten days, not five, and when no one expected them to be cut.

Diab's shouts continued until Massoud's wife arrived leading her buffalo. She was not alone. She turned continually to insult back a crowd of other villagers who had brought their beasts from the eastern sector. Diab tried to enlist their support in his opposition to Abdul Hadi. There was now the sound of voices mixed in anger.

Abdul Hadi again came back to the bank, doing all he could to control himself. With a gentle smile he asked Diab, in the interests of peace, to get back to the village, or go to the field near the canal, as he had always done before, and not try to cause strife among people. Diab refused point-blank to do this: he was not stealing water or anything else, he was taking his rights, while Abdul Hadi was throwing his weight about, as usual.

Some of the men from the eastern sector now broke into the argument, with their wives. They had brought their buffaloes and cows expecting to use the wheel for two days. Abdul Hadi tried to point out to them how things were changed, that the period was reduced from ten days to five, and that if they took two days, as before, other fields would go thirsty. To Abdul Hadi's suggestion that their two days should in fairness now become one, the men and women replied with angry shouts and screams. Diab's rage was the most fierce: the more angry he got, the more release he felt, and carelessly his words tumbled one on top of another. Violent rage flashed between the men of the eastern sector, between them and Diab, between them and Abdul Hadi, and between Abdul Hadi and Diab. In the violence of the argument each felt that the other was trying to deprive him of fife itself. Suddenly Abdul Hadi remembered that no one was in his field, arranging the distribution of water from one part to another; the wheel was turning, the whole field would be drowned.

But a woman shouted to him with a loud mocking cry, that since they had come, the wheel was turning no more!

Rushing to the bank, Abdul Hadi found that his cow was rubbing her head against the sycamore; nearby the little boy stood idle, there was a woman too, and men stood in a circle; in their midst stood a hooded buffalo.

'Bravo, Abdul Hadi, so manly and so clever. A woman has sufficed to stop your wheel.'

Without a thought, Abdul Hadi cracked Diab hard on his cheek.

Trembling with rage, Diab raised his hoe to bring it down on Abdul Hadi's head. But before its shiny blade could fall, Abdul Hadi caught it and flung it afar. The men's shouts got louder, joined by the screams of women.

Running quickly to the waterwheel, Abdul Hadi seized the strong bar to which the animals were tied, and with this stout, squared stick he began to beat the heads of those around him, blindly. In a surge of violent feelings, to protect the land, to give it water, the villagers set upon each other, beating and being beaten, without thought or care: as if they were strangers to each other, as if there had never been between them ties of love, as if it was impossible that they could ever be friends again; as if each could do anything, however terrible, to his brother, cut from him, eat him ... do anything to obtain water. And the women were no better. They picked up stones and hurled them against the men. Blood flowed, mingling from each man's veins with that of his neighbour. A man fell to the ground, then a woman, then Diab, then a man, then another two women, then a fourth man, and a fifth. The sticks continued to whack, the women to scream; the noise of the fight drew children and women, as well as men; women began to scream from far off, not knowing yet the cause. Among the newcomers was the Sheikh al-Balad, stumbling in his long gallabya. Alwani awoke in his melon-field and ran to calm the fighting villagers, asking them to break it up. No one paid him the least attention. He tried to push his way among the men, but the sticks continued to whack. So seizing a stick for himself, he stood behind Abdul Hadi, using his stick to ward off any attacks which might come from behind.

The Sheikh al-Balad tried to stop the men fighting, from outside the range of their whirling sticks. But they heard neither his insults, nor his threats. The sticks continued to whirl, the women to scream. The only one he could detach from the fighting was Alwani, whom he ordered to run as quickly as possible to the village to fetch the guards. Alwani took a short cut between the fields.

Sheikh Shinawi now arrived, panting from his haste, sweat pouring from his face, his belly shaking. He panted imprecations on the men for their blasphemy, on the women for their unfeminine boldness. He beat their backs with his short stick, till his eyes fell on a longer one with which to beat more efficiently, keeping himself out of range of the sticks at the same time. And all the time he cursed them: it was a terrible sin for one Moslem to spill the blood of another!

The last to arrive was Sheikh Yusif, also tired out, carrying a long thin cane, with which he tried to separate the men, at the same time threatening to leave this Godforsaken village and remove himself and his family to some civilized spot.

The shouts calmed a little, though the sticks continued to fly and though men continued to fall. And at this moment a pitiful cry of despair came from the waterwheel. A sound Sheikh Yusif thought worthy of a demon! He ran to the wheel to investigate.

'The buffalo ... Come and save the buffalo ... she's fallen down the well!'

Suddenly the fighting stopped, the sticks and staffs no longer whacked, the women no longer screamed, but all clustered in a silent, breathless throng around the well. Cries mingled with shouts for help. The Sheikh al-Balad's orders were drowned in the noise. But Sheikh Shinawi managed to outshout them all.

'Take care, boy, take care, you! Don't come near or you'll drown her. Recite the Opening Prayer, so that God may rescue her!'

And to give encouragement he began to recite a story of

how once the cow of the Prophet Moses ... But he couldn't complete it, for thrusting him aside, all but pushing him in the well, Massoud burst out: 'Go away, Sheikh ... be off! What has Moses and his cow to do with us? Get in, go after her, please, please, all of you ... lend a hand, save her! This is my ruin, the end of all I've worked for!' And he sat on the grass, beating his face and moaning piteously, in complete despair.

But Abdul Hadi, short of breath though he was, leaped into the well, lowering himself by means of the water-holders, and then put his hands under the stomach of the buffalo, levering against the sides of the well with his feet.

Some of the men who had been lying down by the bank, wounded, crept near the well; even Diab tried to get down to it. But Abdul Hadi urged him back with tenderness.

'Take care of yourself, Diab ... Your blood is still flowing.'

And a third man approached Abdul Hadi, and very nearly fell down the well himself, only Abdul Hadi told him to go further off and rest. The loss of Massoud's buffalo had united them all; a calamity like this fell on them all equally, and they must all confront it, standing side by side.

So now other men got down into the well, manoeuvring their feet against the sides or against the receptacles for water, some with great difficulty, but all working together against a disaster which each felt as his own: their hands together under the belly of the beast, their eyes straining together to see some way to rescue her. And outside the well other men and women pushed and peered in anxiety. The Sheikh al-Balad shouted orders which nobody heard. Sheikh Shinawi invoked the power of God. Massoud's eyes were on Abdul

Hadi, while his hands clutched at the earth. He looked now at the men struggling in the well and now at his wife, sitting yellow as death in front of him. Suddenly he saw the nose of the buffalo as she almost managed to scramble out of the well; the next moment she fell back in again, and his despair increased.

'The buffalo is lost! My life is finished! You have ruined me, woman! Oh that you had fallen down the well, and not her! For where will I ever get a buffalo again? Be strong, Abdul Hadi, Oh, be strong, the rest of you.'

Sheikh Shinawi roared at him, 'Be strong yourself, boy, and call upon your Lord! God curse you if you do not call upon Him!'

And the men in the well continued to struggle, and whenever one had to give up from exhaustion, another one took his place.

But at last the buffalo was lifted out by the efforts of the men. Her hood was removed. She staggered, stretching her hind legs, while the bystanders patted and felt her. And life returned to Massoud's wife, who had felt herself on the point of death, and hope to Massoud, and the wife led the other women in shouts of joy. The Sheikh al-Balad shouted at the women to shut up, but they took no notice. Massoud put his bloodstained head against the buffalo, then turned to Abdul Hadi and embraced him with all his remaining force, and then kissed the hand of the Sheikh, apologizing for his sins.

Abdul Hadi was quite out of breath. He walked in silence and stood under the sycamore by the bank. He wiped his sweat from his face with his hand, and shook his head sadly.

The Sheikh al-Balad began to speak with what he considered was an eloquence equal to that of any city-dweller:

'We have come back to where we started. No modesty among women, no shame among men! Chaos only, chaos in which you beat each other openly, in front of me, in front of the representative of the Government, in front, in fact, of the Government itself.'

A pleasant breeze played upon his face as he spoke.

But on the faces of those who listened played mocking smiles. And people felt a new bond, besides fatigue, and sweat, and the common efforts to rescue the buffalo from the well: this new bond was a common ability to laugh at his pretensions, to greet his attempts to play the ruler and the boss with a sense of humour. And someone began to imitate the accent of the Sheikh al-Balad as he had shouted so ineffectually during the rescue operations.

'Come here, you! Get down that side, you, and you, there, get down here!'

And another added, 'But he's an utter fool, he knows nothing. If it had been left to him, the buffalo would still be there next year. If he'd come near the well, he'd have fallen down too.'

And the general laughter drowned the shouts of the Sheikh al-Balad.

Some men were washing the blood from their faces in the water of the canal.

And Diab murmured to himself in a voice which was all the more wounding for sounding resigned and pitiful:

'So, Abdul Hadi, so ... You took advantage of me when I was alone, when I was all alone on account of Muhammad Effendi's going away, when I was isolated ... I would not have expected it of you.'

And hearing his words Abdul Hadi's heart was suddenly flooded with a sense of guilt, a sense that he had been cruel. He could not bear it, and putting his head between his two hands he began to weep passionately, to the amazement of all who saw. Impetuously Diab ran up to him, and tried to quieten him, trying to kiss him, but Sheikh Shinawi exploded at Abdul Hadi with a cold rage.

'What are you weeping at? May they weep for your death, and soon! You mean, you kill your victim, then walk in his funeral procession? You beat up the whole village, and then wish it well? The Devil take you for your impudent strength! You must be ridden by a Devil stronger than Pharaoh!'

Some of the men laughed, including Sheikh Shinawi himself.

And only now did Abdul Hadi feel, like a breeze touching his heart, a sense of relief, and he too smiled.

The Sheikh al-Balad leant on his stick. He had some advice to offer to the men: they should fill their wounds with dust, it was the best cure.

'Dust, indeed!' said Sheikh Yusif. 'The only thing for wounds is coffee. Let each man buy a small quantity from my shop, for an egg, or two corn-cobs, and plaster his wounds with that. Dust, indeed!'

Some of the men laughed, and one said sarcastically: 'Why don't we all go to the hospital in the town?'

'Or better still,' said another, 'why don't we fetch the doctor here?'

And another, letting fall each phrase with mocking deliberation:

'Are we the Pasha's horse? Or smart effendis? Or Cairo whores that we should be visited by doctors?' Sheikh Yusif interrupted their laughter with a reminder of Abdul Hadi's original suggestion that they should simply cut the bank of the river: let them break the bank and irrigate their lands as they wanted, without any need of waterwheels or apportioning of times. And Diab exclaimed, 'That's the best policy, let's irrigate just as we wish.' Only Sheikh Shinawi raised objections: but Abdul Hadi retorted that this was not a question of Heaven or Hell, and it would be best for him to keep silent.

'But it will be a black day if you break the bank. The guards will in any case come and stop you!'

'The guards? Welcome to them, let them come and drink hot coffee!'

And Sheikh Yusif backed him up. What did the breaking of the bank have to do with sin or religion? And as for the guards, what did they know about irrigation? And as for the Sheikh al-Balad, it was not his job to give useless advice, standing there with his hand on his hip, as if he was a provincial governor!

This made even the Sheikh al-Balad smile; he approved their plan. Let them irrigate as they wished, but behind his back, and he would promise to keep the guards away from them. And as he turned to leave, followed by some of the women, the men attacked the embankment with might and main, and in a short time they had made a huge gash through which the water flowed in a great tide, and merrily the villagers saw to it that all the fields were awash with water, heavy with silt.

'This is the way to do things,' said Abdul Hadi. 'We don't need waterwheels, this flood is more than ten wheels could muster.'

Only Massoud was pessimistic. 'How long will they let it last?'

Abdul Hadi and Diab walked towards the village.

'We must never fight,' said Diab. 'We are each other's prosperity. For us to fight, is like our entrails fighting. We must not shed blood, for we are all of one blood in this village.'

On their way back they saw Abu Suweilim coming towards them. He shouted to them from far off: where was Sheikh Yusif? Abu Suweilim looked older than his years, as though some great worry was in his mind, and at first Abdul Hadi thought it must be because of the fight.

'It's all finished, we've made it up, we're friends again.' Diab enthusiastically agreed. But this was not the matter.

'That's child's play,' said Abu Suweilim violently. 'As for you, Diab, run off and greet your brother.' In delight Diab ran off. The two others walked together, Abu Suweilim beating one fist against the other. Suddenly he stopped, and taking Abdul Hadi by the arm, explained the situation which made him so anxious. The new Petition, which Muhammad Effendi and Mahmoud Bey had taken to Cairo, had nothing to do with irrigation. The Omda had tricked the village, and in collaboration with Mahmoud Bey had forced the villagers to sign a document requesting the construction of a highway, to run across their land, linking the Pasha's new Palace with the main road to Cairo.

Abu Suweilim, seeing Abdul Hadi's astonishment, assured him it was true, not a dream. And as though awakening from a nightmare, Abdul Hadi simply said, 'Mahmoud Bey!'

And Abu Suweilim replied:

'Didn't I warn you? They have cooked up this scheme, to make it appear that they are acting in the name of the village, not against it. They mocked us, and we were silent. They took the Chief-Guardship from us, and we said nothing. They smashed our waterwheels and cut our water, and we were silent. And they will do worse things so long as we say nothing!'

And still in a voice that sounded as though he were awakening from a nightmare, 'What do we do now, Muhammad Abu Suweilim?'

But what could Abu Suweilim reply?

While the little boys invented a new game, the imitation of Abdul Hadi's triumph in beating singlehanded the men of a whole sector of the village, the hero of the morning was escorted to his house by Abu Suweilim, who opened up his little-used parlour for Abdul Hadi to rest in. While Waseefa brought the two men water in a spotless jug, Abu Suweilim remarked that Muhammad Effendi had returned from Cairo on the first train. This took away Abdul Hadi's pleasure at being served by the beautiful Waseefa. He felt he knew the reason which had prompted Muhammad Effendi's sudden return.

While Abdul Hadi was tilting the water-jug to his lips (between jealous glances at Waseefa) Abu Suweilim asked: 'What on earth has kept that rascal, Diab?'

The mention of Diab made Abdul Hadi spill the water, which cascaded down his cheek and on to his neck. Waseefa smiled and put out her hand for the jug.

'Wait ... wait ...' He frowned.

Muhammad Effendi was also complaining about Diab. For though he had begun to run home as fast as he could, he had been stopped on the way. He saw Kadra in a doorway, describing what had happened in her indecent language, with her habitual shameless gestures. The girls were fascinated by her story, but at the same time pretended to be shocked by her way of telling it, hiding their amusement by turning their heads behind each other's backs. As Diab's role in the fight was inglorious, he was naturally incensed by Kadra's account, and he angrily shouted to her to desist.

'You weren't so valiant on the bank, were you, you lord of men!'

Caught by her logic, Diab had only one reply: to hit her with his fists, and kick her in the stomach. She fell to the ground.

The girls were shocked.

Diab's rage left him. He was suddenly conscious that he, the brother of Muhammad Effendi, had been valiant only against a woman, a poor lost creature with no family or influence in the village, a woman furthermore with whom he had tangled more than once in the sweaty embrace of love.

'What's wrong, girl, what's wrong?'

Kadra raised her head from the ground and spoke in the same coldly mocking tones as before:

'So that's what you do to Kadra the Noble?'

And Diab and the girls laughed at her reference to the popular folk tale, and Diab replied with a reference to the Beduin Knight, his tone tender. Kadra murmured in a low voice ... perhaps Diab wanted to bring on an abortion.

'You can make anything into a joke,' said one of the girls, with disapproval.

'And I know what you good girls really want,' replied Kadra tartly, 'conceal your wishes though you may!'

Kadra staggered to her feet, her eyes on Diab. The blood was beginning to cake upon his face; Kadra told one of the girls to bring water and coffee, at the same time scolding Diab for doing nothing about his wounds, but leaving them open to the sun. A girl brought water in a tin mug and Kadra washed his cuts and filled them with coffee. One of the girls exclaimed, 'What will Muhammad Effendi say when he hears all this?'

Kadra turned on her.

'Why this sudden interest in Muhammad Effendi?'

Blushing furiously, the girl turned her head.

Holding the coffee on his head Diab ran home. There he found his brother, in tarboosh, suit and shoes, sitting on a clean mat that his mother had spread on the raised platform by the door. His mother was squatting on the ground, under her thighs a duck to whom she was feeding seeds.

Muhammad Effendi got up in sudden alarm at sight of Diab's wounds. The two brothers embraced with heartfelt warmth, each discovering suddenly how much he had missed the other, and weeping with relief. Muhammad Effendi sat down again, asking his brother to sit beside him. He felt that he must never again desert his brother, but must stay always by him to protect him from the dangers which lay in wait. And Diab said through his tears:

'You shouldn't have left me, brother. What a black day! Without you a man's not worth a piece of firewood in this village.'

Suddenly his mother turned, and asked Diab what had happened by the river. Diab did not know what to say. His mother, who knew the truth, was upset. No one in the village had ever dared to strike her husband! Only once one of the villagers tried to have a row with him. But instead of coming to blows, their father had complained to the Omda, who had shut the man up for two days in the telephone room.

Diab hated his mother's anecdote, and knew that he would have to put up with her scoldings for the rest of the day; so he shouted to her to be silent. His brother rebuked him.

'Don't speak to your mother like that, boy! Hold your tongue.'

When Muhammad Effendi came downstairs again from changing his clothes, he found his mother holding a little box of white wood.

'Come and open these Cairo sweets, Diab. I'm going to bake you some pies.'

Diab's thoughts were at that moment on Kadra, but before he could slip out, he remembered that he had to tell Muhammad Effendi that Abu Suweilim and Abdul Hadi had been waiting for him a long time. Muhammad Effendi was angry that Diab had forgotten to deliver this important message. His head hanging low, Diab followed his brother out of the door. But their mother shouted:

'I missed you so much. Can't you stay a while longer now? Did you meet Sheikh Hassouna in Cairo? When's he coming to visit us? We all long to see the Headmaster again. He's no idea of his prestige in this village.'

Muhammad Effendi was impatient to be off. But he turned to say that Sheikh Hassouna would shortly be visiting the neighbouring town to enquire into the question of the highway, and he would take the opportunity of inspecting his own land, all of which was by the canal.

Sheikh Hassouna, a man in his fifties, had supervised Muhammad Effendi's education. Muhammad Effendi respected him more than anyone in the world. For once he had grown up and joined the Teachers' College, Muhammad Effendi had felt little respect for his father. He had no longer kissed his hand, as he did that of Sheikh Hassouna. When he was studying in the town, Sheikh Hassouna would pay him surprise visits. He would walk into his room and question him minutely about his studies. If he found anything to criticize in his way of life, or any signs of slacking in his work, he would beat him without pity.

Sheikh Hassouna was not really Muhammad Effendi's uncle, being in fact a second cousin of his mother's. He had been at Al-Azhar years ago, and had afterwards taught in Upper Egypt, in villages whose names no one had ever heard of, where he had slept on beds made of date sticks, over nests of scorpions. He had then been promoted to the headmastership of the school in the next village. But when the People's Party came to power, he had stood up to it; particularly when it had held elections, in face of the boycott of all other parties.

Sheikh Hassouna had called on the villagers to abstain from voting. He had allowed his teachers to leave school in protest. Nevertheless, the rigged elections had been carried out and won.

The People's Party deputy visited the village after being 'elected'. Sheikh Hassouna refused to receive him in the school. He sent the children home, and locked the doors. When by chance he met the deputy in the road, he warned him not to visit his own village, where he owned land, or he'd have his neck broken. Another village received the deputy with a hail of stones. No sooner was he back in the safety of town, than he demanded the immediate transfer of Sheikh Hassouna, or if possible, his dismissal. So the Headmaster was sent, as a simple teacher, to a remote village near the Barrage, the one means of access to which was by river-steamer. Sheikh Hassouna vainly tried to incite the village to revolt, as they had done when the English exiled the national leader. 'So he's Saad Zaghloul, is he?' One of the villagers laughed. 'Or William Makram?' And none of them stood in the roads to shout 'Long Live Justice!' as they had done in the glorious days of the past.

This deeply disappointed the Headmaster, and he let his land on a long lease, and swore he'd never set foot in the village again.

With him went his wife and five children. He rented for them a whole house in Shubra al-Balad, while he himself lived in a room at the school, and only came to Shubra at the weekends.

Sheikh Hassouna was still referred to locally as 'the Headmaster'; even his colleagues in the new school insisted on giving him the same title, as a tribute to his brave stand.

When Muhammad Effendi had arrived in Cairo with Mahmoud Bey, he was shown Sheikh Hassouna's house by some of the villagers living in Shubra. He at once told his uncle how Mahmoud Bey had pocketed the Petition, making an appointment to meet Muhammad Effendi in a cafe in Ataba Square. The Bey arrived late for this and every other appointment. Thus two days passed without their having a serious talk. Invariably Mahmoud Bey would receive a cordial welcome from the *gargon*, would present his shoes to a shoeblack; Muhammad Effendi could not help overhearing the shoeblack's whispers: once he caught the phrase 'Turkish, very young ...' another time, 'Yes, only a schoolgirl ...' or 'French ...' or 'She's not Egyptian' ... or 'a real Englishwoman.'

These whisperings, the consequent vanishings with the shoeblack, impelled Muhammad Effendi to ask, very nervously, if Mahmoud Bey would prefer him to return to the village.

Enraged, the Bey mockingly asked what Muhammad Effendi wanted. Plucking up his courage, Muhammad Effendi said, would he be so kind as to read him the Petition? Some of the villagers, he said, had made him promise to read the Petition before it was presented. Mahmoud Bey's answer was to read the Petition in a clear, unemotional voice.

It had to do with the new highway. Muhammad Effendi could not believe what he heard. His eyes glazed as he looked at the trams circling Ataba Square, clanging their way through the crowds. When he tried to ask a question, the Bey answered brusquely.

'You now know the situation. Or are you trying to play the fool? Your Omda told me you were bright. Why else did you give me the money? Or do you take me for a child?'

Without paying for the coffee, the Bey stalked off, muttering insults.

Sheikh Hassouna asked coldly why he had given the Bey money, and how much.

In anguish, Muhammad Effendi swore that it was not true, he had not given him a penny.

'You're a liar, a brazen liar. A dog's tail will never grow straight.'

His nephew was slumped on the pale red plush of Sheikh Hassouna's drawing-room chair. Beating fist upon fist, the old man said, 'So you trusted Mahmoud Bey, the son of that Turkish woman? Now you are tasting what you brewed! Fancy trusting the Bey and the Omda.'

Muhammad Effendi could find no words to answer his uncle. His only relief was that Sheikh Hassouna had spoken of 'you' in the plural, not to him in particular. But his relief was short-lived.

'And as for you, what do you do in the village? Drink tea here and there, preening yourself as a teacher?'

There was a moment's silence.

'If you give way this time, as you did before, if the Pasha's whims are indulged, then all the people by the canal will lose their land.'

Muhammad Effendi had to get up early next morning to take the bad news to the village. Escorting his nephew to the front door, Sheikh Hassouna told him to sleep where he had slept the previous nights, for having daughters past puberty he would not invite any males, outside the immediate family circle, to sleep in the house. Digging into his pocket, he offered Muhammad Effendi a coin for his hotel bill, but the latter refused it: he still had enough.

The Petition, Mahmoud Bey's behaviour, his uncle, all returned him to the village with a despondent heart.

'What about his girls?' his mother asked. 'Are they fully grown? Two years since I've seen them. They must be ripe for marriage. Zaynab was born the year we built the waterwheel, Fatima immediately before her, she's the oldest. Another was stillborn. How old is Fatima now?'

'About fourteen.'

'Fourteen! A girl of fourteen, her face is the fourteen-day moon! She must be as sweet as honey, with all the refinements of Cairo. If you were to marry her ...'

'But my uncle always speaks to me as if I was a failure.'

His mother was indignant.

'You a failure? Why you could sit on a sofa and pick the best! You just decide and leave the rest to me. Fatima or Zaynab,' she said as he walked away. 'I'll fix everything with your uncle.'

Greeted by Abu Suweilim and Abdul Hadi, smiled at by Waseefa, Muhammad Effendi could not help saying, 'I would not have expected it of you, Abdul Hadi. You are so much older and wiser than Diab. To take advantage of the boy when he was alone ...'

Abu Suweilim turned the subject, first by laughing at the story of the townsman's donkey, then bringing up Sheikh Hassouna. When Muhammad Effendi said that his uncle would shortly be coming, the old man exclaimed: 'Excellent, my friends! Now's the time we need him. We're in a time as grave as under the Military Authority!' Abdul Hadi repeated balefully:

'The Military Authority!'

This was Abu Suweilim's cue.

'Yes, the Authority. You were still children then ... They rounded people up wherever they could find them. You've no idea what we went through, Abdul Hadi! Their soldiers conscripted men, camels, donkeys, anything that walked. Sheikh Hassouna was with me, in those days a simple teacher. They handcuffed us, dressed us in khaki, and called us "volunteers". Anyone who refused they put in prison. They took us to Palestine. I went to their villages! A thousand times I looked death in the eyes, there in Palestine. We crawled through snow. Do you know what snow is? We crawled on our bellies through the freezing cold. And when we rested, we asked each other: "What are we here for, lads? What's this to do with us?" No one knew the answer. We were fighting who? We were fighting, why? No one could say. They spoke of "the enemy" ... who was the enemy? And whose enemy? No one could tell us. Bullets whistled over our heads, our friends were shot down without a word. Those were terrible days.May God rob them of rest who sent us! There are corpses mouldering on those mountains still. Men who died far off, but had no idea what it was all about. God forbid such days return again – days when they drag men off to war and call them volunteers.'

Three days passed and still no sign of Sheikh Hassouna. Sheikh Yusif sat on a bench in front of his shop, with him Abu Suweilim. The youths who loitered near the shop had drifted off; Alwani appeared, asking for his night's ration of tea and sugar; but Sheikh Yusif would not move to get it, unless Alwani paid first.

Alwani stood a moment in front of them, then squatted on the earth. Leaning towards Abu Suweilim, Sheikh Yusif asked, in a whisper, what his reaction would be, if he himself wrote a Petition, in his own style, for he knew exactly what language was most convincing to the Authorities.

Before the old man could reply, Alwani leapt to his feet, his face afire with enthusiasm.

'By the Faith of the Prophet, a wondrous suggestion! A petition from Sheikh Yusif will shake the Government!'

Sheikh Yusif, pleased with this flattery, shook his head, sucking in his thin lips:

'Not everyone, it's true, knows how to write.'

But Abu Suweilim belittled the proposal.

'Haven't we had our fill of petitions? Can't you think of something new?'

But enthusiastically Alwani proclaimed that a Petition from Sheikh Yusif would be something different; he could tease the Government with his cold, cutting words. No one could equal him for cold, cutting phrases.

This did not please the old man at all. Angrily he warned the perplexed Alwani to be quiet. Abu Suweilim smiled.

At this moment Diab appeared. Sheikh Yusif nodded to him curtly. Diab greeted them one by one, but no one asked him to be seated. Diab felt he must say something, so burst out with:

'My uncle's come!'

Abu Suweilim was delighted.

'The Headmaster? Where is he? At your house? Are you hiding him?'

Diab remembered his real message.

'No, I meant, he's coming. He's already left Cairo.'

'You donkey! Is that news?'

Alwani laughed, and said to Sheikh Yusif:

'Do you judge everyone to be as clever as yourself? Or that they know how to speak as you do? We don't know how to read, even – no one ever bothered to teach us.' And he turned with a reassuring smile to Diab.

Abu Suweilim, however, shook his head, intolerant of Diab's stupidity; then suddenly noticed an ill-shaped girl in black, coming from the direction of his house, and going into Sheikh Yusif's.

'Girl ...! You girl, there, Kadra! You were at our house? Didn't I tell you to keep away?'

Without a word the girl vanished indoors.

Vehemently, Diab declared that it was not Kadra. At this time in the evening she was always too busy with the young men who were unemployed and had come back from Cairo with their small savings. They attracted girls like Kadra. They had nothing to do except flirt. They couldn't wield a hoe, or even unload manure.

Abu Suweilim, maliciously amused at Diab's anger, turned to the old grocer, and entreated him never to let Kadra into his house. He himself had given her a good beating and driven her out of his house, when she had come, the previous evening, to ask for Waseefa. Sheikh Yusif nodded in agreement, and seeing Alwani trying to eavesdrop on what they were saying, angrily shooed him off.

Abu Suweilim at the same time dismissed Diab, telling him to fetch his brother. 'Where from?' Diab muttered indignantly, going away slowly.

He had not gone far when he passed Abdul Hadi.

Abdul Hadi was depressed and worried.

'Where's Muhammad Effendi?'

Diab shouted that he was on his way to find him.

Abdul Hadi, without a word of greeting, slumped down between the two old men, neither of whom dared to question his black mood. He suddenly asked Abu Suweilim:

'Do you mind coming with me to your house?'

Abu Suweilim took his leave of Sheikh Yusif, and noting the anguish in Abdul Hadi's eyes he asked him, as they walked away:

'What's all this about? What's so private?'

Abdul Hadi continued to walk in silence. When they reached Abu Suweilim's house, they both sat down at the threshold. Then in an earnest voice, Abdul Hadi asked:

'Where's Waseefa?'

'The girl's indoors;' and after this simple answer, he asked in his turn: 'What's the point of your question? What's so private about all this?'

'Take heed when I speak to you, Abu Suweilim.'

Obediently Abu Suweilim turned to take heed of whatever Abdul Hadi might say.

In a gruff, insistent voice the young man asked: could he marry Waseefa? This was the last time he would broach the subject.

Gently and patiently the old man answered him.

'Is this the time for that question, Abdul Hadi? Be patient a while longer.'

'Is that your answer?'

'All right, all right, Abdul Hadi. Everything will come right by and by. Just be patient.'

Abdul Hadi stared ahead of him, hoping for a new answer. None came. Instead, there came the quivering paunch and the clacking beads of Sheikh Shinawi, muttering to himself in a trembling incantation:

'In the Name of the Preserver, I take refuge in God.'

Saluting them breathlessly, the Sheikh sat down. Kadra, the impure, had been found murdered! Her face buried in the mud of the little canal by the river.

'Her life was mud, and her end was mud,' he concluded.

Angry, Abdul Hadi said that all men and women came from mud, Kadra and Sheikh Shinawi, just the same.

Sheikh Shinawi did not notice Abdul Hadi's gibe. Instead, he said that Alwani had murdered her.

'Alwani? But he was with us here, just now. Why should Alwani kill her?'

Coldly the Sheikh answered:

'Because he's a blasphemer, who cares nothing for religion. He never prays. And besides, he's a Beduin,' and he quoted a religious text: 'The Arabs say: "We have believed." But say thou: "Ye will never believe!"' And besides, Kadra was found by the field which Alwani guarded. No one but a Beduin would do such a thing. She was a fallen woman; but to kill her – ah, that was a sin, in God's eyes, the worst sin of all.

In a tired, platitudinous voice Abu Suweilim murmured:

'She's gone where she's gone – leave her.'

But it was best to bury her quickly, before the townspeople heard about the murder.

But who knew that it was murder? Abdul Hadi thought it quite possible that she had tried to drink water from the shallow canal – she had done so before – and while stretched over it, had fainted.

But Sheikh Shinawi was preoccupied with what Abu Suweilim had said about the police. He had just come from the Omda's: the Omda had decided not to inform the police about Kadra. Instead, she would be buried at dawn on the second day as soon as the Health Authorities had sent their permission, as usual, by telephone.

Yet where was she to be buried?

Abdul Hadi flippantly suggested: in Sheikh Shinawi's plot, he and she were similarly propertied, the Sheikh owning nothing in the village except his grave-plot. Naturally, the preacher was enraged, and accused Abdul Hadi of being as impure as Kadra. Never would he sanction the burial of Kadra's corpse in holy ground: she had lived and died in defiance of God. There was no question of her being buried with true Moslems.

Quietly Abdul Hadi replied that Kadra had no relations in the village now, except for one cousin, who worked as cook for Mahmoud Bey; this cook was also a distant relative of Sheikh Shinawi. The Sheikh tried to interrupt, but Abdul Hadi would not be quiet. Shaaban, another cousin of hers, had disappeared from the village, no one knew where; and her only sister, Zenouba, was now running a bar in Cairo, behind Ezbekiah Gardens, in the brothel quarter, where she went under the new name of 'Madame Ihsan'. All this Sheikh Shinawi should know. She had last visited the village five years ago, a plump woman with paint on her lips and gold everywhere – on her arms, her neck, her ears; and on her cheeks a powder the colour of brass. She had driven up from the town in a carriage. She had held a 'night of God', killing a calf for the poor, and she had offered a fiesta to the Prophet. She had given Sheikh Shinawi two pounds to recite prayers for the souls of her departed, and he had prayed God to give her abundance: though her abundance came from a bar, as everyone knew!

But unlike Kadra, Madame Ihsan was a reformed character, the Sheikh protested. She had made her peace with God. She gave alms to the poor, she made fiestas in honour of the Prophet.

'Exactly!' Abdul Hadi exclaimed. 'She's made good, because she's got jewelry and money enough for fiestas and preaching: you're not ashamed to own her as a relation. She has a palace in the Hereafter, and a garden too! If Kadra had not stayed in the village, but had gone to Cairo, and had entertained men, she too would have made good. Instead she stayed in our village, and you call her "impure".'

The only answer the Sheikh could find was his stick; but Abdul Hadi was in no mood to let himself be struck, and he snatched the stick and threw it aside.

'Stop boring us with your sermons, Sheikh. Instead, give us your opinion about this highway, which is going to take our land so the Pasha can make trips to Cairo.'

The old man clapped hand against hand, looking to Abu Suweilim for support.

'This boy Abdul Hadi is an unrivalled blasphemer! God curse him in all his Books.'

Abdul Hadi got up to go but was passed by a group of guards coming down the road.

One of the guards asked Abdul Hadi to wait a moment. Abdul Hadi thought: This means the Omda is going to accuse me of Kadra's death!

Abu Suweilim shouted from the threshold:

'Speak up, Abdul Aati! What new trick of that cunning Omda? What have you come to tell us? If the old rascal tries anything new, I'll break his neck.'

But Abdul Aati respectfully replied that Kadra had died alone, of natural causes; she had stretched herself out to drink from the shallow canal, she had become dizzy; such dizziness was common; she was stifled in the mud, and died immediately.

Abdul Hadi was relieved that for once the Omda had no opportunity for tricks.

But the Omda nevertheless wanted Abdul Hadi and Abu Suweilim at his Residence.

'What on earth for?'

Falteringly, Abdul Aati said that yesterday night an official had discovered that the bank had been broken. The Magistrate had telephoned the Omda, threatening to punish him severely if he did not dictate to him a list of all those whose land was by the river. The Omda had given way, and had included the name of Abu Suweilim, although his land was all by the canal.

'Put my name on the list? I'll break your neck, Omda! I'll put you in irons for lying against me.'

One of the guards muttered that the magistrate had ordered the arrest of everyone on the Omda's list.

'But don't worry, Abu Suweilim, my father ... don't worry, Abdul Hadi. It's just the times that are wrong.'

Abu Suweilim and Abdul Hadi found Diab and many others at the Residence. The space in front of the house was full of people and clamour, insults against the Omda, shouts of encouragement to those who must endure his plots. And shortly after, when night fell, the villagers were led off to the magistrate in the town, by the guards, carrying their guns.

Early next morning Sheikh Yusif sat in his shop, dangling a long flywhisk made of rushes. Those who had not been arrested went to the fields – for the earth could not wait till the others should return.

A boy from the eastern sector came to the shop in tears.

'My mother says, the Government have taken my father. Will you go and find out when he'll be back?'

The crying of this child tore at Sheikh Yusif's heart. For he knew the whole story, that the Government had taken this child's uncle, as well as his father, and many other men who were fathers, brothers, uncles or sons. But if he went to the town, no one would receive him, no one would know him from Adam. There was nothing that he could do. Perhaps if he went, they would even arrest him as well. A tide of misery washed over him as he saw the passers-by, women weeping, boys with bowed heads. It reminded him of the days, fourteen years before, when he had still been a student at Al-Azhar. He had come back to the village in a sailing boat, along the Nile, as the railway had been sabotaged. Those days of struggle had been merrier, he himself had been younger and stronger. He remembered Sheikh Hassouna his friend, shouting beside him:

'Despite the English ... Independence!'

He was woken from his reverie by a woman weeping convulsively.

'For God's sake, Sheikh Yusif, come and read for me the chapter *Ya-Seen* against the Government, for taking my sons from me, yesterday night.'

In those heroic days of 1919 no one spoke of reading *Ya-Seen* against the English. Instead, they acted. Even the village had taken part. He would have liked to curse this silly woman, but she was so weak and defeated, the words stuck in his throat. And instead he said, brokenly:

'Our Lord will make things right. Go home. He will protect and comfort you.'

But the woman continued to weep, drying her tears, as fast as they fell, on her black sleeve. She had not found Sheikh Shinawi to read the chapter for her, though she had been sweeping the shrine of the village saint, Ramadhan, and had prayed to him to avenge her from the tomb. But between her tears, she confessed she did not have the money to buy candles for the shrine, so she had hoped Sheikh Yusif would read *Ya-Seen* without a fee, or perhaps lend her a few candles against the eggs which her hens would be laying that evening.

At this point Sheikh Yusif could control himself no longer.

'Be off with you, woman, be off! The chapter *Ya-Seen*, Sheikh Shinawi, candles for the shrine ...'

Sheikh Shinawi himself, in 1919, had stood by his side in the streets of Cairo waving his hands, shouting like everyone else: 'Long Live Egypt!' His face had been as round and plump as today, with the same white beard; but in those days he had spoken of Tel el-Kebir, of Kafr el-Dawar, of the struggles against the English, and even the Khedive, for the original Constitution.

The only one to have thought of the village Saint was Abu Suweilim. He had just been demobilized, and he urged the villagers to hide arms in the shrine.

Suddenly he felt an urgent need for the company of Alwani. But then he remembered: at this time Alwani would be sleeping, after being on watch all night. There was no one in the street, and Sheikh Yusif felt alone and dismal. Suddenly he had an idea. He delved beneath his cashbox and came up with a large volume in dark yellow paper, and shaking his head he turned its pages. It was the history of Antar, the black slave hero who defeated the oppressors of Egypt, Syria and the other Arab countries. And strength flooded back into his voice, as he read of this black defier of destiny and sultans. A quiver of excitement, of new confidence. He did not even notice when someone said:

'Good morning, Sheikh Yusif!'

He did not raise his eyes from the page, but continued to read, a blush of strength in his yellow cheeks.

'I said, Good morning to you, Sheikh Yusif.'

He looked up at last, smiled, closed the book, and said confidently, no longer sad:

'Good morning, and welcome, Muhammad Effendi.' His normal dislike for his visitor was washed away by sympathy for the arrest of Diab. 'Tarboosh and jacket – where are you off to?'

Muhammad Effendi had first thought of going to the town, to find out what news he could. Then he had heard that no one was admitted to the police-station; if he went he might be arrested himself. So he had decided to call on Mahmoud Bey, and ask for him to intervene for Diab and the others.

'Haven't you had enough of Mahmoud Bey yet, Muhammad Effendi?'

'What else can we do? What other remedy is there?' And leaning towards Sheikh Yusif, he told him the story of the ten pounds he had given, without use, to Mahmoud Bey. He would now risk ten more, if Mahmoud Bey would get the men free. Five on account, five when the men were released.

In his tarboosh and jacket over a clean white gallabya, Muhammad Effendi led his elegant little donkey to Abu Suweilim's house. It was locked. The night before Waseefa had come to his house, and had wept with his mother, who had been weeping for Diab, as he had been too. The night had passed in tears.

Seeing the empty threshold, Muhammad Effendi felt a terrible sense of loss, and for Abdul Hadi a deep affection, as though they had never quarrelled. Then he thought of his brother: were they torturing him? Was he dead? And tears which he could not stifle poured from his eyes, for he knew exactly how the police would treat the villagers.

They were probably torturing them now, young and old alike, forcing them to drink the stale of horses ... this had been the Government's way with the fellahin, ever since they boycotted the elections.

For the first time, doors were locked in the morning, doors that were usually locked only at night. He jumped on to the back of his ass; the fresh sun of the new day was sparkling on drops of dew. He reached Mahmoud Bey's estate. He was kept waiting at a little lodge some distance from the big house. He drank the coffee that a servant brought him, and still he waited. He rehearsed the speech he would make to the Bey. The very thought made him perspire, and he wiped his face with his handkerchief, and cleared his blocked throat ... and went on waiting.

At last Mahmoud Bey arrived, his hair tousled.

Yawning, rubbing his eyes, he spat out crossly:

'What's brought you here, at dawn, like this?'

Looking at his watch, Muhammad Effendi replied that it was ten o'clock, and he had been waiting since six-thirty.

Well, what did he want?

Muhammad Effendi told him about the arrests, and Mahmoud Bey listened with a bored expression, at the same time lighting himself an American cigarette. Muhammad Effendi looked stealthily at the door, then very quickly pulled five pounds from his pocket and handed them to Mahmoud Bey, in silence, for he had forgotten every word that he had planned to say. Mahmoud Bey was pleased, but he too said nothing. He then asked Muhammad Effendi to wait for a few days. Muhammad Effendi pulled out another five-pound note, reminding the Bey of the money he had given already and from which the village had received no benefit. He and the village depended on the Bey; if he helped them now, they would always be his to command. Mahmoud Bey stood up and called one of the men outside to fetch his horse. He turned to Muhammad Effendi.

'Go home and wait for them in the village. Congratulations!'

Muhammad Effendi leapt on to his ass and practically flew back to the village, disregarding the bumps on the road or the hot sun. His first stop was at Abu Suweilim's house, where he found Waseefa behind the open door, her eyes red from weeping.

But her face lit up when she saw Muhammad Effendi.

'Come in, welcome!'

In spite of everything, she was still beautiful. She was delighted to see a friend.

Muhammad Effendi came into the house.

He was face to face with Waseefa, alone.

Where was her mother?

Sleeping, worn out by worry.

Muhammad Effendi felt twinges of conscience, at his own desires, taking advantage of the arrest of the men. Scratching his scalp, he coldly told her that they would be let out today. Waseefa began shouting for joy, clapping her hands, her whole body, from her dimples to her breasts, dancing with happiness.

'Really? The Prophet's truth?'

Without a word, Muhammad Effendi pressed closer to Waseefa, his face flushed, his eyes lustfully staring at her plump breasts. Waseefa leapt agilely to the door.

'Quickly, Muhammad Effendi, quickly! Catch your donkey, she's broken away!'

Crestfallen, Muhammad Effendi saw it was true: the donkey he had left tethered at the door had run heedlessly off to the fields. As he ran off to catch it, Waseefa shouted from the door:

'Your uncle's come, Muhammad Effendi. He arrived in a cab, and called here on his way.'

She raised her voice still more loudly. 'That's someone who knows how to behave with women when their men are gone.'

Her words hit Muhammad Effendi like a whip. Without replying, he stumbled in pursuit of the ass.

Sheikh Hassouna had arrived while Muhammad Effendi had been waiting on Mahmoud Bey.

Sheikh Hassouna had spent a night in the town. He had gone at once to the large chemist's, which was used by

Government employees and well-to-do citizens as a club. And there on the pavement in front, Sheikh Hassouna joined his old friends. They all had roots in the neighbouring villages, and were concerned about the new road which would swallow some of the villagers' land. Everyone of them had some relative who would be made landless if the scheme went through.

The Kadi, who had studied with Sheikh Hassouna at Al-Azhar, pointed out that the Pasha had made the new road coil like a snake, so as to avoid taking the least fraction of land belonging to himself, Mahmoud Bey or any big landowner.

A young man from the Pasha's village, employed in the Survey Department, said this highway would cost the State ten times as much as would the repair of the existing road. (As he spoke, the young man peered along the pavement and inside the shop, as if afraid of a sudden attack.)

Sheikh Hassouna had given his shoes to a shoeblack, and was listening to the conversation in silence. The shoeblack suddenly looked up and shouted: 'If only the People's Party could be destroyed, before it destroys the world!'

Sheikh Hassouna smiled with pleasure, and the others laughed.

At that moment a seller of figs passed, fat, sleazy, vending her fruit with salacious words, and making sly advances to the young employee from the Law Courts, who took refuge from his embarrassment in the pages of a newspaper. The shoeblack cursed her, while the rest roared with laughter. The embarrassed employee murmured from behind the pages:

'They'll sell the whole country to the English!'

'Oh, they did that long ago,' said the Kadi.

'The English aren't omniscient,' another broke in. 'They're only clever when they're dealing with idiots, such as our politicians.'

Later Sheikh Hassouna moved with the Kadi and several others to the Civil Servants' Club. The Club was crowded with men from various Government offices, such as the Irrigation Department, the Law Courts, and the Police, all playing cards. Glasses came in full and went out empty.

The Kadi glared with disapproval at the servants, as they came and went, ferrying alcohol.

'Such, my friends, are our leaders. Alcohol, gambling, every kind of immorality … That's why I dislike the Club, and its leading lights.' He suggested that they go as far as possible from the noise of backgammon counters and clinking glasses. So they sat down in a distant, poorly furnished room, all by themselves.

One of their number suggested that they write telegrams to the Opposition press, protesting against the highway. This suggestion, and one of Sheikh Hassouna's, that they should cable the Saadist Club, were approved. The Kadi suggested they should send copies of their telegrams to the newspaper columnists, and this too was approved. The Kadi wrote the text, and Sheikh Hassouna collected money from everyone in the room. They signed the cables with the names of their farmer relatives who were affected by the scheme.

One of the employees, with great boldness, volunteered to put his own name, reminding all of them of the courageous stand of the employees in 1919. But the Kadi said that prudence was a part of wisdom; the Government would be ruthless with civil servants, and would rigidly apply the law forbidding them to take part in politics. There was no point in getting themselves dismissed, or transferred to remote places. They all had children.

The man who had made the gesture relapsed into a silence of self-gratification, then got up to send the telegrams.

Sheikh Hassouna was told about the struggle of the village against the new irrigation times. He was impressed when he was told of how the farmers had broken the bank. And he said proudly: 'This was a heroic village all its life ... This was their water, they must have it, whatever means they take!'

And his pride was not lessened when he heard of the arrests. He whispered to himself, this was nothing! For the nation's leaders themselves had been arrested, and exiled to distant places, such as the Seychelles. And many people were dying at this moment, under gunfire, in the streets of Cairo and Alexandria, and Mansoura, and Beni Sueif, and Assiut. And he raised his voice, declaring that he himself would send a telegram of protest to the Public Prosecutor against these illegal arrests.

Sheikh Hassouna slept in a simple hotel. In the morning, he went to the station and sent off a telegram in the name of the villagers to the Minister of Justice and the Public Prosecutor, asking for an enquiry into the arrest of the villagers. He sent a copy to the Opposition press. He then took a cab and drove in it by the river road to the village. As he gazed at the river and the fields, he was amazed how people could overlook this fine straight road and choose instead a twisting way, which would please the Pasha, but would cost so much more money and would take away from the villagers so much land.

The cab reached the village. It drove right up to Muhammad Effendi's house, where Sheikh Hassouna intended to stay. The door was shut. Women were watching from behind their windows, frightened that this new arrival might bring some new disaster to the village. But as they peered inside the cab, they could see no khaki uniform, no scarlet tarboosh, no gun: they smiled with relief. The rear end of the cab was crowded with little boys, whom no amount of shouting or swearing could dislodge.

Sheikh Hassouna went indoors, and met his cousin, Muhammad Effendi's mother. She was taken aback by his sudden arrival. Sheikh Hassouna pulled down the sleeve of his kaftan over his hands to avoid pollution, while she kissed his hand and made him welcome.

Where was Muhammad Effendi gone, so early in the morning?

She told him that he had ridden off on his donkey to Mahmoud Bey's to ask for his help in getting Diab and the others set free.

Sheikh Hassouna was very cross when he heard this; smacking fist against fist, he exclaimed that his nephew was an idiot! What business was it of Mahmoud Bey's? The Bey would never do any good to the village! He was on the Government's side.

His words were lost on the woman, whose only thoughts were to entertain the Headmaster. She spread a new mat for him at the threshold of the house, and then killed a duck. She lit a fire to boil water, and squatted down in front of the simple stove, fanning the smoke. How she hoped that Diab would be back in time to share this bird! Suddenly she remembered that she had no wheat bread in the house, only dry maize loaves. Diab had not been able to have any flour ground at the mill. She called to a girl from a neighbouring house and asked her to run to Waseefa's and ask to borrow three, or if possible four, loaves of white bread. But the girl came back empty-handed. So she sent her off again, to the Sheikh al-Balad's wife, and this time she brought three loaves, neatly wrapped up in a white cloth, fresh from the oven.

But Sheikh Hassouna did not dally with his cousin. He must visit the Omda, the man responsible for the arrests. But first of all he called at Abu Suweilim's house. Waseefa kissed his hand, her tears wetting it. Sheikh Hassouna embraced the girl's head, and assured her that she was exactly like his daughter. And he encouraged her mother, urging her to have faith. He offered to lend the two of them some money, if they needed it. But Waseefa's mother, wiping her tears, refused to accept any. He then went off to Abdul Hadi's house, and cheered up his family. Then to several other houses in the eastern part of the village, doing the same thing there.

It was now about nine o'clock. Sheikh Yusif was listening to Sheikh Shinawi, who had come back from the Omda's. Alwani had just arrived. Sheikh Yusif was greeting him with a voice full of tenderness: how he had wanted to see him; he had even thought of sending a boy to fetch him, but had not done so, remembering that Alwani would be tired out, after staying up all night to guard the melons.

Joyfully Alwani shouted that the same thought had occurred to him! He was carrying on his shoulders a sack full of corn cobs; his gallabya was bulging with them too, held in by his belt. He now poured them out in front of the grocer, and having cleared his person, began to empty his sack. He asked Sheikh Yusif to subtract the value of the cobs from the bill which he owed for groceries. And could he meanwhile have a packet of readymade cigarettes?

'You've changed to ready-mades? Wonderful news! The men of the village are taken away from us, and you collect their corn, is that it?'

Alwani roared with laughter. 'I'm a bold one!'

He went on: 'I'm brave! Yes, indeed. But I swear by the Prophet that not one of these comes from a friend, or from anyone whose salt I've eaten, or from anyone who's hard up.'

Sheikh Yusif hesitated whether to take the corn from Alwani. Sheikh Shinawi exploded:

'You boy, you Beduin! This is your road to Hell! Sheikh Yusif, you must not accept these.'

'Hell? You think I'm afraid of Hell? Isn't this Hell, where I live?'

Sheikh Yusif began to count the corn cobs that littered the counter and the ground. Then he took his long account book and turned its pages. A copying pencil in his hand, he turned to Alwani:

'Right! Four shillings off your account.'

'Sheikh Yusif, isn't this sin, to try and cheat me like that? Sheikh Shinawi, isn't that sin? These corn cobs represent a whole night's work. Eighteen shillings ... and that would be cheap.'

Sheikh Yusif examined one of the cobs, handing a small packet of cigarettes to Alwani. Pretending to be angry, he said:

'Right, take your cobs, the bargain's over.'

'No, no ... I'll come to terms. Credit me with twelve shillings. I'll accept that.'

The grocer refused. 'Right, let's make it eight. Good? By God, you are a clever bargainer, Sheikh Yusif. You can't get them for less than this.'

'Six shillings, not a penny more.'

'All right, register them in your book.'

Sheikh Shinawi continued to protest. 'This is sin, man, this is terrible sin. Your honour should refuse such trickery.'

Without even raising his head, Sheikh Yusif said:

'You think so? Don't bother me like this. Your words sicken us.'

Alwani tried to join in, but Sheikh Yusif told him to go some distance off. Sheikh Shinawi went back to the account Alwani had interrupted, of how he had visited the Omda, to read him his daily texts. The Omda had confessed that he had been worn out by Abu Suweilim's insults. Abu Suweilim never referred to him in public except by the adjective 'impure'. For this reason he had included Abu Suweilim's name, in order to get him punished. If the Government now released him and the others, and if he returned to his insulting ways, and if Abdul Hadi returned to his arrogance, and if Muhammad Effendi had any idea of abetting them, then he still had a weapon up his sleeve: the affair of Kadra. It was quite possible she had been murdered. It was well known that Abu Suweilim had banished her from his house. He had even beaten her, only a few hours before her death. Abdul Hadi, too, had struck her, out of his dislike of her influence over Waseefa. And perhaps Diab had made her pregnant, and had feared a scandal? Thus the Kadra affair remained open: the Omda could use it at his convenience.

'And what did you say to this?'

'Why, nothing,' the Sheikh answered, innocently.

'What? You talk to me of sin and unrighteousness, about little details like corn cobs. Yet when this rogue talks to you like this, your God suggests no answer? Or do you consider the Omda one of those on High?'

Sheikh Shinawi covered his embarrassment with indignation.

'You're speaking like this to me? Have you forgotten the saying of the Prophet: "Who taught me a letter, made me his slave?" Didn't I teach you to write before you went to the Azhar? And now you speak to me in this fashion. Shame!'

Their argument was killed dead by the arrival of Sheikh Hassouna. Sheikh Yusif ran out of his shop in excitement at seeing his old friend.

Sheikh Yusif asked Sheikh Shinawi to keep an eye on his shop; he led the Headmaster inside his house, pushing him in front of him in the excitement of welcome. They sat down in the parlour on an old settee covered with a torn, dirty cover. Sheikh Hassouna studied the inscription on the wall: *Expect Evil From Those You Benefit!*

Sheikh Hassouna turned to those splendid days of 1919, when they were young men together, like Muhammad Effendi now, or a little older.

'By God, those indeed were the days, Sheikh Hassouna. I was only thinking of them a day or two ago. How different the village was then – no talk of saintly interventions! Then we knew how to fight the English and their artillery!'

Before Sheikh Hassouna could comment, Muhammad Effendi arrived. His face showed pleasure mingled with anxiety. He was still wearing his tarboosh, jacket and shoes.

He kissed his uncle's hand and then sat down.

His uncle looked at him in a cold silence.

After a few minutes Sheikh Hassouna said that the village could never benefit from Mahmoud Bey; those who had personal experience of his trickery should know this best!

Muhammad Effendi made no reply. He shook his head in silence.

Sheikh Yusif saw his opportunity. Sarcasm was his favourite weapon.

'All that's left is for you to confide in the Omda, too.'

Muhammad Effendi replied softly:

'Oh, no, it wasn't I who walked behind the Omda in the elections, or who helped him get subscriptions for the party newspaper.'

But his uncle would not let him get away with this.

'Strange! You beware of the rope and take no heed of the snake? What is the difference between the Omda, or the Pasha, or Mahmoud Bey?'

Then he raised his voice as his words jumped out, one after

the other. 'The English, what are they? The Government, what are they? They're all one ... one chain, one filthy chain.'

Muhammad Effendi tried to say something to save himself from his embarrassment. 'You are enough blessing for all of us, Headmaster, you are enough!'

'But you, too, in this village can play your part. This land belongs to all of us. If only you have courage, you too can defy the oppressor. After all, who are the people fighting our corrupt regime and their foreign supporters? The students and the railway workers, people like that. Don't you read the newspapers, don't you know what's going on in Egypt?'

Sheikh Yusif prevented Muhammad Effendi replying.

'Newspapers, you say? Newspapers! Who reads newspapers in this village, I ask you? By God, this village has no men in it such as we knew, Sheikh Hassouna.'

Sheikh Hassouna did not agree.

'You are wrong, Sheikh Yusif. This village could rival, even excel what we did. Look at the students in Cairo!'

Muhammad Effendi looked gratefully towards his uncle, but at that moment there was the clattering of cups outside the door. In the half-open doorway stood the daughter of Sheikh Yusif. She waited for her father to take the tray. But suddenly a bright idea came into the old man's mind, and with a quick glance at the others, he said: 'Come in, daughter, come in! No one here's strange to you. Come and say hello to your uncle Sheikh Hassouna.'

His daughter obeyed him. She was an unattractive girl, with the same frowning expression as her father, her cheeks sunken, her figure scraggy, a red dress half-concealing two skinny legs. She put the tray down in front of her father, and then went towards Sheikh Hassouna, who, pulling his sleeve over his hand, greeted her in the traditional manner.

'In the name of God ... God willing, Sheikh Yusif, this girl's ready for marriage.'

The girl blushed, her cheeks trembling. Her lather smiled.

'So ... good ... now go and greet Muhammad Effendi.'

The girl stumbled shyly towards Muhammad Effendi, who saluted her without enthusiasm. She then hurriedly left the room.

Sheikh Yusif poured their coffee, on his lips a smile.

'Well ...'

He then gave a cup of coffee to Sheikh Hassouna.

'Real coffee, from the hand of my daughter. She's skilled at everything, coffee, cooking, baking, as well as religious observances.'

Sheikh Hassouna smiled gently. 'God willing, you will be blessed in her. A fine girl from a fine womb.'

Sheikh Yusif then offered a cup to Muhammad Effendi, who had shown no emotion at all.

They drank their coffee loudly.

Still the men did not come home.

The Omda visited Muhammad Eftendi's house to return Sheikh Hassouna's call. The Omda claimed that the only man responsible for imprisoning the men was the engineer, when he discovered the broken embankment. He had demanded that the Omda should be dismissed unless he gave the names of the men responsible.

Quietly, sarcastically, Sheikh Hassouna asked:

'Was Abu Suweilim one of those responsible?'

Before the Omda could reply, Muhammad Effendi broke in with an angry shout: 'The boy Diab had committed some crime, Omda? That mere boy, what could he do? What did he do to merit prison?'

Sheikh Hassouna turned angrily to Muhammad Effendi, annoyed that he had given way to his emotions in front of the Omda.

'Get up and fetch the coffee, Muhammad.'

As Muhammad Effendi went out, Sheikh Hassouna said gently: 'Prison isn't shameful, prison isn't scandalous. Saad himself was put in prison. Saad lay in gaol, while Adli Pasha sat up all night in his palace with the English.'

The Omda trembled. 'Yes, yes, of course ... Yes. Yes, Headmaster.'

Both men were silent. The Omda contemplated the texts which hung on Muhammad Effendi's walls. '*The Generous Does not Want*'. Another said in interlaced red letters: '*Therefore Of The Bounty Of Thy Lord Be Thy Constant Discourse*'. He only managed to read the first words of a third, when Sheikh Hassouna sighed and looked at his watch. It was time for evening prayer. The evening had begun to cover the village houses with orange light. He unrolled a little mat from one corner of the room. Muhammad Effendi came in with another mat, which he spread on the floor. When they had all finished praying, the Omda said:

'We have prayed together. Now permit me to take my leave.'

Crossly Sheikh Hassouna turned to his nephew.

'Where's the coffee?'

Reluctantly Muhammad Effendi went out, muttering: 'He put Diab in prison, and we offer him coffee! Let him die of poison!'

His mother shared his feelings.

'What impudence,' she said, 'that he dares to drink coffee here. He puts my son in prison, and then comes to drink coffee in my house!'

Muhammad Effendi nevertheless brought in the coffee and poured it for the Omda and his uncle. They drank in silence.

The Omda exclaimed: 'May you always be prosperous, Headmaster! May you always drink coffee in our village!'

Finally he took his leave, Sheikh Hassouna escorting him to the door, at every step the Omda asking him not to bother.

Standing at the door, the Omda turned: 'Pray God that the men will be home again tomorrow!'

The Magistrate had told him in confidence, and he was repeating this in confidence now, that the men were only being detained because tomorrow some Ministers were coming to visit the Pasha, who would be going back to Cairo once again the following day.

The Omda gone, Sheikh Hassouna went indoors and scolded Muhammad Effendi and his mother. Manners were manners, they should not have been so dilatory with the coffee! Muhammad Effendi said nothing; but his mother angrily replied that she could not be expected to be polite when her son Diab was in prison.

Quietly her cousin said that a cup of coffee was a detail; what mattered was more important. He sat down at the threshold of the house, Muhammad Effendi at his side, while the woman went indoors.

Muhammad Effendi asked his uncle about this visit.

Sheikh Hassouna said that the Pasha had invited several Ministers from the People's Party to visit his new Palace. He wanted them to see the state of the present road, so that they would get interested in the new Highway to link his Palace to Cairo.

This was not the reply that Muhammad Effendi was wanting. He wanted to know what connection the visit had with the liberation of Diab.

Sheikh Hassouna smiled: he and Muhammad Effendi were lucky not to have been arrested to form part of the welcome for the Ministers! Orders had filtered down from on high, from the Minister of the Interior to the Prefect, from the Prefect to the head of police, that the Ministers should be given a rousing welcome, a welcome to asphyxiate them! Undoubtedly the Police Chief would force all the thousands in the local prisons to take part in this reception. He would distribute ordinary clothes in place of the prison clothes. He would have them joined by the plain clothes police, and the religious leaders, and the Omdas, and the village officials, and the rural Guards. In fact, anyone who could be rallied from the streets would take part in the popular welcome.

As the Omda came back from his visit, he found a crowd of women waiting in front of the Residence. Some were sitting on the ground. Seeing him, they thronged around him, asking him urgently when a husband or a son or a father would be released.

Silently the Omda pushed his way towards his house. Abdul Aati followed him, continually trying to keep the women away. The Omda had become accustomed during the last few days to the screams of women outside his house, and he had ordered the guards to keep the door shut. From the time that Sheikh Hassouna had returned to the village, the Omda had avoided sitting in the courtyard of his house; he never went into the roads of the village; this was the first time that he had been out. On his way back a woman had accosted him, and asked him about her son. The guard had tried to stop her, but she had stood her ground. Then another girl had asked him about her brother. Again the guard drove her off. A rather beautiful young woman had then approached the Omda, taken him by the sleeve, shaken him, and asked him through her tears about her husband. He pushed her off, while the guard taunted her about her attachment to her husband: would she have been so energetic if it had been her father, only, who had been taken? Even the Omda scolded him for making such remarks in public.

But now there was a wailing wall of dark-clothed women in front of him, blocking his way, thrusting out their hands towards him. The Omda noticed that one was not wearing a black dress like the others. She was slim and of a fair complexion, though she was weeping terribly. Seeing the Omda, she pushed her way till she stood in front of him, despite the guard. Raising his hand above her head, the guard told her to go. The girl screamed: 'Take your hands off me, you urchin! Take your hands away from me!'

'Who is this girl?'

'The daughter of the Chief Guard.'

'Chief Guard?' the Omda shouted. 'He's still the Chief Guard? Ah, yes, you were his protege, he brought you up, Abu Suweilim was your protector!'

Abdul Aati replied: 'I meant, the former Chief Guard, your Excellency.'

Waseefa pushed forward.

'I am Waseefa, the daughter of Muhammad Abu Suweilim. Tell me, where is my father?'

The Omda shook his head. The last rays of evening were spreading from the river over the dark houses and on the girl's pale face. With a feigned calm, the Omda said:

'Good. But isn't it shameful to gesticulate like this? In front of me, a man even older than your father?' Waseefa shouted. 'Shame? You speak of shame? You dare to use the word? Wasn't it shameful of you to have gaoled my father?'

The Omda stared frankly at her body, and then glanced to the other women. Cunningly he said: 'You're the split image of your mother. As pretty as she was, as clever, too, and daring, I don't doubt.'

The women understood what the Omda meant.

A woman said angrily: 'What business is it of yours, to speak about her mother? How do you know that she was daring?'

Another broke in: 'By the Prophet, if the Chief Guard was here, and heard you speaking like that, there'd be two bullets for you and no delay. Speaking about Abu Suweilim's wife when he's not here.'

A third said: 'The Omda's old, sister, but shameful still! Sixty muddy years.'

While the women were protesting, Waseefa tugged at his robe and shouted in a terrible voice:

'You speak about my mother? What is there between you and her? Fetch my father! Where is my father?'

The Omda tried to extricate his thin body from Waseefa's grasp. The guards saw Waseefa attacking the Omda, they heard his cry of distress: 'Hit her, hit her, boys! Why are you doing nothing? Boys, help me, beat them, hit them... They're killing me! Rescue me, guards ... Or you're all dismissed.'

Reluctantly the guards came to his aid. Perhaps he would insult their wives next in the same way, or even worse. All of them knew that it was the Omda who had written down the names of the villagers; he had gone himself to the police-station to do so. He was the same Omda who had cheated them over the Petition. All that he had done was to please Mahmoud Bey and the Pasha, and to harm the village. They all had relations among the men now lying in prison; some of them even owned land which would be taken away if the road was built. How they wished, each one of them, to beat him with a stout stick on his white pate, like a venomous snake.

Lazily one of them imitated the Omda's voice.

'Go ... go ... go away, all of you ... or you are dismissed.'

The others stifled their laughs.

But their laughs hid hatred, not good humour.

The Omda screamed at them, exhorting them in a hissing voice to strike the women. 'What are you up to? Treading on egg-shells? Beat her, boys! Beat her! Good, that's better ...'

Some of the guards burst out laughing. But Abdul Aati raised his stick and began laying about him. The women screamed and shouted. Waseefa took the Omda by his skinny neck. Abdul Aati thereupon seized her by the arm. She turned to Abdul Aati, clawing him. He struck at her, kicking her with his heavy feet. She groaned in sudden pain, and began to weep, thinking how far her father was from her. It was the first time she had been beaten since she became a woman, and by the very boy whom her father had protected. She fell to the earth.

In the scuffle Abdul Aati had been cut by her nails. Seeing him bleed, the guards began to obey the Omda in earnest, and to beat the women off. In retaliation, the screaming women picked up clods of earth with which to pelt the guards.

Seeing the earth flying, the Omda hid behind Abdul Aati.

Now was the time when every evening the beasts returned to the village. Behind them came the nightly procession of women catching their droppings in order to make fuel-pats. On their heads were baskets full of the steaming manure. The procession reached the place where the guards were fighting the women. As they drew level, Waseefa suddenly snatched a basket full of excrement and emptied it with one swift movement, all over the head of the Omda.

The Omda could not believe what had happened. His face and neck were fouled. His spotless turban was a dirty brown. His eyes could hardly peep through the clogging dung. With difficulty he opened his mouth to shout.

'Satanic bitches! Gypsies! You guards, what are you doing, standing there? Your night is like your faces. You are all dismissed! Your night is as dirty as your face.'

All the guards ran to the Omda. One of them said,

laughing: 'Our night? You talk of our night? Our night will be like your face, Omda ... all of it musk!'

All laughed at his sally. They stood by the Omda helping to wipe the dung from his face, and from his robe and his kaftan. The women now hurriedly left, their faces showing their delight. The Omda raved against them in vain. Not a woman remained in front of the Residence. Waseefa left, too, unwillingly, feeling her head and shoulders as she went.

Meanwhile Sheikh Yusif was sitting inside his shop, laughing with all his mouth. Beside him sat Muhammad Effendi, while Alwani stood just outside.

They were all laughing with simple pleasure at the discomfiture of the Omda.

'Congratulations, Waseefa! You are the real daughter of Abu Suweilim! He wore the basket, and all its contents! Wonderful news, friends, a splendid event! And done by women! What were our men doing?' He frowned a moment. 'No, no, our women are worth all our men put together.'

Alwani broke in: 'What we had in our hands we did not use!'

'Enough, boy! Enough, Alwani. What did you have in your hands? Listen to me!'

Leaning towards Alwani, Sheikh Yusif whispered into his ears. Instead of robbing the men in prison, he should break into the Omda's stores. Sheikh Yusif would pay him double for any corn or maize that he stole from the Omda. Sheikh Yusif did not want Muhammad Effendi to hear what he was saying, so he stepped outside and assured Alwani that if he had any trouble with the guards, he would rescue him. The guards protecting the Residence had all worked for Abu Suweilim before, they all had friends among the men in prison.

Alwani agreed with rapture. Sheikh Yusif returned to the shop and got him a big packet of extra-special cigarettes. 'Take these long cigarettes! Enjoy their flavour. Now is not the time for us to be skinflints.'

Sheikh Yusif also handed him a packet of tea, and a large lump of sugar.

'Give me some more sugar,' said Alwani.

Sheikh Yusif cut him another lump. 'Take it,' he said. 'You're a real Beduin, a real gypsy sheikh, not a sheikh of the Arabs. The only thing that'll fill your eyes is dust.'

Alwani laughed.

'You think so, Sheikh Yusif?'

He then turned to go, but at that moment Waseefa arrived, with another woman returning from the fight. Sheikh Yusif welcomed her warmly. 'Bravo, Waseefa! Congratulations!' But he suddenly noticed that she was weeping, very bitterly.

Muhammad Effendi felt a knife in his heart. He wanted to comfort her, but no words would come.

Waseefa approached the shop, stopped by the counter, put her head between her hands, and continued to sob. What upset her so terribly was the shame of being beaten, in public, and by the one man among the guards whom her father had most helped and most protected. She could not understand why her father was in gaol. The only reason was the Omda's treachery. Her tears mixed with unintelligible words.

'Father, Sheikh Yusif, they beat me. That boy, Abdul Aati, dared to beat me, because my father is not here.'

With horror Sheikh Yusif exclaimed: 'Abdul Aati beat you? The boy your father helped? What a black day for you, Abdul Aati! You carry slavishness to the Omda that far?'

Walking into the interior of the shop, he picked up a stick that lay on top of his book of Arab heroes. Alwani said: 'You want me to go and bring you the news of someone's death?'

Sheikh Yusif asked Alwani to go away. He, and no one but he, would beat Abdul Aati, with his own hands. Reluctantly Alwani stood aside, but had not moved two steps, when he froze.

'Abdul Aati is coming, Sheikh Yusif, his hand on his head!'

The guard came up and asked Sheikh Yusif for a little coffee for his wound, and some essence of peppermint for the Omda who had just fainted in his Residence.

Sheikh Yusif laid down his stick on the counter. He stared a long time at Abdul Aati, asking him to come nearer. Waseefa said:

'May your heart be torn out, Abdul Aati!'

Sheikh Yusif asked him to come nearer yet, and when he stood just in front of him, he dealt him a ringing slap on his cheek. As Abdul Aati put his hand to his cheek, Sheikh Yusif struck him again on the other.

'You beat the daughter of Abu Suweilim, do you? You know how to beat Waseefa, you ungrateful guard?'

Abdul Aati tried to say something, but Sheikh Yusif said angrily: 'Get away, boy! Get away! You'd try to bray at me, would you? Shut up! Get away!'

Waseefa raised herself up, feeling much better.

After a moment, Muhammad Effendi coughed. Shouldn't

Sheikh Yusif give Abdul Aati some peppermint, to save the Omda's life? It was a question of common humanity.

'Shut up, Muhammad Effendi! Enough of this philosophizing. Enough of "common humanity". Did your Omda show common humanity?'

Abdul Aati had turned to go.

'You're quite right, Sheikh Yusif! This Omda was a wicked man all the days of his life, by God! After I rescued him, after I was wounded for him, what did he do but show his gratitude by shouting at me, and throwing his slippers at me? That was the last straw!'

Hearing this, Waseefa laughed helplessly, as if she had never wept.

That night Sheikh Yusif was the happiest man in the village.

Alwani brought him two sacks full of the Omda's maize, and a sack of wheat, as well. The Omda had heard footsteps, but the guards had not heard his shouts. Early in this morning, he had summoned the guards. 'You are all in collusion with those unemployed rogues. You, too, are now unemployed, you're dismissed.'

He had then ridden to town on his mule, with Abdul Aati, to take part in the reception.

He had made no attempt to bring any of the villagers with him, as the Magistrate had asked. The men left in the village would refuse. Even Sheikh Shinawi, who had never before refused a request of the Omda, even he would probably refuse.

The Omda, as he rode, thought of the village, so rebellious and disobedient. What would happen next? The women had pelted him with cattle dung. A girl had practically strangled him. Unemployed boys had stolen his maize and wheat! All of this, just after the men had been gaoled. He wanted to discuss it with Abdul Aati, but controlled himself in time; it was important that it should appear in front of people, including Abdul Aati, as though he knew the answers to everything.

The moment he reached the town, he went straight to the Magistrate, and whispered in his ear that the men must be freed, immediately after the reception: for his position in the village had become intolerable.

The Magistrate picked up the telephone to rebuke some police official for not getting the streets fuller of people, then returned to the Omda. He replied that the men would be freed this very day, as soon as the Ministers had left.

The evening sun was low above the western bank, when Sheikh Hassouna, Muhammad Effendi and Sheikh Shinawi were saying their prayers.

Suddenly Sheikh Yusif rushed up to them. One of the boys had ridden from town on his donkey, to tell them that the men had been set free, and were walking home!

They were delighted: only Sheikh Shinawi demurred: 'They've come out? No, no, not yet ...'

Sheikh Yusif asked them why they had not gone to the mosque, but had come to this lonely place.

Sheikh Hassouna replied that any place was suitable for prayer, and any place where one prayed was a mosque! They had come here to greet Abdul Hadi, although he was far off.

Suddenly they heard the joy-cries of women from the

village. They all rushed back to the village. All the doors were open, and the cries increased. Children were dancing in the roads. Everything in the village seemed to be dancing. The rays of the dying sun gave a flower colour to mud lanes. Women were shouting in ecstasy:

'It's true! It's true! The men have come back!'

What had happened to the men was soon known.

It took some days before Diab could stand upright; traces of his beating remained on his back. When for the first time he went to his field, he saw the vast, far-stretching earth, and the shoots of maize sprouting. He smiled as he saw the pods of new cotton hanging on their stems. The cotton was emerging perfect from its shell. At the end of the field, the stable made him feel desolate for Kadra. But he stepped into the growing cotton, bent to the earth, picked up a clod of the dry clay, crumbled it and let its dust spill between his fingers. The people who had beaten him in the town would never understand the earth, neither the policemen nor the Magistrate himself. None of them understood! And he himself found it difficult to explain. No one could put into words what the earth meant to someone whose hoe had broken it, whose feet had trodden it. As he knelt, he remembered that the chief pain he had suffered had been separation from these beloved fields.

He stood up and wiped tears from his eyes with muddy fingers.

Abdul Hadi, however, wasted no time in bed. His first day home he walked round the village narrating what had happened to the Magistrate.

He threw out his chest with greater confidence than before. His voice trembled with robust laughter. Yet every part of his body carried traces of his being beaten and kicked.

Though nobody liked to ask him what had happened, everyone came to know: the men had been forced to drink the stale of horses, whips had flamed on their bodies, they had been forced to sit upon iron spikes. Abdul Hadi had been beaten every time until he fainted; he was the only one who had never exclaimed 'I am a Woman!'; he was the only one who had never been set on a spike, until he was unconscious; who had never drunk the urine of horses, until he fell to the floor and they opened his unconscious mouth. And every time he came to, he cursed his tormentors without fear.

The night before the Ministers were due, the men in prison were joined by a large number of young men, thrown into nearby cells. Some wore gallabyas, others western suits. They kept up a hail of slogans:

'Long Live Egypt!'

'Long Live Freedom!'

'The Constitution: Sole Source of Power!' 'Independence!'

When they stopped shouting, they talked amongst themselves of the English and of King Fuad with his big, waxed whiskers. All night new arrivals were brought in. There was a strange mixture of students, some from the secondary school, others from the Teachers' College, others from the Agricultural School. Some were even university students from Cairo: the same who had made themselves famous for their demonstrations, but were now on holiday. There were also merchants, shoeblacks, street-vendors, lawyers, workers from the Cotton Ginnery, and a great number of unemployed. The villagers recognized the names of some of the people who supplied Sheikh Yusif with groceries for his village shop.

Abdul Hadi learnt from what he overheard many things which till then he had not known: the English, for example, were the real rulers of Egypt. But the English and their stooges would not last forever. In the future, everything would get better, since Egypt would never consent to remain under foreign rule.

Abdul Hadi was impressed by the pure, confident tone in which these people spoke; prison in no way daunted them. He turned, and noticed that new blood was suffusing Diab's cheeks. The three villagers listened attentively. The newcomers spoke with contempt of machine-guns, of death, and of the Egyptian Government. One said that the Government's imprisoning everyone who opposed it was a sign of weakness, not strength. All Egypt was against the People's Party. This was the reason they had to shut up their enemies: they were frightened now that people might ask the visitors about the Constitution, about the rigged elections, and other embarrassing matters. People might ask them about the crisis they had brought, about the fields which were going to waste, about the price of food and cloth, and about the money which no longer circulated in people's pockets, about the factories which were turning workers away, and about the land which was being- bought up by banks.

Diab whispered: 'Now I understand properly! They're not afraid of prison. But we ... we understood nothing of all this before.'

The other two smiled in a friendly way to Diab. They craned their ears towards the nearby cells.

Suddenly the Magistrate came into their cell. He stepped in his heavy shoes, not caring whom he trod on. Behind him were a number of soldiers, with fixed bayonets.

The Magistrate paused a moment, overwhelmed by the stench.

The men stood up and crowded round him, gazing at his face, at the soldiers, and at the guns.

The Magistrate announced that their Excellencies, the Ministers of the People's Party, were honouring the town with their visit at ten o'clock. The People's Party had paid the farmers' debts; its newspaper was the voice of the People.

Before he could go on, a villager spoke up to say, simply, that the People's Party had paid the debts of Mahmoud Bey, nobody else's. Mahmoud Bey had been penniless; now he was well off. But the farmers were still in debt, and their land was taken to make a road for the Pasha.

A farmer from another village broke in, swearing that the Government had confiscated land, against tax, while it had left untouched the land of a foreigner who owned the biggest bar in town.

Very coldly, without showing anger, the Magistrate remarked that these farmers had all spoken like donkeys, and like donkeys they would be stabled for the whole day with the horses. He looked at the faces of the farmers, worn out with suffering, their bodies marked with whips. In the same quiet tone, he then explained the procedure for welcoming the Ministers. He told them what their role would be. They would leave the gaol under a police guard and be distributed along the route the Ministers' cars would take on their way to the Pasha's estate. The Lieutenant would signal to them when the cars were approaching. It would be their duty to shout enthusiastically.

'What do we shout?' asked a villager naively. 'Long Live Justice? or Long Live The Nation?'

Still in a quiet voice, the Magistrate pointed at him: he too would spend the rest of the day in the stables.

He returned to the villagers. They must shout: Long Live His Glorious Majesty! Long Live the People's Party! And above all, Long Live Sidky! And this last shout must be intoned rhythmically, many times.

The Magistrate began to demonstrate how to shout Long Live Sidky, in a dancing rhythm, accentuating the notes by clapping his hands.

A villager whispered that the Magistrate would make an excellent drummer! All tried to stifle their smiles.

Raising his voice, the Magistrate began to curse the villagers. He shouted to the police to give these fellows a good beating before locking them up in the stables!

The Magistrate had been almost stifled by the smell. But before leaving the crowded cell, he wanted to repeat his instructions about cheering Sidky. They should practise the slogans now.

In a toneless voice, the villagers recited: 'Long Live the King! Long Live the People's Party! Long Live Sidky!'

In a rage the Magistrate stamped on the ground and began to coach them. They must put enthusiasm into their voices, to show their pleasure at the visit! He warned them that if he caught any of them shouting without enthusiasm, or slovenly dressed, his fate would be black.

He turned to leave. But a new thought occurred to him.

'You must shout in rhythm. You know what rhythm is? You have your beledi drums. You must shout rhythmically, as to a drum! Just as you used to do, in 1919. Didn't you shout, Long Live Egypt very musically? Long Live Egypt! And in the elections, you used to shout Long Live The Wafd! Didn't it go like that? Now you must shout Long Live Sidky in the same rhythm. Just the same!'

An hour later, the villagers were led out in groups and stationed by the police along the road. The sun was beginning to rise above the roofs. The shops were not open as usual, however. So the police dragged their owners into the roads, ordering them to open their shops at once. The police broke some of them open. They then put little flags up as a decoration. But no one tended the shops with their fluttering flags.

In the same way the streets were strangely empty. But hour by hour the pavements began to fill. The rays of the sun brightened the city bit by bit.

Abdul Hadi, Abu Suweilim and Diab recognized some faces. They had seen them above a whip, yesterday, or the day before; but now their owners wore gallabyas, not uniform. Abdul Hadi recognized the face of Shaaban, a man who had been absent from the village for a long time. He saw, too, someone from the eastern sector, an old friend of his, who had been gaoled for three years on a charge of poisoning sheep. He no longer wore convict's clothes.

The whole road from the station to the limits of the town was crowded with convicts and police, but all in gallabyas. There was the sound of music from far off, from the police band, and the reform-school band, as well as from beledi drums. Banners were strung across the road with flattering descriptions of the heroes of the People's Party. The roofs of houses were crowded with women. The Magistrate waved to them from his white horse: 'Shout for joy, all of you women!'

Obediently a few joy-cries broke out.

He rode up and down on his horse. Suddenly he ran into a group of newspaper-sellers, hawking the opposition papers, fresh from Cairo. He ordered his men to confiscate their papers, and make the sellers join the Popular Welcome.

Suddenly the Magistrate gave the order for the demonstration to start. The bands began to play, the drums began to beat. The men on the pavements began to shout their appointed slogans, orchestrated by officers standing in front.

'Raise your voices a little! Show some enthusiasm. Wave your hands in the air! Put joy into your words! Dance and shout. You're men, not sheep.'

The sun was now hot on the crowded pavements. Backwards and forwards rode the Magistrate, telling police to go to every corner of the town and drive the people to take part in the welcome. He then galloped to the station to inspect the notabilities and Omdas. He then repeated the whole route, inspecting carefully both sides, muttering as he went: 'Nobody could do better than this! A splendid popular welcome. There's no other Magistrate in Egypt that could arrange such a reception. I should emerge a Chief of Police, at least.'

The Magistrate reached the outskirts, turned his horse's head, and rode back to the station. 'Well, we're ready. The train should arrive any minute. At attention, everyone! Raise your voices, clap your hands, chant properly, on the right note, with real enthusiasm!' He looked up at the housetops. 'And I want cries of joy from you. Make them resound properly!'

After a few minutes the Ministers' train drew in at the station. They got into the waiting cars, and a crowd of important people, as well as police, gave them a warm send-off, as they drove towards the Pasha's palace on his nearby estate. For the first half of the drive, the cars were edged by applauding crowds. Long Live His Majesty! Long Live The People's Party! Long Live Sidky!

The cars drove with arrogant slowness. On the pavements hordes of people waved and clapped. On banners cheap poetry eulogized the visitors. Women's joy-cries came from the roof-tops. The Magistrate rode proudly alongside the cars, thoroughly pleased with himself and his steed. He waved to the people as they shouted. Here and there men were still shouting Long Live Sidky, others were beating their beledi drums, and the two bands added to the noise.

These rhythms were not new to them. They had put the Magistrate's slogan to their old tune. Suddenly, no one knew how, they reverted to their old words ... Long Live Egypt! Long Live Egypt! they sang in chorus. The whole city broke into one shout. All hands were in the air. The chant ran like a revolution through the town. From streets, from lanes, from every quarter through which the official cars passed, came the cry: 'Long Live Egypt! Long Live The Wafd!'

The cars accelerated.

The Ministers scowled at the transformed crowds.

The Magistrate on his white horse felt more exposed than the Ministers inside their cars. He spurred his horse, which reared amidst the crowd. Loud cries were raised, the forbidden slogans reverberated. The police began to lay about them and women's joy-cries turned to funeral cries. The Prefect got out of his car, ordering his officers to arrest anyone they could lay hands on. The Magistrate got off his horse and stood slapping his cheeks. The Public Welcome was the funeral of his career.

Abdul Hadi's admiration for the men was unstinted: they had borne themselves like heroes!

But Abu Suweilim was a changed man. To him the ignominy of having been beaten, defiled and insulted in front of the other villagers was something from which he could not recover. He sighed and groaned, and though his wife soothed his physical hurts, massaging his swollen body, his spirit was unsoothable. It was true that at the height of his torments, beaten and humiliated, he had yet mustered his last reserves of strength, and had spat all his saliva into the eyes of the Magistrate. He had then been beaten and kicked into unconsciousness by the police.

But despite his courage, he felt defeated. He felt as if he had been stripped naked in front of the other villagers, that he had lost his prestige. He had been treated worse than an animal. If the Magistrate had beaten a cat or a dog as he had beaten Abu Suweilim, the Society for the Prevention of Cruelty to Animals would have intervened.

The worst blow was the behaviour of Abdul Aati in his absence. And though the guard came with tears in his eyes, imploring him to beat him with shoe or slipper, and though Waseefa herself forgave the boy, and asked her father to forget, Abu Suweilim could not forgive him.

Sheikh Hassouna was upset at his old friend's state of mind. After all, Abu Suweilim had suffered no more than Abdul Hadi or Diab. Yet Abdul Hadi remembered only his own resistance, and that of the villagers. Even Diab could laugh, now that it was all over, when the story of his torments was told. But Abu Suweilim was perpetually downcast, as though he carried the world upon his head. He no longer went to the mosque, no longer visited anyone, nor encouraged visits.

Every morning at dawn he went to his field, and stayed there all day. At noon Waseefa would bring him his food, and at dusk he would go home, to stay indoors till another dawn.

One afternoon after prayer Sheikh Hassouna decided this could go on no longer. He and his nephews found Abu Suweilim lying on a heap of dried earth, under the shadow of a mulberry tree. When he saw Sheikh Hassouna coming, he got up to welcome him. Sheikh Hassouna climbed the pile of earth and sat down beside him. Abu Suweilim wanted to go and fetch a sack to put on the soil, but Sheikh Hassouna refused.

'No, sir! Dust we are, and unto dust we shall return! The Good Book says: "We have created you from dust".'

Muhammad Effendi laughed, and he too sat down, beside his uncle. Diab squatted a little way off in the evening shadows.

Despite their insistence, Abu Suweilim got up and cut a large melon. He slapped its cheeks, inspecting it carefully, then handed it to Sheikh Hassouna. Muhammad Effendi brought out a pocket-knife, and cut the melon in four; then he put the open pieces in the sun for a moment, before giving slices, first to his uncle, then to the others.

Sheikh Hassouna blurted out: 'Tell me, Muhammad, my brother, why are you so depressed? Are you carrying the world on your head? Really, you should be very happy. Hasn't the Magistrate been transferred? You and the others did something never done before. You ruined the police. You upset the Prefect. You will, I hope, upset the Government too. What other village can rival you? You should be happy. What is prison? What if the soldiers did rough-handle you? They have no manliness. That was no defeat. No, no, my friend. ... A beating is the reward of every patriot. Think what you have accomplished. Who could have foretold the Ministers' welcome?'

Abu Suweilim opened his eyes. He remembered the rage of the Ministers, when the slogans changed, when the cry Long Live Egypt! thundered through the city.

For the first time since his return, a faint smile spread on his yellowed cheeks. He confessed in a low voice, that indeed they had done something that had not been done before, indeed they had defeated the Government, and they would be able to give the same medicine to the Omda.

Diab, busy devouring his slice of melon, threw away pith and rind. He exclaimed: 'Omda! What Omda? My greetings to the Omda! With what we did to the Government, you talk about the Omda? Hah! By the Prophet, the next time he tries to annoy us we'll throw him down the well. We can get rid of the Government. So why bother with the Omda?'

Abu Suweilim laughed at Diab's bravado. Sheikh Hassouna finished his melon and wiped his lips.

Very slowly, he said that everything that had happened to a man could be an instructive experience. Abu Suweilim was a man who had endured mud and ice for long days when he had fought in Palestine. He had left many friends there, dead in a war without point. And after that, he had come back to build a new future for himself and his wife. His two sons had died, one after the other. Yet despite these miseries, he had contrived to build a new life, and had begotten a new daughter, Waseefa. A man such as he was undefeatable! His experiences in the war had equipped him for the struggle of 1919, and that struggle had given him courage to insult the Magistrate.

Abu Suweilim's blood grew warm as he heard these words. They gave him new pride, new confidence in his powers. A moment before he had felt ready to die.

Sheikh Hassouna finished. 'Perhaps next they will try to take our oxygen from us, too?'

Just then, a lad arrived from the village, running. He kissed Sheikh Hassouna's hand: Sheikh Yusif wanted him urgently in the village.

'What news? What's the matter?'

The boy said that he knew nothing, but that the Government had arrived: they were sleeping in the Omda's house and at dawn they would mark out the new road with iron pegs. Sheikh Yusif was very upset. The arrival of the Survey people was a disaster.

'What a black day!' Abu Suweilim exclaimed. 'Once more. They will drive their road like a plough through wet earth. Yes, yes ... the new road has come ... it will ruin us all. Two more days, and our land won't be our own.'

The men walked back to the village. Abu Suweilim came last, leading his buffalo. Faced with this new threat, the old man remembered a story about another village. This village, no different from their own, had been visited one evening by a detachment of foreign troops. They came on mule-back and camped in a field of corn. The villagers knew from experience that crops, beasts, women – all would be at the mercy of the soldiers. They held a council of war, secretly, at night. They then collected all the cats and dogs they could lay hands on, and tied to their tails pieces of cotton dipped in petrol. Shortly before dawn, they set fire to their tails and then released the frantic animals amongst the corn. In the ensuing conflagration the foreigners were put to flight, and never came back again.

Catching up Shiekh Hassouna, he said, his tongue regaining its old fluency:

'Action's what we need. Saad Zaghloul, before he died, told them to stop talking ... told them there's no use in words.'

Diab blundered into the discussion:

'Right! You're quite right, Abu Suweilim. We are like a solid wall.'

Sheikh Hassouna nodded his head in agreement.

But Abu Suweilim said: 'Yes, but a wall broken by time.'

His sense of defeat returned to him. He murmured sadly a line of poetry:

'A robust camel am I, but my driver went sick;
My bridle was twisted, my new load was thick.'

They reached the outskirts and saw Sheikh Shinawi in front of them, clicking his rosary. He was shaking his head, as though in amusement at some secret joke. He was on his way to the mosque, to chant the evening call.

Abu Suweilim shouted his name, and the Sheikh turned.

'Have you heard the news?' he shouted. 'Have you heard what that fellow Shaaban has done with his slippers? What a son of sin ... to beat them ... to beat them with a slipper!' His words were made incoherent by his laughter. Sheikh Hassouna shouted, what was all this about the men from the Survey Department?

Still laughing, Sheikh Shinawi stood where he was. 'That boy Shaaban ... he'll kill us with his tricks! He chased them out of the village and along the road they came by ... with his slipper!'

Abu Suweilim shouted in astonishment:

'Haven't you told Sheikh Yusif? He sent for us, tonight, he had something important to tell us.'

Sheikh Shinawi replied, between guffaws: 'You don't

believe me. Yet I told you – that mad boy Shaaban attacked them with his slipper! Come now, offer some prayers in thanksgiving.'

Abu Suweilim pointed to his buffalo.

'What about her? Can I bring her to the mosque?' They all laughed, and Sheikh Hassouna asked Sheikh Shinawi to tell them the details. There was still plenty of time before prayer. But Sheikh Shinawi refused to wait, and hurried off to the mosque.

The others went with Abu Suweilim to his house. Waseefa came out, having heard her father's voice. She glanced briefly at Muhammad Effendi, then bent gracefully and kissed Sheikh Hassouna's hand.

Sheikh Hassouna withdrew his hand quickly, and caressed Waseefa's shoulder, and looked at her beautiful face. 'May God guard you from the evil of time!'

Waseefa replied, laughing gently: 'Have you heard what happened at the Omda's? Sheikh Shaaban, have you heard what he did?'

'So Shaaban has become a Sheikh, has he?' Muhammad Effendi asked. 'This is news!'

Waseefa shyly glanced at Muhammad Effendi, her wide eyes beautiful, as she shook the long thick tresses of her hair, dark as a veil. She then took the bridle from her father, and led the buffalo indoors, while Sheikh Hassouna scolded his nephew for cross-examining her, as if they were in a law-court.

The three men continued to Sheikh Yusif's shop. He ran out to invite them into his house. But they preferred to sit on the bench in front of his shop, in the evening breeze.

'So I hear that Shaaban has come back from the salons of Cairo!'

Everyone laughed at Abu Suweilim's sally.

As soon as he had got rid of Alwani, Sheikh Yusif told them what had happened.

Three men had arrived suddenly at the Omda's, from the Survey Department. They asked him to appoint three of his toughest guards to protect the iron pegs which would be brought next day to outline the new road. The Omda was surprised that they had come all this way, when a simple telephone call would have been enough. Was there something else?

One of them unrolled a large map; parallel lines marked the road.

The Omda tried to probe further, but was cut short. 'Your job is to obey orders, without questions!'

The men prepared to take their leave. The Omda detained them: they must drink coffee first!

Contemptuously, one replied that they had not come to pay a social call. Hiding his feelings, the Omda insisted that they could not go without a cup of coffee.

They fidgeted on the sofa, while the Omda again looked at the map. The Omda whispered something to a guard, and then raised his voice: 'Make haste with the coffee!'

The guard went out.

A moment later Shaaban walked in. He saluted those present; the Omda pretended to be annoyed at this intrusion, but at the same time gave a sly wink.

Shaaban noticed the open map. He studied it, then

wheeled round to ask if the road was going to affect the shrine of Ramadhan, the village saint.

'Get out of here!' the Omda shouted.

Shaaban stepped forward and picked up the map. He gazed at it, then shouted wildly:

'By the day of Resurrection ... Ah!'

The three officials glanced at him with disgust.

Shaaban staggered towards them, shouting that the land they were taking contained the shrine, just by the canal.

No one said a word.

He again examined the map. He asked the Omda to show him where precisely the shrine was.

With a wink, the Omda again scolded him.

Shaaban stepped back and swore with a great oath that he would beat with his slipper anyone who dared to touch the shrine of Ramadhan. Then his body began to shake convulsively, as in a religious dance, and he screamed that there was a special bond between him and the saint, and by God it would be honoured! He stretched his hands palm upwards in front of his face and began to pray. He noticed that none of the men stood up. So he prodded them fiercely. They too must say the Prayer with him!

The men were distinctly uneasy. They asked the Omda to get rid of this madman at once, and one of them cursed Saint Ramadhan and all his tribe. The Omda warned them confidentially that Shaaban was one of those dervishes, touched by God ... no one knew who he was, or where he came from. The villagers believed he was under God's protection. Secretly the Omda gave Shaaban another wink. 'Get out of here, madman! Pick on another village. You're a crow of ill omen. Be off with you! You're upsetting our effendis here.'

Shaaban pushed up to one of the men: let him apologize for what he had said against Lord Ramadhan. Shaking himself free, the man said:

'May your shrine fall on your head! To hell with you and your saint. Take your hands off us ... or you'll tear our suits. We saved up to buy them.' Falling almost to the ground, as if in a fit, Shaaban screamed insanely: 'You insult Ramadhan? Blessings on you, Saint Ramadhan! They're insulting you, Saint!' He took off one slipper and struck the employee on his head. And like a dervish in his dance he shouted: 'Oh thou who seest and art not seen. Oh thou who gavest its wings to the gnat!'

The man was terrified by this assault. He rushed out of the room, shielding his head with his hands, while Shaaban followed with his hard-soled slipper. Another of them shouted: 'Rescue us, Omda! You're responsible for all this. You kept us waiting on purpose. It was a plot, and by God, you'll lose your job! Hell take your house!' Shaaban turned on him, his slipper raised, and rained vigorous blows on his back, as he ran to his donkey and clambered on to its back. The first victim had already ridden off down the road, his hand on his head.

The third official had vanished the moment Shaaban had started his attack. The Omda shouted with affected rage.

'What shame, boy, you have brought on our village! You dare to strike a civil servant? This is not the way to treat effendis. Fancy striking an effendi with a slipper! They would prefer a lady's slipper, not a peasant's.' and as the engineers got safely out of earshot, he said under his breath: 'Damn your effendis.' And to the guards he shouted: 'Arrest him, arrest him: but take care! He may fly off – he's a Sufi!'

But as if by a miracle, Shaaban escaped before any guard could touch him.

The Omda meanwhile prepared his reply, should the Magistrate complain. He would say this was a madman with no land or family in the village, a vagabond who begged from place to place. The Omda had tried to have him arrested, but he had got away. He was a Sufi, perhaps he had magic powers.

His listeners laughed uproariously as Sheikh Yusif told his story. 'That was a real Omda's trick,' said Abu Suweilim. 'If only he could use such trickery for the right cause, Egypt would be free.'

Sheikh Hassouna shook his head.

'These tricks made you happy, but not me. Tomorrow you'll see I'm right, and if I live long enough, I'll remind you of my words.'

Silently they stared at Sheikh Hassouna's face: so often he had proved right. After a little, Sheikh Hassouna said: 'Why should the Omda want to beat the officials? Why should he bring that filthy Shaaban here? Tell me: what is Shaaban up to? When we last saw him, he was in the town, welcoming the Ministers. Abu Suweilim, I'm sure he is playing some secret role.'

Sheikh Yusif, suspicious by nature, had been turning over the same thoughts; he had kept them to himself, lest he be laughed at. But he knew that Shaaban was firmly in the Omda's clutches. He had once poisoned the cattle of an enemy of the Omda's; whenever he got into trouble, the Omda got him off. Some years before, Shaaban had been accused of setting fire to the wheatfields of a landowner in the northern sector, another enemy of the Omda's. But he had come back for no apparent reason, when the men had been in gaol. On the day of the popular welcome, he had gone to the town.

When he came back, he had been wearing a turban wreathed with a green shawl, the emblem of Saint Ramadhan. He had never prayed before; now he described himself to everyone as a converted sinner.

Abu Suweilim said: 'Nobody knows who Shaaban's father was, perhaps he has now come back to burn down my house or steal my buffalo, or poison it.'

Opinion about Shaaban was divided. Some people said he really was a reformed character, others were incredulous at so sudden a conversion.

Shaaban had originally come from the village, but he knew nothing of farming. He had never wielded a hoe, nobody knew where his mother came from. She had married an elderly shoemaker and had settled down in the village. Six months after her wedding the shoemaker had died; a year after that Shaaban had been born. She left the village one day, but returned with a young woman whom she described as her sister. She left Shaaban to her care, while she herself went out to wash clothes in various houses, and to light fires.

When Shaaban grew up, his mother wanted him taught her husband's trade. She sent him to a cobbler in a nearby village. But the boy was no good, and came back to steal whatever he could find in the village fields.

His voice broke and, now adolescent, he began to beat his mother and his aunt. The aunt got married and left home, but the son regularly rough-handled his mother for no known reason.

When he was sixteen, he joined a cargo boat that happened to be moored at the embankment. He was away for three years. When he came back, he brought with him nets and fishhooks and set up as a fisherman. He married a village girl, who bore him a daughter. But he deserted them both, and when he next came back, he lived apart from them, not in a house, but like a wolf, and the village became accustomed to seeing him, flitting among the fields.

He excelled in seduction. Any girl knew that if he waylaid her, he would drag her to some lonely spot; if she tried to scream or struggle he would kill her with no more emotion than if she were a large fish.

Then he took to going off for a few days and coming back with a sack of hashish which he would sell quite brazenly to anyone who wanted it. One day a gun he was cleaning went off in the direction of a guard. By accident, said Shaaban. But people looked at him with new suspicions.

Another of his activities was sending girls to Cairo to work as maids. Most of these never came back. Zenouba, the sister of Kadra, who came back from Cairo bronzefaced, swollen with fat, decked out with gold, and her lips scarlet – she was one of these, although she was also his relative.

If ever there was a fiesta or a religious dance, he would

import, from far off, men with yellow complexions and long hair who would whirl under flags, himself in their midst, dancing as wildly as they, shaking himself in convulsive gestures and shouting nonsensical sentences which would be acclaimed by the watchers: 'Syriac, that's what he's speaking!' And at the climax: 'Look, he's arrived!' using the mystical term.

Shaaban was tall and thin, a man of strange movements, or nervous twitches: his complexion was dark, indented with pockmarks; his teeth, many of them broken, were a dirty black, he moved his hands whenever he spoke. So much so, he reminded people of the wriggling snake which his name recalled; one of his boasts was also that he had rid the village of snakes, simply by whistling. More than one villager said he would prefer to keep a snake or two, and lose Shaaban.

Now he had a new persona, that of a holy man, in a green turban, 'Sheikh' Shaaban. One of his first objectives was to try and become friendly with Abu Suweilim. Waseefa, who happened to be at the door, asked him not to call on her father's absence. He laid his hand on her breast, pretending to be blessing her, muttering 'Allah' as he did so. She sprang away, angered by his touch, and took refuge in the house, slamming the door in his face. He sat down at the threshold in the evening sun. When Abu Suweilim came back, after the evening prayer, and found him there, he greeted him brusquely, telling him to stay away from his house in future, and Shaaban never dared to come there again. He took to visiting Sheikh Yusif's shop instead. He would stand in front of it with the young men, telling them stories of his adventures. His open disrespect for the Omda at first perplexed his listeners. He said things about the elderly Omda and his youthful wife such as they had never heard before. Sheikh Yusif himself was surprised at such open attacks. Even Abdul Hadi had never criticized the Omda so brazenly.

He spoke so much of what he had done, and what he would do, that people began to expect some new prodigy.

While Shaaban was making a legend of himself, Sheikh Hassouna had gone to the town. He met his friends, such as the Kadi, on the pavement in front of the chemist's. They were joined by the young lawyer who had once been the Deputy for the town, before the People's Party had come to power. There were also a number of people from the nearby villages, who worked as clerks in the Prefecture, the Survey Department, the Court, or the school. He learnt from them that work on the road would soon start. Nothing they could do would stop it, so long as this Government was in power.

Meanwhile, the new irrigation period was to begin. Abdul Hadi went out to work his waterwheel the first day. At his wheel, he was accosted by Shaaban, who warned him that some young men from the eastern sector were planning, with Diab, to beat him up; they would wait their moment one evening to attack him near his wheel.

At the same time, Alwani told Sheikh Yusif one evening, very merrily, that Shaaban wanted his help in a plot to kill the Omda. Alwani had told Shaaban that nothing would be easier, and it would not cost more than twenty-five pounds. Shaaban would pay ten, and the rest could be provided by Sheikh Yusif, Abdul Hadi, Abu Suweilim and Muhammad

Effendi. These would be the fees for the job. Sheikh Shaaban would arrange everything.

When the grocer heard this, he was alarmed and blurted out that he wanted no part in this! Nor did he want to hear another word about Sheikh Shaaban – or Sheikh Monkey!

Alwani was taken aback by this violent reaction, for he had of course kept no secrets from Shaaban.

Sheikh Yusif rubbed his hands together in dismay. 'Sheikh Shaaban! Be off with you.'

No sooner had Alwani left Sheikh Yusif than he was arrested by some of the guards. He was marched off to the town, and there accused of having murdered Kadra.

Sheikh Yusif was astonished that his fears should be so soon justified. He had not expected Shaaban to show his hand so soon. Why on earth should Alwani have killed Kadra? Had she been killed, after all? And if so, who was her killer?

Suddenly a face flashed into his mind: the face of Shaaban. How typical of the Omda's tricks, if he was behind this. And then another face was before his mind's eye: the wretched Alwani, kicked, beaten, forced to drink the stale of horses, thrown on the ground beneath the boots of soldiers, and then led to a scaffold, a rope round his neck.

This last picture obsessed him, of the pathetic Beduin boy, who had neither family nor home nor anyone to concern himself whether he came or went.. Sheikh Yusif buried his face in his hands. When the old man raised his head from between his hands, there were tears pouring down the wrinkles of his withered face.

The Omda would never forget how the village women

had poured dung over his head: and to defeat them and their menfolk, he had imported Shaaban, who shared his resentment against the village, but now posed as a devout servant of the Prophet.

Shaaban's first task was to gain the trust of the village. His exploits against the engineers had established his bona fides; never before had anyone achieved anything so spectacular. His next move was to make bad blood between the villagers, and at the same time to learn of any move they might be planning against the Omda.

His first discovery was that Alwani had been responsible for robbing the Omda's stores. The Beduin youth had then been arrested for killing Kadra.

Waseefa, who knew Kadra very well, who had been Kadra's confidante, said it was just not possible that Alwani had killed her; not possible at all. Alwani could not have done it, nor any other of the village boys.

Her mother, seizing one of the ducks by its tail, told Waseefa to be quiet, bring her a sharp knife; she was going to kill the duck for dinner, as Sheikh Hassouna would be visiting them that evening.

Waseefa brought a knife and said again how unthinkable it was that Alwani should have killed Kadra!

Her mother looked up and shouted acidly that she should never speak of any man, Alwani, or anyone else.

Waseefa could not understand her mother's rage and her accusing look.

Her mother in a broken voice explained that Shaaban – God remove him from the village! – had put it about that

Waseefa was becoming another Kadra, first with Alwani, then with Muhammad Effendi, and now with Abdul Hadi, and even Diab.

Pale-faced, Waseefa let out a terrible cry.

'Sheikh Shaaban? Sheikh Shaaban said that about me? May his tongue be cut, may his body sweat with fever. ... If only he could stand before me this minute!'

She rushed to the open door, while her mother shouted to her to come back and be quiet. Then lowering her voice, the duck in her hands as she squatted by the oven, she said: 'Shut the whole story in the oven ... Let's leave it to God!'

While her mother sharpened the knife to cut the bird's throat, Waseefa could not sit still; she walked backwards and forwards in the centre of the house, her eyes glaring through the open door for any glimpse of Shaaban.

Suddenly Abdul Hadi appeared, and Waseefa hid herself; she felt she was about to collapse, and did not know what to do.

'Hullo, Waseefa,' he said.

She stood there trembling, unable to reply, or look him in the eye.

'Well, what's wrong with you? Have you got the plague or something?'

In truth, her tremblings were like the convulsions of someone seriously sick.

She mustered strength to say:

'Go, please, Abdul Hadi ... It's not good for Shaaban or someone else to see us together like this, or even you standing there. It would give weight to his accusation.' And she rushed inside the house, tears falling freely from her eyes.

Abdul Hadi realized immediately that Shaaban must have said something dishonourable about him and Waseefa. His eyes glared with predictions of evil.

For despite everything, Abdul Hadi was still determined to marry Waseefa. The crops coming to ripeness in his fields brought him joy, only because he was confident that one day they would belong to Waseefa too, as his wife. The cotton would soon be ready. The foreign buyers would come, as they did every season, to make their offers for his crop. He would postpone paying his taxes, and would pay for Waseefa instead.

On his way to the Omda's house, in quest of Shaaban, Abdul Hadi passed by Sheikh Yusif's shop. He heard the old man shouting at one of the boys who had come back without a job to the village. He was scolding him for the length of his hair, as long as a girl's ... as well as for the effeminate ways he had picked up in Cairo. The object of his mockery smiled back at him, shrugging his shoulders. Smoothing the dyed streak in his otherwise jet-black hair, the boy further enraged Sheikh Yusif by saying that the new road would actually help the village: men would be needed to build it.

Sheikh Yusif burst out: 'What? What craziness is this, boy? The Government wants to help you? You think they're building this road for you unemployed villagers? What about the townsmen without work? Wouldn't they think of them ? You worked as a servant in Cairo. Do you know how to pick?'

boy's face was brazen, his eyes were shifty, and he thin shoulders carelessly. Abdul Hadi glared at

'And what about the bits of land that belong to your father? Aren't they in the line of the new road? You with your long hair and your Cairo accent ... don't you understand? Your father's land will be eaten up by the road. What will you eat, what will you give to your buffalo? I suppose you'll buy hay for her, without sweat, by some miracle? You'll buy bread too? and even cheese.'

Sheikh Yusif laughed, striking hand against hand.

'Honestly, these fellows – are they human? They're all ridden by a phantom called "jobs": this creature Shaaban has given them to understand that they will be employed on the road.'

Abdul Hadi growled through his teeth. 'Shaaban? I'll cut his life in bits, and spread it like manure on my fields!'

The boy spoke as he drifted off. 'What's wrong with Shaaban? Didn't you hear what he did to the men from the Government? Whoever struck a tougher blow than that?'

His Cairo accent enraged Abdul Hadi.

'The toughest blow, you say? Stop mincing like a whore.'

'You're jealous,' the boy shouted. 'Compared to you, Shaaban's red pepper.'

Sheikh Yusif exploded. 'Red pepper? May your tongue be cut in pieces and peppered. You're a whore, a dancing girl. Listen, boy! Pepper, toughest blows, Sheikh Shaaban There's only one place you need pepper.'

The tall gangling youth walked off, shrugging his sho carelessly, patting his greasy locks into place.

Sheikh Yusif had been outraged at Shaaba to belittle Abdul Hadi. This weakling who h

206

boasted to Sheikh Yusif that even he could outfight Abdul Hadi at the stick-game.

Abdul Hadi laughed when Sheikh Yusif told him this. But the old man was angry. He went on to say that the whole village was being led astray. That very morning a short, fat man from the northern sector had said that he'd heard Abdul Hadi had acted as a police informer in prison; this was why he had not been punished by the Government, even though he had been the first man responsible for breaking the embankment.

This tale, too, only amused Abdul Hadi: until Sheikh Yusif told him that its teller was someone whom Abdul Hadi had benefited, taking his part in a village fight.

This was too much for him: Abdul Hadi recognized the man. 'He said that? If he was here now, by God I'd teach him gratitude. And as for you, Sheikh Shaaban, and your Omda, if I don't break your necks, my name's not Abdul Hadi.'

Sheikh Yusif told of other instances.

Only three days before some boys of good character had come to the shop; they had all been sacked from a Cairo factory. Shaaban suggested that they should steal the iron used to mark the new road. No sooner had this been agreed, than the boys were arrested, and sent as conscripts to guard the Nile against floods, on a far-off sector. Sheikh Yusif pictured them now, with no proper place to sleep, no good food, under firstbroiling sun and the whips of their guards. They were only wield st contingent: who knew if others would not be taken

The bone excuse?

shrugged hi adi paled at this threat. The Omda had a new him: against anyone he disliked: the corvee!

Sheikh Yusif picked up a small jar, raised it to his mouth, drank, wiped his lips on the back of his hand and said:

'And you heard what happened between Abu Suweilim and Sheikh Hassouna?'

Abdul Hadi shook his head.

Their conversation was momentarily interrupted by the arrival of a woman. She wanted to exchange a corn cob against some salt. He took the ear of corn and examined it critically. 'Bring me another,' he said, 'this is not a cob, it's a runt.'

'But it's all I have,' she said, 'please, Sheikh Yusif.'

In an ill temper, he agreed, and chucked the skinny ear on a pile of others at the back of the shop, and gave her some salt.

He then turned to Abdul Hadi and told him what had happened the night before.

Abu Suweilim and Sheikh Hassouna had practically come to blows in Sheikh Yusif's own parlour. From the moment they met, it was clear there was some irritation between them. Sheikh Hassouna had spoken first. Why had Abu Suweilim spread the rumour – despite their long friendship – that when Sheikh Hassouna had gone to the town, it had been to convince his town friends that the road was all for the best, since it did not take any of his land?

Abu Suweilim was astounded at Sheikh Hassouna's story.

'I said that about you? What on earth are you saying? Sheikh Hassouna, what is your tongue up to? Do you believe I could say such a thing? Please, Headmaster, please.'

Calmly Sheikh Hassouna replied, 'Those were your very words. Are you now trying to ridicule me?'

Abu Suweilim said, 'It's not me who speaks idle words.

You do your worst. If there's wind in your sails, sail where you want to! To the ruin of our friendship, if you wish.'

'You think I am a false friend. What bad manners even to hint such a thing.'

'Bad manners? And what about you saying cheap things about my daughter, despite your education? I've heard what you said.'

'I said something about your daughter? Are you in your second childhood? But I'm wrong, not you: I should never have come back to this village, to try and help it.'

Their speech had become so furious, their arguments so bitter, that if their friendship had not been old and tried, they might have been turned into irreconcilable enemies. But luckily, both of them had enough sense left to realize that all these tales stemmed from one person – Shaaban, and were to the benefit of one person – the Omda. Their dispute turned into an embarrassed recognition of how they had let themselves be misled.

'I was wrong to believe him for a moment,' said Sheikh Hassouna.

'And I, too,' said Abu Suweilim. 'I know that my daughter's honour is as precious to you as to me.'

Just as Sheikh Yusif had finished, Sheikh Shinawi arrived with the news that the building of the road was about to start: the tools had arrived, and were under guard. Shaaban was with the Government engineers. The iron pegs were already being laid in Muhammad Effendi's field, and the one next to it. Diab had wanted to resist. Shaaban had whispered something in his ear, but pushing him aside, Diab had threatened the men, ordering them out of his field. Muhammad Effendi, however, had called him back, and the boy had reluctantly obeyed: his face yellow with rage. The men had begun to trample over the growing cotton and the fresh green maize. When Diab saw this, he had burst into tears.

Sheikh Shinawi's news brought a crowd of screaming women into the roads. Their tragic cries annoyed the old preacher, who shouted to them to be quiet. But they continued to denounce the Government and the Omda. Only the intervention of a fat, middle-aged woman managed to do what the Sheikh could not do, with all his slaps and shouts, and disperse the women. She hinted that when they said they would go out and defy the engineers, the real reason was a lascivious desire to jostle with the townsmen! Hearing this, the women stumbled off in embarrassment.

Sheikh Shinawi said he had heard a rumour that Shaaban would be the next Chief Guard.

Abdul Hadi clenched his fists. Frowning, he grabbed his big stick and got up to go, despite Sheikh Yusif's entreaties for him to stay.

He went first to Abu Suweilim's house. He found Waseefa there, crouching by the brick oven and weeping bitterly. She already knew the news. Everyone knew that the land was no longer theirs. Abdul Hadi himself did not own land by the canal; all of his land was by the river. He was not threatened with loss. Nevertheless he was as sad as though the menaced land was his. He felt that if one man was struck, then the whole village was stricken. If land was taken from one man, it was taken from all. If he was silent today, when

Abu Suweilim's land was taken, and Diab's, he would be the sufferer tomorrow. He loved the land of the whole village. He could not bear that this green and fertile earth should become a barren surface for the wheels of traffic. Seeing Waseefa's tears, he determined this time to do something.

He took the canal road and came on a group of engineers standing in a field. There was a cool breeze carrying with it the first hints of autumn. Black crows hovered above the fields.

At one end of the field Abu Suweilim was standing on a pile of earth. Sheikh Hassouna, Muhammad Effendi and Diab were sitting beside him. Abdul Hadi left the road and strode towards the men. Abu Suweilim felt that Abdul Hadi might attack them, in an excess of rage. So he jumped down from the top of the mound and ran after his friend and seized him by the arm. Let them talk things over: now was not the time to be rash! Abdul Hadi shook him off, refusing to be held back. But Abu Suweilim said:

'Be patient a while longer.'

Reluctantly Abdul Hadi let himself be led to where the others were sitting; but he smiled at no one.

They were eating roast corn cobs. Calmly, Sheikh Hassouna offered one to Abdul Hadi. 'Take one, my boy, it's good! Eat it, before the highway eats it.'

Abu Suweilim pushed a laugh through his sighs. But Abdul Hadi stared, unsmiling, towards the officials and their gear. Standing near them with Abdul Aati, the Omda's favourite, was Shaaban.

Quietly Sheikh Hassouna said, 'Patience a moment, my brother. All's going to be put right.'

'Who's going to put it right?'

Abu Suweilim whispered something in Abdul Hadi's ear. As he listened, Abdul Hadi's face relaxed, his frowns dissolved, and by the time the old man finished, he was smiling. Seeing his change of mood, Abu Suweilim laughed. 'The Headmaster and I, we're old hands at this sort of thing. We learnt our lessons in the days of the English.'

Lights burnt late in the Omda's house. When they at last went out, the village doors were quietly opened to the creeping steps of men. All looked alike: dressed in black, moving silently. The only sounds were those of barking dogs and a few whirring insects evoked by the cooler nights. By starlight the men reached Abu Suweilim's field.

Abu Suweilim whispered to a tall man in black, pushing ahead of the rest. 'Steady, not so fast, Abdul Hadi! Come back ... that's better. Or they'll see you and perhaps shoot.'

Lying near the strips of iron, Shaaban rubbed his eyes, and raised his head a little. 'I take refuge in God! This place is haunted. Do you hear that muttering, Abdul Aati? Demons are after us.'

Shaaban was silent, conscious of the pounding of his heart.

'Don't you see their flaming breath, Abdul Aati? Abdul Aati! Answer me.'

But Abdul Aati said nothing. Shaaban began to curse him, then changed his mutterings to holy texts.

Abdul Aati was apparently fast asleep, snoring loudly.

The men seized on a length of iron and carried it to the canal, where it plopped into the water.

Shaaban knew now that it was men he had to fear, not

demons. But Abdul Aati was lying on top of Shaaban's gun, as well as his own, as if by accident, but really in obedience to instructions from Abu Suweilim. Shaaban reached for a piece of iron, to use against the men's heads. But Abdul Hadi blocked his way and picking him up, threw him over his shoulders, like a sack of maize.

Shaaban on his back, screaming with terror, Abdul Hadi ran to the canal. He held him high in his hands for a moment, then threw him with all his force into the deep water, still clutching his iron.

Shaaban's screams echoed from the water. Some of the men stood laughing on the bank. If he came back, they would squash him with their slippers like a cockroach!

They did not know that Shaaban, an experienced fisherman, had dived deep and swum off underwater to a remote spot, thence to emerge and carry on living in another village.

When all the iron had gone, the men burst into shouts of joy.

All this time, Abdul Aati had been snoring.

Abu Suweilim laughed. 'You deserve a hiding, Abdul Aati! You're a fox ... no, a monkey! A perfect monkey.'

They returned to their houses, chattering about their exploits. The road rang with their cheerful voices. Before they arrived home, doors opened with welcoming joy-cries of women.

Suddenly a cry of grief punctuated the rejoicing.

The news spread like wildfire: the eighty-year-old Omda had died.

'Every evil has an end,' exclaimed one man. 'Why on earth are they wailing? He must have been at least a hundred and fifty!'

Another agreed. 'Yes, true, every evil ends. To think that we've rid ourselves of the highway, the Omda and Shaaban, and all in one night!'

Cries of joy began to resound through all the lanes; women sang with men an old refrain:

'A splendid night is this. A night of wondrous bliss!'

Only Abu Suweilim shook his head sternly. 'Boys, is it right to gloat at death? But still, congratulations, village! Everything has an end.'

The Omda's relations received condolences in the village guestroom. The Sheikh al-Balad took his place at the head of the relations, sitting aloof among gilded chairs on a pale red carpet. Abu Suweilim had chosen a humble place among the wooden benches, at the other end of the guestroom. These benches stood on the bare earth, and lacked any covering. Between them and the gilded chairs were rows of beledi sofas, borrowed from the relations' houses.

The Sheikh al-Balad was sitting on a gilded chair, quite near the door. He kept thinking of what the Magistrate had said to him on the telephone: he was now defacto Omda, and the Omda's responsibilities were his. He had already begun to act like the previous Omda: he would half get up, or get up completely, or walk a few paces from his place, depending on the rank of those who came to condole; it was clear to himself that he was now the most important person in the village. Yet he felt he must try and imitate the manners of his predecessor, who was so different from himself, being venerable, whitehaired and self-assured. For most people, he would never stir from his seat; when he did get up for someone important, everyone else got up, too.

The Sheikh al-Balad, however, got up, stepped forward, and sat down again, but nobody moved.

So he now reached a decision: he would stay seated for everyone, except those who arrived by carriage from the town.

He must act like an Omda, with an Omda's dignity!

He turned his gaze to the people on the benches. They were listening entranced to Sheikh Ibrahim, the most famous reciter of the Koran in the district. They were uttering shouts of encouragement, and making requests for him to prolong certain verses, just as if it were a fiesta and not a funeral! The Sheikh al-Balad was very angry. Pulling his cashmere gown around him, he strode a few paces towards the villagers, and asked them peremptorily to be more reverent, for they were hearing the Koran!

Diab nudged his neighbour:

'Why's he shouting at us like that? What does he think he is? The Government?'

His neighbour whispered back: 'What do I care for this yellow-faced creature? We don't have the chance of hearing Sheikh Ibrahim every day. It's five years since he was last with us.'

No sooner had the Sheikh al-Balad gone back to his seat, than Sheikh Ibrahim began to chant a new verse in his loveliest tones. One of the farmers from the rough benches shouted, 'Ah, Sheikh Ibrahim, you nourish us! Please repeat that verse in all the Seven Ways, and sway as you do so.'

The farmers nearby smiled, and so did Sheikh Ibrahim himself.

Another whispered, 'He's the real reciter, Sheikh Ibrahim. Not like the ones we have here, they croak like frogs at us. This is the real Koran, not something from the sedge, like Sheikh Shinawi gives us.' Though angry, even Sheikh Shinawi assented to the praise of his rival.

All the villagers listened entranced. Only the Sheikh al-Balad edged forward on his golden chair: he wanted to hear what some men were saying who had come from the town and were now sitting with Sheikh Hassouna. All of them were whispering together. He gathered that they were discussing some newspapers which had been banned by Sidky, and which had now appeared under new names. He heard them talking of people who lived in Cairo and about whom people in the village knew but little. The owner of the chemist-shop was speaking enthusiastically about Taha Hussein, the famous writer, and about the newspaper, *Al Jihad*, as well as something called 'democracy', and freedom of the Press.

The Sheikh al-Balad moved his chair forward, craning towards the speakers. The lawyer was speaking, who had previously represented the district in Parliament, before the People's Party came to power. Almost falling off his chair, the Sheikh al-Balad blurted out, without any respect for Sheikh Ibrahim:

'We have heard your words, Sir! They were splendidly

informative. What you say is news to us, here in this ignorant village!'

The lawyer obligingly spoke more loudly. He attacked the regime for the way in which people were transferred hither and thither, the way the farmers were treated, and the way in which freedom was suppressed.

The Sheikh al-Balad had never heard speech like this before. He had always followed his kinsman, the Omda. He was troubled to hear now that there was no future for Egypt, until parliamentary government was restored.

He did not know how to pose the questions that arose to him. But he suddenly said, 'Good, Sir, and what is your idea about cotton? Will it get as it used to be?' The lawyer shrugged his shoulders, a little contemptuously. He said, ironically, that Sidky Pasha had many skills; one of them might be in economics; the English depended on the skills of such men!

Sheikh Ibrahim's voice, meanwhile, rose louder as he recited verses in the seven approved ways. The farmers showed their appreciation with increasing fervour. One said, 'Allah! Allah! Sheikh Ibrahim! We can't be living.'

'Oh, Sheikh Ibrahim,' said another, 'if only we could have an Omda die on us every day, so we could listen to you.'

There was the noise of a carriage arriving outside. Someone was heard cursing the farmers' donkeys tethered by the entrance. There was the noise of animals being pushed out of the way. Then wheels crunched to a halt at the guest-room door.

Before the carriage stopped, the whisper ran round: 'It's the Magistrate, with Mahmoud Bey!'

The Sheikh al-Balad ran to the door, discarding in a flash all the dignity he had assumed so carefully.

Behind him clustered Muhammad Effendi, Sheikh Shinawi and other notables, all eager to welcome the Magistrate.

Everyone rose, except for the lawyer and his entourage. The lawyer said acidly that he was not going to greet anyone who represented the Government or its agents.

Sheikh Ibrahim continued to recite the same verse as before.

As the Magistrate passed through the door, all eyes were on his paunchy figure in its military uniform. At the same moment came the Koranic verse: 'And behold thine ass!'

The Magistrate paused in the doorway. The voice repeated: 'And behold thine ass!'

The Magistrate stepped towards the chair of honour; at his side stood Mahmoud Bey in a high, brilliant tarboosh; the white folds of his beledi gallabya shimmered elegantly.

The Magistrate sat down, in the Sheikh al-Balad's chair. On his right sat Mahmoud Bey and Muhammad Effendi. There was a general re-shuffling of seats. Some who had previously seated themselves on the gilt chairs, moved to the sofas, while some on the sofas moved to the hard benches. Sheikh Shinawi sat down amidst the villagers. The Sheikh al-Balad himself sat at the very end of the gilt chairs, to the Magistrate's left. Sheikh Ibrahim continued to recite in the Seven approved ways, repeating the verse, 'And behold thine ass!'

The Magistrate turned his head towards the reciter as if

to ask him to change the verse. But Sheikh Ibrahim was pre-occupied with exercising the beauties of his famous voice in every musical trick which he knew.

The Sheikh al-Balad was still basking in the glory of his proximity to the Magistrate. He took from his pocket a packet of cigarettes, bought by the relatives of the Omda for important guests. He bowed in front of the Magistrate and offered him a cigarette, and another to Mahmoud Bey. He then withdrew to his place at the end of the line, shouting, 'Coffee for His Excellency the Magistrate, boy!'

Sheikh Ibrahim continued to intone:

'And behold thine ass!'

The visitors from the town, sitting with the lawyer, all smiled; the lawyer whispered in his neighbour's ear and smothered a laugh. They all stared at the Magistrate and Mahmoud Bey. All ears took in the words of the verse. There was a ripple of stifled laughs.

The Sheikh al-Balad suddenly realized what was happening, and in embarrassment looked to the Magistrate. He saw that he was puffing smoke ahead of him, his face slowly losing whatever colour it had had in its mounting rage.

The Sheikh al-Balad went and whispered in the reciter's ear:

'Please find us some verse other than this. No need to recite this one in all the Seven Ways. "Behold thine ass!" Everyone's staring at the Magistrate.'

The reciter glanced up at him in stern disdain and putting his hand on his cheek in the manner of Koranic reciters, he sonorously repeated, 'And behold thine ass!'

Now open laughs reached the gilt armchairs with their green velvet cushions.

Mahmoud Bey exploded in anger. 'Enough, Sheikh Ibrahim! Is there nothing in the Koran except this verse? For the hour we've been here, you've given us nothing but this. Who put you up to this?'

Laughs broke out from the wooden benches. The Magistrate stood up and said in an angry voice, '"The verity of the Almighty". My friend, that's the phrase, to conclude your recitation, or to say something else, such as "We have crowded the Wafd into Hell".' The Magistrate misquoted a verse from the chapter 'Mary'.

The laughter ceased. Stern-faced the Magistrate sat down.

There was a breathless silence. Then the Magistrate pointed at the benches. 'Very good; aren't you the men of the iron bars? Aren't you the ones who shout Long Live the Wafd!?'

The lawyer answered calmly, 'Not them only, all Egypt shouts that, your Excellency. You would prefer them to shout "*Long Live Sidky* or *Long Live The People's Party*"? No wonder you're angry! You think you can rule Egypt forever? This country belongs to its people, not to highwaymen and thieves.'

The Magistrate was taken aback. But the benches were delighted at these bold words from their former deputy. And as the lawyer continued to protest, the Magistrate, not wishing to get involved in a political dispute in the midst of a funeral, allowed a few moments of tension, then demanded threateningly:

'Which of you was responsible for taking the iron?'

A farmer murmured, 'Is this a funeral or an interrogation?'

His neighbour said to him in whispered mockery, 'Look! Look! Behold thine ass!'

Many tried to control their laughter in their sleeves, while others remained expressionless, their eyes switching from their previous deputy to the Magistrate, afraid of what might happen.

The Sheikh al-Balad swore to the Magistrate that he did not know whom to blame, as the guard who had been on watch said that it was demons who had thrown the iron into the canal. The lamented Omda, he added, had been in good health, until he heard of this outrage: thereupon he had died immediately. Fawningly, he offered a second cigarette to the Magistrate. The Magistrate got up.

'Good! I shall make this village an example to others.' Sheikh Shinawi ran after them, making excuses for the village: then came the Sheikh al-Balad. Muhammad Effendi was going to join them, but caught a glare from his uncle Sheikh Hassouna, who hissed at him, 'Have some respect for yourself, Muhammad!' SoMuhammad Effendi joined his uncle abashed.

The Magistrate took his seat in the carriage, Mahmoud Bey at his side. The Sheikh al-Balad and other relatives of the Omda stood at the door, touching their foreheads with both hands in gratitude to the Magistrate. But the Magistrate made no response, and neither did Mahmoud Bey.

Sheikh Yusif had a new problem: who would be the next Omda? It must be someone not from the old Omda's family.

His relatives were all at odds with each other; besides, none of them owned the stipulated amount of land that an Omda should have. Nevertheless, this divided family would agree on the election of the Sheikh al-Balad. Like a pack of squabbling dogs, they would bark together against an intruder.

Sheikh Yusif went to the town and bought a new outfit: a shawl for his turban, a cashmere robe, and a new undervest of pure wool. Proudly he shook out his sleeves, showing the undervest. He happened to be visited by Sheikh Hassouna. Offhand, as if in jest, he spoke of his hopes. 'Look, Headmaster! My Omda's outfit. Do you like it? Wouldn't I make a fitting Omda? I'm cut out for the role! You'll be His Excellency the Headmaster. I'll be His Excellency the Omda!'

Sheikh Hassouna spoke to him so snubbingly that Sheikh Yusif did not dare to broach the subject again. Alwani was the only person who, if he had been there, would have enthused over the idea. But alas, though guiltless, Alwani was in prison, beaten and humiliated, and Sheikh Yusif had no one in whom he could confide. So he took off his splendid new clothes and locked them away. To console himself, he began to read the exploits of an Arab hero famous for his patience, whose star, long occluded, finally rose.

Days passed, and still no one knew who the new Omda would be. The ordinary villagers did not much care. Whoever it might turn out to be, he would not be able to improve the price of cotton. There were three or four candidates, each with his own interests in mind. The villagers were more concerned with what the Government might do about its vanished ironware.

One evening, the Sheikh al-Balad and some relatives of the Omda, mostly children, sat on reed mats by the Omda's tomb, situated in the more distinguished part of the cemetery, apart from the poorer graves. They were reciting in a rhythmic, excited manner passages of the Koran, for the repose of the Omda's soul. It was almost a picnic, with things to eat.

The time came to go. On the road back the Sheikh-al-Balad confided that the Magistrate had telephoned him, as deputy Omda, to inform him that the Camel Corps were coming to the village. They would enforce a curfew, beginning that very evening.

This news stopped the men in their tracks. They encircled the Sheikh al-Balad; what did this curfew mean? The Sheikh al-Balad explained that everyone would have to stay indoors all night, to prevent any interference with the road.

The sun was now low in the west; crows wheeled and cawed in the darkening sky. The Sheikh al-Balad strode arrogantly, his hands clasping a cane behind his back. These were Government orders, he said; he was the Government's deputy, and a new era was beginning.

The rays of evening were pink as the Sheikh al-Balad led the reciter and the children towards the village.

Suddenly cries rang out. Before they could move aside, a buffalo ran down the lane, followed by a donkey thudding its hind legs in panic, and children colliding with the sturdy wings of ducks and geese.

'The Camel Corps are here! Their whips are at work in the village. Run, boy!'

Some men ran panting from the stables. The Camel Corps

had laid about them: men, women and children, they had beaten everyone they met, including Sheikh Yusif, whom they had beaten in front of his shop.

The Sheikh al-Balad tried to encourage his group; no one dared touch them while they were with him; for he was the representative of the Government, as they knew, and as the Camel Corps would know too.

At this very moment the Camel Corps appeared from round the corner, cracking their immense whips. The men were hypnotized by the long leather whips bound with golden wire.

The Sheikh al-Balad stood his ground. 'I am the Government representative here. Take care, Mister Sergeant. What is your name?'

But the Sergeant in charge of the soldiers raised his whip and cracked it at the Sheikh al-Balad, ordering him to get into his house, at once. He was Sergeant Abdullah, and he didn't like people who answered him back!

The Sheikh al-Balad screamed with pain and took to his heels, far in front of the other men. One of these said mockingly:

'They've beaten the Government's representative! He ran off, boys! The Government has beaten its own representative.'

Everyone took refuge at home, and when night fell, every house was filled with foreboding, but also with mirth at what had happened. Sheikh Shinawi's neighbours also had something to laugh at; for he had been on his way to the mosque for evening prayers. No sooner did he hear the cracking of the long whips, than he fled home, forgetful of the mosque, and those who were praying.

In the morning the village found that new ironware had been brought for the road. At the same time, Alwani was released from prison.

When Alwani heard what had happened, the first question he asked was where had the Camel Corps slept? No one knew. He next asked where they had drunk tea. To the villagers this seemed an absurd question. But Alwani said he regretted that he had long since sold the tent in which he had been born. For if he had still had the tent, pitched behind the houses, he could have invited the Camel Corps men to tea. 'If I had been here, none of this would have happened. I am an Arab, like them. They'll soon get used to you fellahin.'

At the same time, Sergeant Abdullah was sitting in the Omda's Residence, thinking of his distant home south of Aswan, and his father and mother. He was filled with regret. He had beaten men like his father, women like his mother, and even children like those he had loved at home. Why had he beaten them, pitilessly, without cause? This was a question he could not answer.

He patrolled the roads of the village with his men, as the villagers hurried home, driving their beasts from the fields, the women, as usual, collecting the manure for fuel. And the villagers passed the place where the new iron bars had already broken the white-crowned cotton and the fresh green maize. The sight filled them with gloom. And soon every man and woman and child was at home, behind locked doors, every one of them afraid of Sergeant Abdullah and his Sudanese whip.

PART THREE

AUTUMN HAD COME to the village. The new maize was not yet ripe; the village stores were running short of last year's corn.

Every evening I used to sit by Abdul Hadi's waterwheel, thinking of the secondary school to which I should be going in two weeks' time, in Helmia Gadida, that quarter of Cairo so melancholy in Autumn. I recalled, too, the books and novels I had read during the holidays.

I would return home each evening as the sun sank behind trees topped with white birds, fluttering hither and thither till their wings dissolved in the dark. I was not allowed to stay out after dusk, ever since the time I had met Waseefa by the sycamore.

With the coming of Autumn, the maize had grown as tall as men. The lofty stems, heavy with new ears, revived in us children fears of the unknown, and stories of mysterious men skulking in the protection of maize groves, waiting to attack their foes. But this year, I had books to remember, as well as legends.

During the summer I had read *The Days* and *Ibrahim the Writer* and *Zaynab*. In my village, as in the village described by Taha Hussein in *The Days*, I saw children whose eyes were eaten up by flies. How I wished that my village could be a village without troubles, like the village in which Zaynab lived. The farmers there had no troubles with their irrigation water, the Government did not take their land away, nor send men in khaki to flog them with whips. The children's eyes were not consumed by flies. In Zaynab's village, men did not pass blood and pus in their urine, nor were they convulsed with pains which did not leave them till they were silent, finally.

Yet my village was every bit as beautiful as Zaynab's; its sycamores and mulberries were interlaced along the river bank. The river's pale surface glistened like silver till the evening turned it to gold; and at night it trembled darkly, faltering on its journey to the unknown. And in the fields by the canal - where the Government were taking the land - the earth was thick with cotton and in the fields by the river, plains of maize waved blond summits as far as the eye could see. The women in my village carried their pitchers in the same picturesque way as in Zaynab's, and were beautiful, too. Waseefa was lovelier than Zaynab, fair-skinned and young. Yet even she had a certain pallor that prophesied the withering of her youth, the slow conquest of her cheeks.

Zaynab's village had never tasted the whip, as my village had. On the other hand, Zaynab's village had never known the thrill of defying destiny, the foreigner, the Omda, the Government, and of winning, too, at times.

Zaynab had never wept with the bitterness on Waseefa's face one morning, the first time that I saw her after our meeting under the tree.

At this time I heard a great deal about Sergeant Abdullah, and his doings. I had not seen him, however. I pictured someone as tall as a door, as burly as a bale of cotton, tough, black as soot, his teeth white as cheese ... someone who never smiled or spoke, but excelled only in flogging. The people spoke of him so much that he entered their proverbs and their legends. For example, if a very fat woman-hawker should come to the village, people would say, 'Sergeant Abdullah!' And even children playing with sticks would call the toughest of their number 'Sergeant Abdullah', until another would reply, 'Good! But I am Abdul Hadi!'

Abdul Hadi had not crossed sticks with Sergeant Abdullah. But the boys liked to imagine what would happen if he did.

I was kept at home all summer. And with autumn the end of the holidays was in sight. I heard now that the Sergeant no longer beat people, and some people even said that he was a fine fellow. A boy told me he had seen him laughing. I heard too that he had visited Sheikh Yusif in his shop, and had joked with him. He sat at night with Sheikh Hassouna, Muhammad Effendi, and Abdul Hadi at Abu Suweilim's door, and Abu Suweilim told Waseefa to bring coffee for Sergeant Abdullah. But the Sergeant had asked for tea instead, and when he tasted it, had exclaimed:

'Long live joy, Oh you Arabs!'

Everyone laughed, smiling delightedly because they knew they were with a man just like themselves.

Sergeant Abdullah allowed Sheikh Shinawi to go to the mosque for evening prayers, and Sheikh Yusif to keep his shop open till dusk. And after that, he would sit with Abu Suweilim and tell his three soldiers to escort people politely to their homes, and then come and join him. There was even a rumour that Sergeant Abdullah wanted to marry Waseefa, though her father was said to have refused permission. I longed to see him! I wanted to know how he talked, this man who had flogged all the village the day he had arrived. How did he laugh? Did he have a wife and children like other men?

I also had a great desire to see Waseefa. I might not have another chance for a long time.

One morning I went to her house. Her door was open like all the doors in the village at this time of day. Before I went in, I heard her mother telling her to fetch some corn to roast for bread. I stepped forward. Then I saw Waseefa coming back from the storeroom, in her eyes tears that had not had time to fall. I heard her say, 'There's no corn in the store, Mother!'

My heart trembled as I saw her crying.

I remembered my father's words when I begged him to give me a new suit for my new school. He had looked at me tenderly, sadly:

'My boy, even bread's hard enough, let alone a new suit.'

As I retreated from her house, I heard her mother say: 'Well then, take this duck and find someone to buy it for ten pounds of corn. Try Muhammad Effendi, or Sergeant Abdullah. Oh, Lord! Oh, Lord!'

And I wondered to myself when Our Lord would give them corn or me new clothes. When? and how?

My first chance of meeting Sergeant Abdullah came one evening. It was lonely by the river, as the villagers hurried their cattle home. On my way back, I heard from far off a rasping voice:

'Fire of straw forever. Fire of love not a day!
Fire of straw goes out. Fire of love will stay!'

I recognized Abdul Hadi's voice. He was preparing a bonfire of stubble and straw. There was a pile of corn cobs. He called to me, asking me to share the corn which he was going to roast.

I had to be home before dark. Then a thought came to me: perhaps he could get my father's consent for me to stay out, this once? Delightedly, he agreed to try, accompanied me home, had my father's permission and took me back to the fire he was preparing.

Night fell, the glistening surface of the river grew dark, and we were joined by Abu Suweilim, Muhammad Effendi, but not Sergeant Abdullah. Sheikh Hassouna was leaving in the morning, for the start of his school term.

'Are the holidays already over?' asked Abdul Hadi.

'Yes,' said Muhammad Effendi, 'our school, too, will start at the same time as the Headmaster's.'

Abdul Hadi laughed. 'You talk of working? All you do is to earn wheat bread and sweetmeats, while we poor fellahin exist on maize bread and whey.'

Alwani arrived. But I was impatient only for the Sergeant, about whom I had heard so much. Alwani fanned the flames with the skirt of his gallabya. The cobs began to crackle in the fire.

All at once, out of the darkness, strode Sergeant Abdullah.

Abdul Hadi, knowing my desire to meet him, called me to sit beside him. I was thrilled to be sitting by someone so important, and I could not restrain my curiosity, staring at the huge whip dangling from his waist. He must have noticed, for he gripped its handle as though about to use it. I shivered with delight and fear.

Then suddenly he smiled. His dark face lit up with smiles. It was impossible to believe that it was he who had been beating the villagers but a few days before. I could not believe that this was the selfsame whip that had rained blows on men, women and children.

The Sergeant asked me where I went to school. I told him that I would soon be going to secondary school. He told me, smiling, that he had a brother, like me, who wanted to go to the secondary school in Aswan, but he doubted if this could ever be possible. He was silent, staring ahead of him into the night.

Abdul Hadi then offered the Sergeant a roasted corn cob. The Sergeant took it and handed it to me. I dropped it, my fingers burning. Thereupon the Sergeant picked it up from the earth and wiped it with his fingers, simply. But it must go back into the fire: 'Everything is improved by fire.'

Everyone smiled.

Abdul Hadi offered the Sergeant another cob; he took it without flinching. Everyone else gasped from the heat, laughing.

I could not help thinking of all that the Sergeant had done in the village; I wanted to ask him why he had beaten the women, the children, and the men. But everyone was happily munching, and I did not like to ask.

Suddenly we heard a boat moving on the water. Sergeant Abdullah walked to the bank. None of us knew what the boat was, or where it was going. I found myself remembering the night at the beginning of the summer, when I had sat here with Waseefa, and of the boat that had passed then. Waseefa had dangled her feet in the water, had asked me about Cairo. She had wanted to wake up in the morning with a jar full of florins by her bed. And now she did not even have enough to eat.

All was silent. Suddenly a sad voice was heard from near the river:

'Why are their necks white, and our necks red from the sun?
Why is their fortune good, while we are beggars, every one?'

It was Sergeant Abdullah. I did not have the chance any more to ask him questions. The men continued to eat, and Abu Suweilim said:

'Strange, isn't it? He came as an enemy; but now he's one of our best friends, our dearest.'

Again silence: the only sound the crackling of the fire, into which Alwani inserted his teapot. From the farther bank came the straining sound of a waterwheel. I wanted to speak to Sergeant Abdullah, but could not: he was listening to the wheel. I heard Muhammad Effendi talking to one of the soldiers. The soldier said that where he came from, the Nile was wide, the father of our small stream. There they knew nothing of waterwheels or fields, for the Nile flowed rapidly between sand and wilderness, and people knew nothing of greenery or life.

The Sergeant asked the soldier if he was homesick here, amidst this greenery.

The soldier murmured from his heart, 'Ach!'

Under his breath Sergeant Abdullah muttered sad words we could not hear, he was far from his mother and father, in a village where he had no relations or friends, and to which he had come with whip in hand, yet he was now sitting with people he had attacked!

Before I could question him, he suddenly asked me if I knew English. When I said, Yes, he insisted that I should teach him it.

I was silent. He was silent.

The tea had begun to boil. Alwani picked up the pot to pour it.

Suddenly one of the guards loomed out of the darkness. He shouted:

'Your Excellency, Sergeant Abdullah!'

Abu Suweilim said, 'What's brought you here, Abdul Aati?'

In great distress he replied, 'The Magistrate's come!'

Everyone got up, astonished, except Sergeant Abdullah.

He calmly replied, 'Good, Abdul Aati. You go.'

Abdul Aati stood rubbing his neck, and then spoke hesitantly.

'I wanted to tell you ... I ... I mean ... he dashed into the village, three soldiers with him, on horses ... they beat people in the field ... I mean, he was angry when he didn't find you ... I said you were in another village.'

Abu Suweilim said crossly, 'Can't you stop rubbing your neck?'

Sergeant Abdullah smiled at Adbul Aati kindly. 'Has the Magistrate been killed, or something? Good ... you go off!'

Abdul Aati went. The rest of us waited to see what Sergeant Abdullah would do.

He told his soldiers to accompany us to our homes. But he himself strode in front, his shoulders back, his whip in his hand, with steady steps across the dusty earth. His eyes gazed heavenwards.

We walked after him, proudly; we were eager to see what would happen next.

What happened we heard in the morning.

The Magistrate, trembling with rage, had met Sergeant Abdullah and had begun to scream insults at him. Without a moment's hesitation, the Sergeant had raised his Sudanese whip and cracked it down on the Magistrate's back. According to Alwani, Sergeant Abdullah had then picked up the Magistrate and thrown him like a bundle over the back of a horse. But as for Sergeant Abdullah, he said nothing. His calm, gentle face remained silent amidst the speculation of the village. The only thing he said was that he was sorry Sheikh Hassouna had left the village.

That evening as he was sitting with his soldiers, a telephone message came from the town that he and his men were to be transferred immediately. The village knew that they would never come back.

Before sunrise, while the Government men were busy trampling the maize and cotton, a crowd of villagers by the embankment said good-bye to Sergeant Abdullah. Alwani shouted through his tears:

'What a loss to us, Sergeant Abdullah. You are the best of the Arabs – our champion.'

Sergeant Abdullah wiped his eyes and rode off, saying nothing.

Sheikh Yusif said, 'What an unlucky village we are.'

The camels of the four men raised a cloud of dust. Abu Suweilim's words did not ring true, 'Friendship excludes goodbyes.' For it was goodbye. Sergeant Abdullah never came back to the village again. He and his friends rode off along the riverbank, and new men came to trample on the maize.

That evening four policemen and a Sergeant-Major arrived from the Prefecture. They let it be known that they would be staying at the Residence, until a Police Station was built for them. The mention of a 'Police Station' reminded the older people of the war. An old woman asked Sheikh Yusif if this meant that they would begin confiscating food and beasts, as during the war, and if they would take men as 'volunteers', never to come back.

He did not answer her, but looking to Alwani said bitterly:

'You see what our evil deeds have led to? Our pointless quarrel with the Government. Why do you all weep for

Sergeant Abdullah? For the pennies you wasted from giving him tea?'

Alwani was outraged. 'What's a penny to me? Weren't you sincere, Sheikh Yusif, when you wept at his going? Or are you angry because they'll not be needing an Omda, if they open a Police Station?'

The old woman went off, Alwani stayed.

He wanted Sheikh Yusif to buy him a sheep, which he could earn his living from; now that the melon season was over, he was desperate for a job. 'Where can I go? Who will employ me? Do you think Abu Suweilim might buy me a sheep, or Abdul Hadi, even!'

Sheikh Yusif gave him no encouragement.

His mind was taken up with one thing only: the establishment of a Police Station would ruin his hopes.

If there were police, there would be no need of an Omda. The Sheikh al-Balad was just as alarmed by the news of the Police Station.

Someone like Abdul Aati cared little whether there was an Omda, or a Police Station. In neither case would his patch of land by the river grow any bigger, that gave him some corn in summer, beans in winter. His thoughts were taken up by the plump young widow of the Omda. She had never loved her elderly husband, who had kept her locked up since the day he married her. Now that she was a widow she took to flirting with Abdul Aati through the open window.

The Sheikh al-Balad found them exchanging snatches of songs. He quivered with rage.

'What is this "beauty" you're singing about, Abdul Aati? It would be better if you minded your "duty". Come here!'

The pretty widow vanished from the open window.

Abdul Aati sauntered indifferently towards the Sheikh al-Balad. But when he raised his hand to slap him, Abdul Aati caught his wrist and pushed him off. 'Don't you dare lay a finger on me. You're not the Omda, you know!'

And Abdul Aati strolled off, then turned. 'What's wrong with you, Sheikh al-Balad? What are you afraid of? *Two* baskets of dung on your head, perhaps?'

The Sheikh al-Balad sat down, shaking his head in anger, muttering under his breath.

Night fell. The doors of the houses were locked, there was silence. But indoors there was apprehension in every heart.

Suddenly five men rode up on horseback, in tarbooshes and khaki, guns slung over their shoulders. Four of them, dark-complexioned, rode white horses, while the fifth, thick set with a ruddy face, rode a black stallion. His uniform was open at the neck, a pistol dangled from his belt, and his eyes flashed.

From chinks in their doors the villagers saw the arrivals. They whispered to their children, 'The Government! The Government has descended on us, riding horses!'

When they saw the Sergeant Major, 'What a black day! He's the split image of an Englishman. What a dreadful year!'

The men rode to the Residence, where the Sheikh-al-Balad had prepared them sleeping quarters, as far as possible from where the women slept. He sent them in food, carried by a smiling Abdul Aati. The Sergeant Major raised each raffia lid, sniffed, and said disdainfully, 'I'm not in the habit of eating with Omdas.'

So Abdul Aati carried the food back to the kitchen, where he plonked down the dishes in front of the Omda's widow, then stood without speaking. The Sheikh al-Balad called him back. In a rough, coarse voice the Sergeant Major shouted, too:

'Boy ... Come here, you lazy guard!'

After a moment's rest, the Sergeant Major got up and patrolled the village, followed by his policemen, with Abdul Aati at the rear. The lanes were empty of all life. Arrogantly, the Sergeant Major produced an empty packet of cigarettes. Wasn't there a grocer who sold cigarettes?

Abdul Aati ran and asked Sheikh Yusif to open up for the Sergeant Major.

Sheikh Yusif unlocked his shop and reluctantly dusted his cigarettes. The Sergeant Major arrived and quickly snatched a packet and without asking the price placed a small coin on the counter. There was nothing for Sheikh Yusif to do but accept this half price.

When the Sergeant Major was back in the Residence, he sprawled on a large sofa while the police stood at attention. Finally he gave them permission to sit, too. He then handed Abdul Aati a florin and asked him to fetch him wheat bread, fresh eggs, and a sesame cake. No one in the village sold wheat bread, but Abdul Aati went back to Sheikh Yusif's. The latter was delighted at the chance of recovering what he was owed on the cigarettes. He gave him dry village loaves, some eggs and a large hunk of sesame cake. Abdul Aati took them

Now that the road was under way, with many men working on it, Sheikh Yusif had changed his views. He was as eager for trade as he was for the Omdaship. And as for the land he would lose, he did not care a fig: the Government would pay him compensation, and he would prefer the cash. When Muhammad Effendi rebuked him for accepting the trade of the young men working on the road, he replied coldly:

'They bring business, they pay. If they don't buy from me, they'll buy from someone else.'

Muhammad Effendi, once so servile to Mahmoud Bey, had changed. He had genuinely hoped that all the money he had given to the Bey might bring some good to the village, for which he himself could take credit. He was now completely disillusioned, and he was nauseated by Sheikh Yusif's opportunism.

Alwani broached the subject of sheep to Abdul Hadi. He was agreeably surprised when Abdul Hadi showed interest in the project, but added, 'So long as you don't cheat me as you used to cheat Mahmoud Bey, Sheikh of the Arabs.'

'How could you think such a thing?'

'I was only joking.'

I had drifted up to them as they were talking. Abdul Hadi asked me when I would be travelling.

'In four days time.'

'Oh, dear, what a loss! I never had time to sing you my ballads. We were so busy with the Omda's tricks.' And in his rough, but melodious voice he sang a line of verse:

'Chances are many ... tomorrow improves ... sorrow will go.'

The whole village had been surprised by the speed and the skill with which the Government men were building the road. Abu Suweilim was anguished. He had hoped to salvage his crops before the iron broke the earth. Feverishly he had grabbed pieces of his cotton and his maize, bitter at the village girls who had been hired for the new road. His cotton was his one hope of getting food for his family.

In despair he turned to the Overseer:

'What's a day or two to you? Can't you just wait till we've picked our crops?'

'You think we should hold up Government work', the Overseer was scornful, 'just for your cotton?'

The Overseer continued to direct the destruction of Abu Suweilim's crops. Waseefa shouted tragically:

'You're ruining us, and it means nothing to you.'

The Overseer tried to be reasonable. 'What was your cotton worth anyway, old man? Only dust! You know the low prices which the foreign buyers are offering this year. Be sensible, let your daughter come and work here with the other girls. He stood up, caressing his paunch. His eyes suddenly brightened as he took in Waseefa's beauty. 'Ah, you are lovely, lovely as a moon ... we'll pay you extra ....' There was something obscene, not only in his eyes, but in the way he patted his stomach. He continued to gloat. 'Pretty ripe, you come and work with us.'

Abu Suweilim was horrified at the thought of his daughter working like the other girls, meeting men in the fields. The idea was unbearable, the very depths of humiliation. There was the sudden sound of a young man's laughter. It was the ex-disciple of Shaaban, whom Sheikh Yusif had once banished from his shop, for belittling Abdul Hadi, but who was now a valued customer. 'She's worth an extra florin a day,' he taunted.

Before anyone knew what had happened, Abdul Hadi, Diab and Abu Suweilim had raised their sticks against the Overseer and his men. The insolent boy took to his heels, followed by the Overseer. Suddenly the atmosphere changed. It was like harvest in the old days. The young men and the young women began with all speed to gather the cotton, making straw girdles round their gallabyas, and stuffing their breasts. They even sang the traditional harvest songs, verse answering verse.

One said to Abdul Hadi, 'Your destiny is honey, Abdul Hadi ... isn't that so, Waseefa?'

She blushed.

'Who'll be best man, Abdul Hadi? The Sheikh of the Arabs?'

Abdul Hadi was flooded with joy at such a prospect.

Everyone brought their cotton to Waseefa, which she skillfully packed into sacks. She asked Abdul Hadi to help her stamp it into its bales.

They had collected quite a large quantity, when suddenly the Sergeant Major rode up on his horse, his soldiers and the Overseer trotting by his side. Still on his horse, he shouted:

'This land belongs to Abu Zift, no?'

Abu Suweilim stood his ground. 'I am Muhammad Abu Suweilim. Don't you insult me in front of my daughter. Would you like someone to insult you in front of yours?'

The Sergeant put his hand on his pistol. 'Take care, old man, or I'll shoot.'

Abdul Hadi said, 'You not only take our land, but shoot us, too?'

'Yes,' said the Sergeant, 'if you interfere with Government property.'

Diab blurted out, 'Government property? This land is ours!'

'It's mine,' said Abu Suweilim, 'my cotton and my life.'

'What's its total worth, do you think?' the Sergeant asked. 'A pound? Right, a pound. And that's what you'll pay for stealing this.' He jumped off his horse, which began to graze.

'Ah, I understand, you want a bribe?'

In fury, the Sergeant advanced on Abu Suweilim and gave him a ringing slap. The old man fell down. Waseefa cursed the Sergeant with all the insults she knew, at the same time looking at his thick neck and his broad back, wondering where to strike. The police held her off, while the Sergeant ordered them to shut the men in the telephone room, till the road was completed. Waseefa lay on the ground where she had been thrown, while the men were led off to the village. She saw the Sergeant Major ordering the cotton to be collected: it was now Government property. He then turned and followed his prisoners to the village. The men were shut in the telephone room. The Sergeant Major jumped down from his horse and bolted the door from the outside. He then stood with his back against the door, seeing Waseefa following him.

'Would you like someone to insult you, Effendi, in front of your daughter?' she shouted.

Strangely, her words upset the thick-set, burly Sergeant, and after a few moments he got on his horse and rode off to town, having first told the Sheikh al-Balad to keep the men under lock and key.

Abdul Aati went to collect the cotton. He had been distressed to shut the men in the telephone room, in particular Abu Suweilim. He was yet more sad to be the one to rob the old man of his last cotton.

He was slowly tying up the sacks when Muhammad Effendi approached him.

'Bring the sacks to my house, Abdul Aati. I'll buy the cotton, and give the money to his family. If the Sergeant asks you, say you didn't find any.'

Delightedly Abdul Aati agreed and began to collect the cotton with enthusiasm. The Overseer strode over to ask what they were doing. Confidently Muhammed Effendi replied: they were carrying out orders; this cotton belonged to the Government, they were taking it to the Residence. The overseer was satisfied, and the girls working on the road rushed over and helped. Altogether there was well over a hundred pounds. Abdul Aati then carried the sacks, with the aid of some men, to the courtyard of Muhammad Effendi's house.

'You've done a good job,' Muhammad Effendi whispered to himself, 'a brave piece of work.'

Abdul Aati ran off to the telephone room to tell what he had done.

Abu Suweilim said quietly, 'Thank you, Muhammad Effendi!'

Meanwhile, Muhammad Effendi returned from the field, his head bowed in thought. He was composing the text of a telegram to send to the Public Prosecutor complaining against the way villagers were illegally imprisoned. He thought of making copies of the telegram: one for the Opposition press, another for the Ministry of Justice, and yet another for the Court of Appeal. One to the Lawyers' Syndicate, too? No, that would be pointless: the Lawyers' Syndicate was now a closed shop for Government supporters.

He reached home to find his mother weeping. He asked her to cook a duck, and bake special wheat bread to send on a tray to the men imprisoned in the Residence. She raised her hands to Heaven ... imploring the release of Diab and the others.

Muhammad Effendi went to his room and dressed. Wearing his tarboosh, shoes and cashmere gallabya, he went to Abu Suweilim's house. In front of the house he stopped to look at some weeping women; they were commiserating with a newly married wife. He did not hear Waseefa's voice. He could not discern her face among those of the women.

He thought again of his telegram, and decided on some fiery phrases in place of milder ones. He would even sign the telegram with his own name, whatever the consequences.

Waseefa came from the inner part of the house. She approached him, her face pale with worry, her body exhausted from anguish. Muhammad Effendi walked a few sad paces with her, unable even to look her in the eyes. She asked in a broken whisper what he wanted. Equally broken, Muhammad Effendi whispered that he had bought the cotton, and wished to pay her for it. For a moment her eyes opened wide, then lowering her head, she said, 'Let me ask my mother – you can't consult my father, he's not here.' Her voice was tragic with grief. He quickly turned and ran for his donkey, to ride to the town to send his telegrams.

I tried myself to speak to Waseefa, but in vain. I went into her house, picking my way past the women in black. I found Waseefa clutching the knees of a prostrate woman. I could think of nothing to say, and ran quickly out again.

Time was pressing. After one more day I would leave for Cairo. I wanted to talk to people about Waseefa. The only person I could find was Kassab, the cabdriver. But he was taciturn, smoking cigarette after cigarette, silently shaking his head. Suddenly he said that Abu Suweilim, like himself, could start all over again.

But this was not what I was wanting. But this was all that he would say: it was the chief lesson he had learned from life, that men could always start up again.

He then got up and wiped down his horse, before taking it down to the river. My mother brought me some baskets which she had carefully packed with food and clothes. I could not bear to speak, so I walked into the road. I found myself approaching Sheikh Yusif's shop. He was sitting with Sheikh Shinawi. They were reading together from Sheikh Shinawi's sermon book. Sheikh Yusif was wearing a clean new shawl round his fez, a cashmere robe, and an undervest of wool – his Omda's outfit. A barefooted young man was standing in front of the shop, astonished by what he saw. I saw Sheikh Yusif raise his hand from the book and say, 'Yes, that's the way, sir, but shout a little more loudly at that point ... Sheikh Shinawi, God bless you, and His Prophet! For the Omda, as you say, deserves obedience; the disobedient are blasphemers! Mahmoud Bey assured me, a little moment ago, that I shall have his support for the Omdaship.' Lowering his voice, he added, 'But what an appetite he has for cash.' Sheikh Shinawi answered, 'God give you success, Sheikh Yusif! The blessing of Muhammad upon you, and prayers, and peace. Meanwhile, let's pray.'

The young man joined in the prayer with them. When they had finished, Sheikh Shinawi said to Sheikh Yusif: 'This village – it needs a strong hand.' And the Sheikh then launched into a vicious attack on Muhammad Effendi; he was using his opportunity, the men being in prison, to seduce the village girls. The girl herself had told him how she had been offered money ... He had told her to refuse it.

Before he could continue, the barefooted youth rushed into the shop. The two of them were hypocrites, he said. His violent words infuriated the two old men. 'You call me a liar?' said Sheikh Yusif. 'May your tongue be torn out! Do you want a taste of my foot? Abdul Hadi pulled your buffalo out of the well, so you trot behind him like a dog?'

Massoud, for it was he, replied, 'I walk behind Abdul Hadi like a dog? How do you walk behind the Omdaship, while Abdul Hadi is in prison? You need a couple of his best blows.'

I went home to get ready for my journey.

Waseefa had told her mother about Muhammad Effendi's offer, and that Sheikh Yusif had told her this was all wrong; she must never accept a farthing from Muhammad Effendi. Her mother pondered, before saying, 'He's right. What would people say if we took money?'

Sheikh Yusif had also advised her to work on the road; he was ready to put in a word for her with the overseer.

'Good ... go and ask him to get you a job. We must have money if we are to eat. I pray you get a good wage!'

Waseefa did not at all relish the idea of working alongside men who cared nothing what they said. A new idea occurred to her: that she and her mother should go and live with her sister in the town. But this would mean leaving her father in prison – something impossible.

Sheikh Shinawi encouraged her to work; he too would talk to the overseer. After all, the men wouldn't eat her! Perhaps she could begin work next morning. The work was light. She would be independent of Muhammad Effendi's charity, and safe from scandal.

Waseefa looked at the dust beneath her feet. She was ashamed to work beside men destroying her father's fields. She could not decide, but Sheikh Shinawi joined Sheikh Yusif in saying that this was the right course. When she looked up, she saw that Sheikh Yusif's face had suddenly grown pale. She heard from behind her a thunderous voice.

'What wicked things are you saying, Sheikh Yusif?'

It was Muhammad Effendi. It was his first visit to the shop for a long time. He spoke fiercely, deliberately not greeting the men first.

Sheikh Shinawi pretended to be very offended. Taking no notice, Muhammad Effendi fixed his eyes on Sheikh Yusif and coldly rebuked him for what he had told Waseefa. He ended his denunciation by threatening to beat Sheikh Yusif with his shoe. He then left the shop, and passed Abdul Aati carrying the tray of food for the men.

Sheikh Yusif regained his courage. 'Just wait till tomorrow, when you have a new Omda. Then you'll see who'll use his shoe ...'

Abdul Aati carried the tray to the telephone room. He laid it on the ground and uncovered the roast duck and the loaves of white bread.

Alwani squatted as near the tray as possible.

'This is meat and hot and cooked!'

Diab joined him, the host. 'Eat, all of you, wheat bread. Eat! No one must stop till he's ready to burst. Get busy, boys, get busy. The fattest duck ... grab at it ...' Everyone laughed.

Abdul Hadi said to Alwani, 'When we get out, I'm going to buy you a sheep, Sheikh of the Arabs.'

Abdul Aati, while they were eating, told them of the incident between Muhammad Effendi and Sheikh Yusif. As they laughed, Diab said, 'You see how brave my brother is.'

'By God, he is,' said Abdul Hadi. 'Bravo, Muhammad Effendi.'

Alwani leant towards Abdul Hadi, still laughing from his story:

'A duck like this needs tea.'

Abdul Aati got up, scratched his head, thought a moment, and went to the Residence. The Omda's widow called to him; she was wearing a black dress with a low neck; Abdul Aati stared at her visible and invisible charms. Could he have some tea for the men? She led him into the kitchen, flirtatiously, while he told her the story about Sheikh Yusif. Suddenly, the Sheikh al-Balad called him, and getting no answer, thumped on the door with his stick. He, too, thought of himself as a new Omda, but Abdul Aati was undismayed. 'Omda? Omda? I know you Omdas ... May Hell take you all.'

The yellow pods of corn were ripening: the September mists evoked mosquitoes. My father went to the town. I waited for his return, hoping for a new suit; the village hoped he would get the men free.

The sun set. I took a last look at the river. I turned, hearing the noise of cab wheels. My father must have come. The cattle were passing along the embankment towards the houses; the road was emptied as the women followed their beasts in the growing dusk. I went home.

Kassab was sitting up in front of his cab, his head high, his chest thrust out, looking happy. My father jumped down, handing me a parcel. I took it from him, my heart beating. Quickly I tore it open. It was my older brother's suit that had been cut down.

My mother was now stitching up the parcels of food and clothes in sacking. She took my suit and packed it for me, telling me to go to bed; Kassab would be coming early in the morning; we had to catch the first train.

I was depressed that I would not be going in a new suit. I walked into the road. Kassab had got down from the cab. He smiled when he saw me. The village had seen the last of the Sergeant Major, thank God! The men would probably be set free this very night: they were waiting for a telephone call. The Prefecture had been turned upside down on account of the imprisoned men; telegrams from the village had had much effect in Cairo. The evening papers had all run accounts of how men had been gaoled without having committed any crime. 'An excellent piece of work from Muhammad Effendi. He's not running after Mahmoud Bey anymore. He's begun to understand. If he had seen what I have seen, in Alexandria, as well as other places, he would never have taken notice of Beys and pleadings.' He spoke vividly of his experiences; the secrets that I had not learnt in school, but that were more important than longitude and latitude. I had not noticed where we were walking. Suddenly we stopped at a door; Kassab walked in, and I followed.

It was Abu Suweilim's house, and Kassab went in boldly, without making the warning cough that people usually made in our village before entering a house. The entrance was dark, but from the far end came a feeble glow. Otherwise the house seemed uninhabited. Kassab advanced, calling Waseefa. She came out, her head defiant but sad. In the pale light she gently smiled, and my heart beat faster. I noticed that she had been crying.

'Your father's coming out tonight,' Kassab's voice was tender. 'We're expecting the telephone call any minute.' She was overcome with joy, and danced in her delight. 'Really? By the Prophet? God's truth?'

Her face had suddenly grown young again. She turned to shout the good news to her mother, who came out of the shadows. She had been busy making fuel pats. Now she joined Waseefa in thanks to Kassab.

Suddenly I saw something I had never seen before in my village. Kassab affectionately put his hand on Waseefa's shoulder, and not only was she not indignant, but she smiled back at him.

kissing his hand, and feeling suddenly depressed. We got aboard and the train moved out.

The train passed through wide fields. Fields white with cotton or green with maize, just like the fields in my village, then through an immense expanse of clover, dotted here and there with girls at work. The train rushed ahead without stopping, past donkeys and buffaloes; suddenly the railway ran parallel to the highway and my brother leant towards me. He pointed out that children were waiting on the highway for the bus to take them to primary school in the neighbouring town.

I went on staring through the window, thinking of my own village.

The train slowed down and the words of a song floated up.

'May I meet my beloved on the broad highway.
From night to night with him on the broad highway ...'

The train gathered speed and interrupted the words. The highway had entered the repertoire of this village. My brother said, smiling, we, too, should profit from the road, not abuse it. I told him of Kassab's plan to build a mill, and he agreed that Abu Suweilim could soon buy better land than he had lost with the profits he would make. People would be able to build cleaner, newer houses on the highway. But when I asked him how, he remained silent.

The train continued its monotonous rush. Suddenly we saw the domes of Cairo on the left, and faraway to the right, three pyramids. My heart was still brooding on Waseefa, Abdul Hadi and my village.

The train drew in to Cairo station. We walked into the sunshine of the square, a porter behind us. We took a cab to Helmia Gadida. The driver cracked his whip and swore in a way which I had not heard throughout the summer. My brother's cheeks went red, I saw him looking at me out of the corner of his eye, for he felt responsible for my moral welfare. But I had heard such words every day in my four years at primary school.

I stared at the busy streets, excited by the tumult of carts and donkeys and luxurious cars, by the women in their dresses, by the men in suits, and by the barefoot poor in gallabyas of every shade, not all blue, as at home. It thrilled me to see Cairo again after four months; it was like seeing it for the first time. Parents were buying books and pencils for their children in the crowded shops. My brother turned and said:

'Back to school.'

I was surprised. Kassab was not a handsome man, and I could not help comparing his thin face and greying hair with the sturdy good looks of Abdul Hadi, of whom the boys said that he grew one lion's hair behind his waistcoat.

No one looked at me. I suddenly said I was leaving for Cairo in the morning. But still Waseefa had eyes only for Kassab. I felt left out and thought it best to go. I dragged my steps towards the door, but as I reached the threshold, I heard Kassab whisper something to Waseefa, and she raised her voice:

'Go in safety ... Read the Opening Prayer for us in Cairo. May you pass your exams and turn into an effendi!'

And as I went, I heard Kassab saying gently, 'No, no, that's not work for you, on the highway. Forget Sheikh Yusif and Sheikh Shinawi. Listen to me.'

In the morning, early, Kassab drove up with his cab and loaded on to it my luggage and that of my elder brother. My mother kissed me, gave me a handful of silver coins, and told me to study hard. I then took my place between my father and brother.

All the way to the town I was absent-minded. My father and my brother never stopped talking; my father was indignant that the telephone call had not come, and the men were still locked up. My brother said that governments were like this, they never gave way except out of fear.

I looked admiringly at my brother, already a second-year student at the Medical College.

When we approached the town, they both teased me about my long trousers: I was a man now!

My father and brother had business at the Prefecture; Kassab took me to wait at the station. I could not get Waseefa out of my mind. I asked Kassab suddenly if Waseefa had gone to work on the road.

'Yes, this very morning, broken-hearted.'

He spoke quietly, factually, then lit a cigarette.

I could not get out of my head the men I had seen working on the road. Perhaps Waseefa would become like other girls? Perhaps she would learn to speak in the same coarse way as the rest? She would mix freely with men ... even walk off into the fields, behind this one, or that.

I asked Kassab: was it possible that Waseefa could become corrupted?

He said nothing, slightly shaking his head.

But the men on the road – like the policemen – had money to spend, our girls were all poor, and who could resist money?

Again I asked if it was possible that she could become corrupted.

He saw my impatience for an answer.

'Ah, well, you've asked me.'

Again he paused, then repeated a saying of the Prophet:

'Hunger is blasphemy.' He had to leave the station to fetch my father and brother.

As he went off with his big whip, I suddenly thought of Kadra. Would Waseefa become another Kadra? Would there be between her and Kassab the same kind of thing as there had been between Kadra and Diab?

I paced backwards and forwards. I reassured myself: Kassab was old enough to be her father.

The station was beginning to fill. I gazed at the rails which seemed, far off, to meet; but I knew this was an illusion; they would not meet ... ever.

I thought again of school, and of what I should do in Cairo; I thought of the demonstrations. Perhaps the Constitution would be restored, perhaps Abu Suweilim would be Chief Guard again, Sheikh Hassouna would come back to the village, and everything would be all right. My eyes stared at the receding rails.

My father and brother joined me, with Kassab. My father bought our tickets and made sure of the train's time. Kassab told me that the message had now reached the village, the men were to be set free at once. Suddenly his face was convulsed with laughter, showing he had something more to tell.

His news was hot: he had just come from the Prefecture where Sheikh Yusif had had a terrible clash with Mahmoud Bey. He had gone to the Prefecture confident that after the money he had paid, Mahmoud Bey would support his candidature. Sheikh Yusif wore his complete Omda's outfit. He had with him two or three followers from the village. The Sheikh al-Balad had also arrived with a small retinue and the same hopes. But when they were shown into the appropriate official's bureau, they were at once asked if they all agreed that Mahmoud Bey should be their new Omda. 'No, no,' Sheikh Yusif had screamed, 'we don't agree. The man's a cheat, he offers to help people, takes their money, but only helps himself.' Whereupon Mahmoud Bey had set upon Sheikh Yusif and given him a severe beating. Sheikh Yusif left the office bedraggled and cursing. The Sheikh al-Balad went after him and whispered that their only chance of stopping Mahmoud Bey was for the Omdaship to go to him. 'After all, Sheikh Yusif, you still have your shop....'

Ready to do anything to defeat Mahmoud Bey, Sheikh Yusif agreed. But meanwhile the official had postponed the election to another day.

This exciting news made me wish to postpone my departure. I wanted to see the reactions of my friends to this news, I wanted to see Abdul Hadi. I could go to Cairo next day, instead. But the next day was Friday, and my mother thought it unlucky to travel on Fridays.

Now the train was arriving. Kassab took our luggage in his two hands and turned to me. 'Go in safety. God grant that when your next holiday comes round I'll have a new house by the highway, and Waseefa brightening it!'

I was astonished, and asked him to explain what he meant.

He told me his plan. It was to use a plot of Abu Suweilim's land by the highway, and to get the old man to go shares with him in a mill, which would be far more profitable to Abu Suweilim than the land he had lost. The train stopped beside us. Kassab added that when he got back to the village he would take Waseefa away from the road, by force if need be.

I tried to imagine what Abdul Hadi would say when he heard of Kassab's intentions. For he had told me that he hoped to have his home made bright by Waseefa by the time I next came home. But then perhaps Abdul Hadi might not want to marry her, if she had worked even an hour on the public road.

The train was about to go. We said goodbye to our father,

THE EARTHQUAKE
Tahir Wattar

What do the thoughts of a religious Sheikh, whose inner-self cares only for cash and land ownership, revolve around – apart from himself?

One afternoon, Sheikh Abdelmajid Boularwah embarks upon a journey in search of distant relatives. His immediate family are ruthless, rich and collaborate with colonial authorities. He hopes his long-lost relatives, who are unknown to the new communist government, might be better placed to help him defraud it. Through a labyrinth of back alleys and memories, Boularwah makes his way from Algiers across the seven bridges of Constantine, battling the forces of a rapidly changing society alongside his own demons and traversing the difficult road of colonialism to independence, tradition to modernity, hope to despair and from one failed ideology to another.

The Earthquake offers a surrealist vision of post-colonial Algeria — a society in chaos, a world turned upside down. Written in the early 1970s, this classic work by pioneering novelist Tahir Wattar presciently foretells the dreadful events which would later besiege his country.

'One of the modern Arabic classics.' *World Literature Today*

978 0 86356 963 0   £9.99

RIVER SPIRIT
Leila Aboulela

1880s Sudan. When Akuany and her brother are orphaned in a village raid, they are taken in by Yaseen. His vow to care for them will tether him to Akuany throughout their lives. As revolution begins to brew, Sudan begins to prise itself from Ottoman rule, and everyone must choose a side.

Yaseen feels beholden to stand against the revolution, a decision that threatens to splinter his family. Meanwhile, Akuany moves through her young adulthood and across the country alone – sold and traded from house to house, with only Yaseen as her intermittent lifeline. Their struggle will mirror the increasingly bloody struggle for Sudan itself: for freedom, safety and the possibility of love.

River Spirit is the unforgettable story of a people who, against the odds and for a brief time, gained independence from foreign rule. This is a powerful tale of corruption and unshakeable devotion – to a cause, to one's faith and to the people who become family.

'Dazzling ... Aboulela has written a novel of war, love, faith, womanhood and – crucially – the tussle over truthful public narratives. *New York Times*

'Aboulela's narratives glow with a rare beauty, a shining sensual awareness of the joy of life.' *The Scotsman*

978 0 86356 904 3   £9.99

A MOUTH FULL OF SALT
Reem Gaafar

The Nile brings them life. But the Nile also takes away.

1970s. A small farming village in North Sudan wakes up one morning to the news that a little boy has drowned. Soon after, the camels die of a mysterious illness and the date gardens catch fire and burn to the ground. The villagers whisper of a mysterious sorceress who dwells at the foot of the mountains. It is the dry season. The men have places to go, the women have work to do, the children continue to play at the place where the river runs over its own banks. Fourteen-year-old Fatima yearns to leave for university in Khartoum.

1950s. In Khartoum, a single mother makes her way in a world that wants to keep girls and women back. As civil war swells, the political intrudes into the personal and her position in the capital becomes untenable. She decides to leave for the village.

A Mouth Full of Salt uncovers a country on the brink of seismic change as its women decide for themselves which traditions are fit for purpose and which prophecies it's time to rewrite.

'Insightful, elegant and compelling, with a profound sense of place. Gaafar shows brilliance in the ways she weaves destinies together and shares truths like all the best fiction writers.' Karen Jennings

978 0 86356 772 8   £14.99

WILD THORNS
Sahar Khalifeh

A young Palestinian named Usama returns to his homeland from the Gulf to support the resistance movement. His mission is to blow up buses transporting Palestinian workers to Israel.

Shocked to discover that many of his fellow countrymen have adjusted to life under Israeli military rule, Usama exchanges harsh words with his friends and family. Despite some uncertainty, he sets out to accomplish his objective ... with disastrous consequences.

First published in Jerusalem in 1976, *Wild Thorns* was the first Arab novel to offer a glimpse of social and personal relations under Israeli occupation. Featuring unsentimental portrayals of everyday life, its uncompromising honesty and rich emotional core plead elegantly for the cause of survival in the face of oppression.

'An impressive narrative of life in the West Bank in which simple profundities are asserted powerfully and poetically.' *Morning Star*

'We highly recommend this book which has already become famous and much-discussed in Palestinian and Arab circles.' *Jacobin*

978 0 86356 986 9   £9.99

DIARY OF A COUNTRY PROSECUTOR
Tawfik al-Hakim

Who shot Kamar al-Dawla Alwan? Why? What does the beautiful peasant girl Rim have to do with it? And is mysterious Sheikh Asfur as mad as he seems?

1920s Cairo. A young and ambitious prosecutor is dispatched from the bustling city to a provincial village to investigate a serious crime. Armed with his European education, the prosecutor is confident that he will dispense justice in this rural outpost. But as he becomes engrossed in village life, he finds himself increasingly befuddled by an alien legal system and the clueless bureaucrats who enforce it. As he teases out the facts of the case only one thing becomes clear: justice is never as simple as it seems.

First published in 1937, *Diary of a Country Prosecutor* takes aim at a self-interested ruling class and the hapless public servants at their disposal. Both a comedy of errors and a trenchant social satire, this classic by one of the Arab world's leading dramatists has lost none of its bite.

'A satirical tale of country life under a repressive and far-away Cairo legal system.' *Literary Review*

'Touching and yet savagely funny.' *The Bookseller*

978 0 86356 981 4   £9.99

THE QUARTER
Naguib Mahfouz

Meet the people of Cairo's Gamaliya quarter. There is Nabqa, son of Adam the waterseller who can only speak truths; the beautiful and talented Tawhida who does not age with time; Ali Zaidan, the gambler, late to love; and Boss Saqr who stashes his money above the bath. A neighbourhood of demons, dancing and sweet halva, the quarter keeps quiet vigil over the secrets of all who live there.

This collection by pre-eminent Egyptian writer Naguib Mahfouz was recently discovered among his old papers. Found with a slip of paper titled 'for publishing 1994', they are published here for the first time. Resplendent with Mahfouz's delicate and poignant observations of everyday happenings, these lively stories take the reader deep into the beating heart of Cairo.

'[Mahfouz was] a master of both detailed realism and fabulous storytelling.' *The Guardian*

'Naguib Mahfouz's legacy as Egypt's greatest novelist is sustained with these engaging short stories ... their themes are timeless.' *New Statesman*

978 0 86356 375 1   £10.99

back to the Residence. The Sergeant was furious that there was only this dry bread. The Sheikh al-Balad was standing with him, and when Abdul Aati tried to make excuses, the Sergeant said:

'I'll teach you a lesson, you impudent rascal.'

The Sheikh al-Balad backed up Authority. 'You're badly brought up, Abdul Aati. Speak to the Effendi properly.'

The Sergeant glared at Abdul Aati from the sofa.

'What's your name, boy? What's your mother's name?'

Abdul Aati could not believe what he heard.

'My mother? What has my mother got to do with this?'

The Sheikh al-Balad intervened.

'His mother's name is Zehana, Effendi.'

Abdul Aati gasped.

'My mother's name is not Zehana. What gave you that idea?'

The Sergeant replied, 'Zehana ... Hebaba ... What difference. I'll teach you a lesson, after supper.'

So Abdul Aati brought back the original dishes. When he was in the kitchen the Omda's widow questioned him about the Effendi; but he was in no mood to reply.

When supper was over, and Abdul Aati had brought the ewer to wash the Sergeant's hands, the Sergeant, having by this time finished most of the cake, told Abdul Aati to take back the remains, as well as the eggs, and get back the florin. With a shrug, Abdul Aati wrapped up what was left and set out for Sheikh Yusif's. On the way, he opened the package and ate a bit more of the sesame cake.

Sheikh Yusif was furious at being disturbed, and still more

at having to restore the florin. But there was nothing he could do.

Abdul Aati went back with the florin. The Sergeant was blowing his nose and clearing his throat after his meal. One consolation for Abdul Aati: the Sergeant was now in as bad a humour with the Sheikh al-Balad as with himself. Shaking his arms, the Sergeant said he would take a nap. He detailed his men to take up various positions in the village, while he himself stretched out on the sofa and went to sleep.

As the holidays were nearly up, I had to make one more visit to the oculist. As usual my father discussed politics, while the oculist examined my eyes and prescribed me medicine. We had been driven to the town by Kassab, a withered man of middle age who had been imprisoned for his radical activities when he worked in factories and on the Egyptian railways. I wanted to discuss my father's opinions with Kassab, while the cab waited outside the Prefecture. (My father had gone in to see what he could do about the new road.) But though Kassab usually loved to talk politics, he was now preoccupied with the danger of our village women working on the new road. Kassab, despite his radical opinions, was conventional in his attitude to women. He was alarmed at the thought that our girls might be corrupted by the strangers. From the way in which he spoke of Waseefa, I guessed that he, too, might be a possible suitor. She had always insisted that she wanted an Effendi for her husband.

The last days of the holidays passed quickly, my mind divided between my dreams of school, and the events of the village.